FEARFUL SYMMETRY

Tash Fairbanks

Published 1996 by Onlywomen Press, Limited
Radical Feminist Lesbian publishers
40 St. Lawrence Terrace, London W10 5ST

ISBN 0 906500 54 0

Cover design © Tyra Till

Series cover format © Tyra Till

Typeset by Columns Design and Production Services Limited,
Reading, Berkshire, U.K.

Printed and bound in Great Britain by Redwood Books,
Trowbridge, Wiltshire.

For Sue
for being there

Chapter One

Sarah's kid leather boots were coated in mud and damp leaves. Her hair, teased by twigs and made lank by dew, would have to be completely restyled tomorrow and she had been only halfway through an exceedingly luscious lobster dinner when she had been paged. But all that was immaterial. To have an assignment like this fall into her lap was truly a gift from the Gods. And it was solely by chance. It was chance that Don had asked her at the last minute to take his weekend shift because of girlfriend trouble. It was chance that she had not been going to London as usual this Sunday and had agreed. Not that she believed in any of that Karma stuff particularly. On the contrary, she was a very material young woman. But modern life was eclectic and one took bits from diverse philosophies as needed. New Age was one of them. Sometimes, in certain situations, the whole of Nature seemed to gel together, to her advantage.

"Couldn't I just have a word with your daughter?" Sarah had never minded being pushy. If you were afraid of hurting anyone's feelings this game was not for you. You'd end up like Don – thirty and still mouldering on a local.

"No, she's in shock. The doctor's giving her something." It was a mellow Sussex burr. There weren't many of them around any more. Especially in the villages. Now most of the rural accents were upper middle. Or thereabouts.

"But maybe she just imagined it all?"

"No, she did not! And don't you go saying that."

"Come on, you know what kids are like. I bet she was just having you on, spinning you a yarn for a bit of attention." Push them till it hurt, that was Sarah's philosophy. It usually got results.

"My daughter's never told a lie in her life." The voice bristled with resentment. The police had, no doubt, suggested much the same.

"She knows what happens to people who tell lies."

"Poor little cow," thought Sarah, her mind and pen racing in two different directions simultaneously.

"'Course she does, Mr Gatwood," Sarah veritably cooed in agreement. "But if I could just have the teeniest little word with her in private ..."

"She's not to be disturbed ... "

"I did see it! I did! It was in the woods!" The girl's voice was breathless, her chest heaving as she pushed through the crowd. The brown eyes were round, large and staring. "Like dinner plates". Sarah thought fleetingly of her lost lobster supper. The adolescent face was streaked with tears, dirt and what looked suspiciously like the remains of some jammy confection.

"Sandra, get away from here and back to bed, like the doctor told you!" Gatwood moved angrily toward the girl.

"What exactly did you see, Sandra?" Sarah interposed herself expertly between man and daughter.

The light from the street lamp fell on the girl alone, as though from a theatre spotlight, starkly illuminating the whiteness of the face and the intense dark pools of the eyes.

"I saw a little baby. A little dead baby. It were a tiny thing, no bigger than six inches long." Her voice rose in pitch and volume, till it became a wail, seeming to reverberate through the treetops.

"And what did it look like, Sandra?" Sarah's voice was gently insistent. But the girl needed no prompting.

"I'll tell you what it looked like." She took a sobbing breath that rattled in her throat. A hush of excitement and expectancy fell among the assembled crowd. They had heard the story already, knew it by heart, perhaps, but, like children themselves, were thrilled to hear its retelling.

"It had the head of a human child and the body of a goat!"

"No sign of it, sir".

"I could have told you that an hour ago". Detective Sergeant Walsh should have been off-duty now, watching rugby union with a can of lager in his hand and the smell of roasting meat in his nostrils. Just his luck for the call to come twenty minutes before changeover.

"We've had the dogs right through this lot."

"O.K. let's call it a day."

"Abandoning the search already, Sergeant? Would that be in the public interest?". The young woman was squatted cautiously atop the stile. He wondered how long she had been there. Not that it mattered. There were no police secrets here. More's the pity.

"There's been enough public interest round here already," Walsh's eyes swept the untidy crowd with distaste. "We've spent an hour combing the place and found sweet FA."

"So you think the foetus was moved before you got here?"

"I think the whole bloody thing's a pubescent fantasy. Girls of that age imagine babies all over the place."

"Not half-animal ones, surely?"

"Just an added touch. Needs a psychiatrist, not a policeman."

"Looks as though we've got both in you."

"Do me a favour," but Walsh was flattered nonetheless. She had dextrously hit a private vain spot of his.

"Wouldn't like to do an interview on the new breed of educated rozzer, would you?"

He looked up sharply. She was laughing at him now. But no, her smile was friendly rather than mocking and, perched there in the shadow of the arc light, small and dark, she resembled a mischievous leprechaun. He smiled back.

"Too bad there's nothing for you here."

"Don't you believe it!" She closed her notebook and slid gingerly from the stile, mindful of the deleterious effect of wood splinters on pure silk.

"Oh come on! You'd really be scraping the bottom of the barrel."

"That's where you find the juiciest bits. Surely you know that!"

He watched her thoughtfully as she moved off through the trees. Without turning she raised her arm in a lazy wave.

"See you around, Sergeant."

"Detective Sergeant. Walsh," he called after her, but the darkness had swallowed her up.

The first stars were pricking a cloudy blue sky as the single figure appeared on the brow of the hill. The figure stood still for some minutes, looking down on the cluster of houses below, its form gradually losing solidity as the night sky thickened around it. Had any of the villagers spared a thought from the evening's diversions to glance upwards or any of the uniformed police officers taken a break from their labours long enough to direct a searching glance toward the hilltop, they would have seen the lone silhouette, the slender figure of a young woman, a travelling bag slung over her shoulder. But they did not and she slipped unnoticed into the village of Lower Hannerley late that autumn evening. Straddling a garden fence, she crept stealthily towards an open back door. She moved without sound, almost without displacement of air. She had had plenty of practice.

Sarah was exultant. It was the chance she had been waiting for.

"Is there a public phone in this place?" How tacky of the Herald not to run to a mobile.

"One opposite the post office."

Good. Superb. In her excitement she fumbled the change, spilling it on the floor. She had just one important call to make before writing the story. A call to the Hunt Genetic Engineering Laboratory. After all, as they were less than two miles from here it was only fair to ask them for their comment on the affair. And as it was past 9.30 on a Sunday evening she was guaranteed to find nobody there. She picked up the receiver and dialled. Oh, life was very sweet sometimes!

The phone on the reception desk rang three times. The third ring was cut off abruptly by a click, followed by a thin, breathless voice racing at top speed through, "This is the Hunt Laboratory. Sorry there is no one to take your call. Please leave your name and number and ...," here

4

the pace doubled as air ran out, "someone will get back to you as soon as possible." The voice took a grateful, and very audible, gulp of air, which the beep mercifully cut short. The voice on the machine this time was full, confident, with a suggestion of suppressed excitement, even gloating, in it.

"Hello, this is Sarah Ginsberg of the Brighton Herald. There's been a chimera, a genetically-produced monster, discovered in a wood near the Hunt Laboratory. Would you care to comment? No? No comment? Thank you very much. Byee."

A click, a whirr and then silence settled on the moonlit desk. From the shadow of a filing cabinet a figure detached itself and prowled across the room. For a brief moment the channel of pale white light from the window threw its form into relief. It was a man, or a tall woman, of sturdy muscular build. There was an animal quality about the movement, as of a powerful force held just in check. The figure glided through the door, which was pulled noiselessly shut behind it. The click of a key turning and silence again. From several streets away a church clock chimed the half hour.

Chapter Two

"Dear God, that we should come to this!" The Reverend Harold Beamish slapped a copy of the Brighton Herald down onto the table, causing his cup to rock perilously in its saucer and his son to jump visibly.

"Have you seen this morning's paper, Doreen?" he demanded of his wife. Doreen, who had spent the two hours since rising loading and unloading the washing machine, hanging the nets and frying the Reverend's breakfast, had not.

"Man playing God and making monsters in the process … finish that sausage, Ian!"

"I can't. I'm full up," his son pushed the remains of his breakfast to one side.

"There are children dying for lack of food. They would give anything for what you're discarding," he jabbed a sticky finger in the direction of his son's plate.

"It's my fault. I gave him too much," Doreen Beamish swooped to remove the offending object, but was intercepted by her husband's hand on her arm.

"You're too soft on him. He's got to learn to eat what he's given."

With infinite slowness, Ian began to slice through the sausage. As his knife split the skin of the pale pink cylinder of congealed grease and gristle, he saw in its place his father's neck protruding from its dog collar and his spirits surged. The knife sawed and sang.

"Now eat it."

Beneath his father's watchful eye, he speared the lump of inert flesh and, transferring it to his mouth, began to chew. Dust and filings. Grey and drear.

"And the last bit." The Redeemer's earthly representative was merciless.

Ian's mother stood beside him, her big hands clenching and unclenching in rhythmic sympathy with his jaws. He swallowed. It was gone. Under the tyrant's unswerving gaze, mother and son let out a soundless sigh in unison, in secret complicity with the unchained air around them.

"That's more like it," his father belched comfortably and turned his attention back to the paper.

"Shame on them! Calvinists and Cannanites," he cursed haphazardly through history.

Ian left the room quickly, running upstairs, into the bathroom. Kneeling over the toilet bowl, he stuck two fingers into the back of his throat. Even against the worst of despots, it was possible to resist. With a retch of bile the contents of his stomach gushed from his mouth.

Soft fingers rubbed gently but insistently at Jo's shoulder. She shrank away from them, pulling the covers up over her head. She was in bed at home, holding on desperately to nighttime and sleep. But there were no covers and the sun was bright through her closed lids. The hand tugged at her arm. Reluctantly, Jo opened her eyes and squinted up at the face above her.

"You want to be my friend?" The woman was a few years older than Jo, about eighteen or so.

"You want to be my friend?"

"Sure," Jo yawned, "why not? I haven't got any friends round here."

"I've got loads. Loads and loads." The woman sat heavily down on the bench beside her.

"Lucky old you," Jo rubbed sleep from her eyes.

"I'm going to see my friend, Maurice. Want to come? He always gives me a cup of tea."

The word 'tea' had a magical effect on Jo. She got up immediately and followed the other woman out of the park.

She had spent a fitful night in a barn, sharing it with at least half a dozen rats who had been throwing an all-night party. They had quieted down by daybreak, but by then the cold had bitten in, the kind of cold that comes in with an east wind as the sky melts from midnight blue to pastel green. Jo knew that kind of cold very well. She had become an expert on early dawns.

"My name's Cynthia and I live at 57 Holmes Park Crescent. What's your name?"

"Jo."

7

"Where do you live?"

"Nowhere."

Cynthia opened her brown leather shoulder bag.

"Look what I've got. Chocolate biscuits. Yummy yummy."

"Mm," thought Jo, "Yummy yummy."

Sarah slowed to a halt. On the pavement ahead was a gaggle of people. Accident, mugging, whatever, it was a rare perk to be first on the scene. Not that she had any stomach for blood or violence, but they sold newspapers and so were definitely not to be sniffed at. As she opened her notebook in readiness the singing reached her. A hymn! What the hell was going on? There were ten or twelve people on their knees, singing "Stand up, stand up for Jesus!", the irony obviously lost on them. Grouped around them, a half dozen women chanted in competition, Demo and counter demo. As she drew nearer she saw the blown-up photographs on the placards. Foetuses. An anti-abortion lobby at Glennings Pregnancy Advisory Clinic. Was that all? She closed her notebook in disappointment and then reopened it. It was worth a column or two, given the right angle. Till she could get a follow-up on her big story, the story that was splashed across the front page of the Herald this very morning.

She studied the scene. Perhaps a satire on fashion was the angle. Why did the God Squad dress so badly? Was dowdiness next to Godliness? Nice line. Not that their opponents were any better presented. Jeans, leathers, spikey hair. They never learned. To put a point across you need pazzazz. She could show them how. Indeed, if she hadn't moved up to one of the nationals by the time she was twenty five she would quit journalism for a public relations consultancy. Life was too short for treading water.

Rapidly she wrote some thumbnail sketches of the protagonists. She was good at that. Merciless, but bloody good. She moved through the crowd.

"Where are you all from?"

"St Saviours," came the reply. Bigot Beamish's lot.

"And why are you here this morning?" her eyes raked

the actors in this comic little scenario. Wasn't that Gatwood on the edge there? As she stared across at him the man moved away.

"We're praying for the souls of the innocent little children being murdered in there today." A xeroxed leaflet covered in tiny coffins was thrust into her hand.

"Tell your readers about the genocide under their noses."

"Right, right. Will do," she moved off toward the rival group, binning the leaflet on her way. Better not spend too long on this. She nearly fell headlong over a placard. 'A woman's right to choose.' Hmm. Why didn't they choose to do something better with their time?

"Hi, I'm from the Brighton Herald. Want to tell me why you're here today?"

"Not really." A woman of around forty with a long auburn plait gave her an unfriendly glare and turned back to her companions. "Then how can I put your point of view?"

"You can read the placards," came from one of the other women.

"Come on, girls, don't you want a bit of publicity? I've got their side. What am I going to say about yours?"

The woman turned to look at her, treating her to a slow, steady, head-to-toes stare that made Sarah feel most unaccountably ill at ease, though God knows why when her pullover was hand-made cashmere and must have cost ten times the amount of the other woman's entire outfit.

"Why, make it up, of course. Like you usually do." There was general laughter and the woman went back to her conversation.

"So anyway, now she's going to try in vitro and see what happens."

Sarah's heart began to pound with exitement. "Oh sweet Jesus," she thought, in conscious parody of those who knelt nearby, "thank you for dropping this heavenly morsel straight into my lap."

This was the follow up story, of course. Genetic engineering needed genetic material. And what better place to get those precious building blocks of life than from an egg and sperm bank? And that's exactly what Glennings possessed. Within two miles of the Hunt Lab there was the perfect original material for their experiments. It sounded good. It sounded true. And if it wasn't, why then, make it up, like the woman said.

Judith Ginsberg nibbled at cold toast and flicked rapidly through the latest copy of The Lancet. It was her regular weekly check for any mention of Hewitt's Disease. She knew others were in the race. At least two teams of geneticists in California and one in Basle. She was sure none were at her stage, but one could never rely on that. Sudden breakthroughs were the name of the game in scientific research. One moment you were nowhere, floundering in seas of mismatched data, and the next you found yourself holding a piece of the puzzle, there in your hand. There was nothing like that high. Nothing in the world.

No, no article on Hewitts Disease this week. Relieved, she flung the magazine aside. Not that it mattered who put the final pieces together, discovered the cure to that terrible wasting illness, so long as it was found. And fast. But still, by rights it should be her. She had dedicated sixteen years of her life to the search. At no small cost. It was she who should claim the prize. Would, one day. Everyone said so. She took a second bite of her toast and chewed mechanically, without tasting, her mind roaming restlessly over the tests she would begin today. Her mistake last week was to use the saline solution. Very well, today she would try another tack. She was close, she knew it. Achingly close. One just needed patience. Last month she had thought she had it, the answer, but it had been a mistake, a chimera, born of tiredness and tension. Rest was a stranger to her now. She slept badly, her nights spent fleeing down the echoing hallways of dark caverns, searching, always searching for an exit, a way into the light.

She pushed the half-eaten toast away and poured another cup of coffee. Caffeine, that's what she needed, on a drip would be ideal. She pulled the morning paper towards her, glancing briefly at the front page. She never usually got much further. The headline seized her by the throat.

"You cow! You bloody little cow!" She snatched up the phone, punching her fingers viciously at the buttons. Two rings and the familiar voice over the line, "Hi, this is Sarah Ginsberg. Sorry I'm not in ...". She waited, drumming her fingers, punishing the table till she could have access to the real object of her fury. The tone; she let rip. "What the hell are you playing at, Sarah? Is this some childish way of getting back at me? The whole thing's ludicrous and you damn well know it!" She took a breath. "You could put my entire research in jeopardy with stupid fairy tales like this. Is that what you want? Is it? What have I done to deserve this, Sarah? Just get off my back, will you!" She slammed down the phone and rummaged across the table for cigarettes. Empty, shit! Her eye caught the headline again. "Frankenstein foetus seen near Hunt Lab!"

"You little cow!"

Vanessa Hunt woke abruptly from a dream of falling and reached out in her panic, as she had done in all the years since her childhood, for a furry animal. Any one of the array of teddies and dogs and pandas around her pillow. This morning, rushing headlong from sleep, it happened to be Mr Bonzo into whom she blundered. She held the bear tightly, let out a long drawn sigh and opened her eyes. The room was dark, but that meant nothing. No matter how bright the morning, the thick, tasselled drapes kept any rogue sunbeam severely at bay. She liked that. She liked dark places, just as she liked soft things. You could sink into softness as you could sink into darkness. They yielded. They enclosed you.

She leant back against the satin headboard and stroked Mr Bonzo and rehearsed, like a catechism, all the nice things that were going to happen that day. She did this every morning and every morning, if she had prepared herself enough treats, it gave her the impetus to get out of bed. That and the 10mg of valium she swallowed with her tea.

Chapter Three

"This is my friend Jo."

"Hello Jo. Pleased to meet you," said the tall, stooped old man in the porter's uniform.

Cynthia had led them through the kind of terrain that was rapidly becoming familiar to Jo, a mixture of council estate and light industrial complex that was common to every town she had been through. For some reason she had imagined Brighton would be different, that she would breast the top of a hill and walk straight down to the lapping sea, to fishing boats and a pier and a promenade with arcades and ice cream, to a memory of childhood. Her and mum on the beach. Together. Just the two of them. Like a photograph. Like a postcard from Brighton. But the sea was at least two miles away still. Never mind, she would be there soon. And then what?

Time later to think about that. For now she had followed her new acquaintance, (she could not say friend for unlike Cynthia, she did not make friends easily), through streets bounded by a sprawl of drab yellow brick housing and grey factory wall.

Maurice's place turned out to be a pleasant, square, red brick building, set back from the road in neat grounds of regulation rose and geranium. A sign announced it was The Hunt Laboratories. At the main gate, Cynthia stopped abruptly, put a warning finger to her lips, adopted a curious, half-crouching waddle and, beckoning to Jo to follow, made her way around the perimeter fence. It was comical. It was playing silly buggers. It made Jo want to giggle out loud. Instead, she tiptoed after the other woman till they reached a sizeable gap in the fence that was partially covered by overhanging branches.

"If they knew, Maurice'd get into trouble, see," Cynthia panted as she squeezed her bulk through the hole. Before them was the porter's lodge, with its bright green door. And inside was tea and chocolate biscuits. And warmth.

Hugh Manders was jolly disgruntled. And what made it worse, he dared not show it. Sarah emphatically did not like men who whined and, as any expression of discontent on his part was automatically assigned to the 'whine' category, Hugh dared not give utterance to this spikey ball of resentment that was lodged uncomfortably in the area of his solar plexus and which was threatening to dispel all the pleasurable effects of the rainbow trout with almonds and mushrooms he was at present consuming. It was all very unfair. He had bought her lunch in the newly-opened French restaurant in the Lanes, partly to make up for the ruin of the (incredibly expensive) lobster supper he had bought her the night before and partly to celebrate her first-ever front-page scoop. It should have been an occasion for the exchange of those kind of looks of melting tenderness that one usually only associates with the best sirloin steak, or for those supreme moments when hand accidentally brushes against hand, synchronistically emitting ten thousand volts of empathic electricity. But they had barely made eye contact the whole meal. She had polished off a breast of lamb with rosemary and well over half a bottle of the best Macon Rouge as though it had been a Big Mac and coke, all the while scribbling away in that bloody notebook of hers, or now and then barking out an impossible question and tut tutting irritably when he didn't know the answer. But how could he be expected to know? Crime was not his speciality. As junior partner in the established and substantial firm of Manders, Cape and Manders, he was more often called upon to untangle the mysteries of Capital Gains than illegal gains. Sarah did not seem to appreciate this distinction.

Now if only they could be like that couple in the far corner. The woman was one of those elegantly sculptured brunettes who could be any age but the man was, like himself, in his mid-twenties. He had something of the hombre look about him, with the kind of lean, unshaven face and muscular build usually only seen wedged into Levis or Peugeots on the telly. He didn't care for the type, but they were undeniably successful with women. He could imagine (he was not wearing his glasses, for obvious reasons), the looks of unrestrained desire that would be the natural currency of their relationship. Taking a bite of trout, he was filled with a sudden and immense sadness that seemed woven in with the very flesh itself. He picked a bone from his teeth. If only Sarah would look at him like that. Just once.

"We'll have to break into the lab." Hugh was jerked forcibly back to the here and now, as his mind attempted to straddle the statement. Her unaccustomed and welcome usage of the first person plural had to be weighed against the preposterous and unnerving nature of the rest of the sentence.

"We! Break into the lab?"

"Yes, Hugh. That's what I said. Do pay attention. You've been miles away all afternoon." Hugh smothered a protest with the facility of long practice.

"No, I was just ... surprised, Sal, that's all."

"I know the joint's wired up, so a jemmy won't be any good."

Hugh felt inordinately relieved at the dismissal of a jemmy from the proceedings.

"I suppose I could go and see mother and eat humble pie. Then I could nick the keys while she's out of the room."

"But what would happen when she found them gone?"

Sarah only partially suppressed her impatience.

"Haven't you ever heard of wax impressions?"

Hugh had, but only in detective novels.

"What do you want to get into the lab for exactly?"

"To find out if they really are doing illegal experiments, of course."

Of course.

"Honestly, Hugh, you really are thick sometimes."

His resentment flared suddenly.

"How would you know, anyway, even if an illegal experiment was staring you in the face?"

"I wouldn't. That's why I need you to come with me."

Hugh, whose sole claim to scientific excellence was an evil-smelling sulphurous brew he and another boy had

14

concocted in the Third Year, decided not to disillusion her as yet.

"But your mother wouldn't do illegal experiments …"

"Don't you believe it! She'd do anything, and I mean anything, to find a cure for Hewitts Disease. That's the only thing she's ever cared about."

Hugh stared. He was used to Sarah's truculence whenever she talked about her mother. But this time there was a different note in her voice, an edge that in anyone else would have sounded like pain. Lifted heavenwards on a wave of tenderness, he reached out and touched her hand.

"You alright, Sal?"

"Yes, of course I am. Order some coffee, will you?" and she pulled her hand away and resumed her scribbling.

He felt a sudden and overpowering urge to protect, to enfold. Not that she would have any of that. She was not that kind of girl. She was like no other he'd ever met. That's what he loved about her. She was special. And they had a very special relationship.

"You can keep your cloying intimacy and heavy sexual vibes," he mentally addressed the couple in the corner, "this woman and I have something of far greater value and rarity than that. Something that," here he availed himself of a lingering mouthful of Macon, "few people in these sordid times would even know how to appreciate."

He looked defiantly across at his intended audience. But the woman was gone. And as Hugh gazed, the man reached into his jacket pocket and pulled something out. After a quick glance around him he snapped open a handbag on the table in front of him (if only Hugh had his specs on), and dropped whatever it was into the bag. It happened swiftly and seamlessly, but Hugh was left with that uncomfortable feeling of having witnessed something he ought not, something of significance, the meaning of which entirely escaped him.

"Christ. It's Vannessa Hunt!" Sarah dived behind the folds of menu. Hugh looked around, the sculpture was returning to the table. A little uncertainly as far as Hugh could make out, which wasn't very far.

"You know her?"

"Yes, it's Roger Hunt's missus," came from behind the Starters.

"What, you mean your mother's partner, at the Lab?"

"Yes, pea-brain. Don't talk so loud."

"It's alright, they're going."

Sarah slid down her chair and underneath the table as the pair walked past them.

"They've gone." Sarah slowly emerged.

"Why didn't you want her to see you?"

"Too embarrassing for words. Like catching someone with her knickers down. I mean he was hardly favourite nephew, was he?"

"Sal, you won't .. I mean, you're not going to mention it in the paper, are you?".

"No. Credit me with a bit of female solidarity."

Hugh felt a rush of pride, like a mother hen with her favourite chick.

"Anyway, since his wife went off with the builder, our editor's gone right off infidelity stories."

"I didn't touch your damned experiment, Roger! I haven't been near that lab," Judith really was not in the mood for this. She had work of her own to do, an experiment that needed hourly monitoring if it were to have any chance of working this time. Roger had just flown back from a three-day trip to Geneva and his first words had been far from welcoming.

"What the hell's been going on while I've been away?" She had at first thought he had seen the local paper, had read that ridiculous article of Sarah's. She'd been about to utter a disclaimer, she had no maternal authority over her daughter at all. But he had not seen it. With any luck he never would. Roger read nothing but the Telegraph and a quantity of scientific journals. The whole thing would be forgotten in a day or so. No, the cause of Roger's wrath was of a different and wholly inexplicable origin as far as she was concerned.

"I'm not saying you did touch anything, but you're the only other person at the lab with keys to that part of the building."

"Are you calling me a liar?"

"All I'm saying is you must have left your keys around and .."

"I keep them on me all the time. What about you? Maybe you left your keys around? Where did you leave them while you were away?"

"At home."

"Well then."

"What do you mean, well then?"

"They were out of your sight. Mine were never out of my sight."

There was a pause, a temporary lull in the firing. Roger pulled at the ends of his moustache, a thin, gingery affair that matched the sparseness of his hair. He was a fussy little man, obsessed with detail, Judith reflected. Yet he was one hell of a businessman. It was almost entirely due to his grasp of the market that they'd been able to attract so much in the way of finance from the industry. Roger always seemed to know a few years ahead what would be flavour of the month in the genetics world. He had prophesised years ago the present frenzied race to map the human genome. In addition, he had a way of putting across an idea that made it sound apocalyptic. The Hunt lab had an international reputation for quality and a keen eye to the future. Money put into the Hunt was a gilt-edged investment in the twenty-first century, as their new, glossy brochure told you. The problem had been, lately, the money just wasn't coming in. If only, Roger had said, she could drop her Hewitts project, just for a short time (he had added quickly, forestalling her objections), let them get a contract for some really "sexy" research under their belt. But she could not hear of that. Time was of the essence. If she allowed herself to be distracted now she would never get there. But the money ...? Something would turn up. Roger was so good with the money. He would come up with something.

"Are you sure the keys were never out of your possession? Even for just an hour?"

"Not for a second! Look, perhaps they broke in, through the lav window or something."

"There's no sign of a break-in. And, anyway, they would have had to disconnect the alarm first."

Which was true enough.

"What's been taken?"

"Nothing."

"Then for goodness …"

"But things have been moved."

"What things?"

"The stool. I left it flush with the bench."

"Roger, you've been away for three days. How can you remember the exact position of a stool?" But, of course, he could. It was just the sort of detail he did remember. She had to admit that Roger, being the supreme perfectionist he was, would not be mistaken about a thing like that. And, if someone had got into a locked lab, that someone had presumably been up to no good. Furthermore, that someone may well enter again and do some damage. And, next time, it may be to one of her experiments. Not that she wasn't concerned about Roger's of course.

"We'd better have a word with Maurice. He might have seen someone hanging round. Anyway, what happened in Geneva? You haven't told me."

"Well, I had the meeting with Van Dreyden."

"And?"

"He had two proposals. There's a big job he could offer us if we had the extra lab and manpower." Meaning if she set aside her own research for a while.

"And the other one?"

"The money's not nearly so good."

"But it's money nevertheless."

"It would help, I suppose," he sighed, already sensing defeat.

"And we *might* be able to attract other funding to it." But he was not keen, she could tell.

"What's the project?", she prompted.

"Well, it's a novel one. I'll say that."

"A rare disease?"

"No, not rare. As for disease, well … I'd always considered it to be a psychological, rather than genetic defect."

He was infuriating.

"Roger, what is the project?"

"To find the genes responsible for sexual deviancy. Apparently they've already found the gay male one. He wants us to find the one that causes lesbianism."

"For heaven's sake why? No one's died from it yet. And, anyway, surely there are other behavioural abnormalities far more important."

"Not for him. Van Leyden's daughter's a lesbian and doesn't keep quiet about it. Bit embarrassing for a pillar of the Lutheran church, wouldn't you say? He's got a lot of money and he's willing to spend some of it stamping out the cause of his embarrassment."

Chapter Four

"Dear God, it has been brought to our notice that there are people not three miles from this very church, who, in their wickedness, have appropriated for themselves powers which belong only to You." Here the Reverend Beamish passed a tongue across his lips as though savouring the combined attention of two hundred souls.

The church was packed, which was unheard of for a Monday teatime service. They had come from miles around with troubled minds. They had come for guidance, for a sign from God, through him, that something would be done about this Evil in their midst.

"People who have taken upon themselves powers invested in You alone, Oh Lord. The power to give Life. And to take it away. In this kingdom that is legal .."

"Shame!" called old Mrs Beaver from her pew at the front.

"As you say, sister – Shame! But in God's Kingdom it is not permissible. Are we to stand aside and allow his kingdom to be violated?"

The question was rhetorical, but an answering "NO" rippled through the assembly like wind through swathes of corn. The Reverend Beamish heard it with satisfaction, knowing he had only to reap and gather in.

"Or are we going to do something about it?"

They had left Maurice at eleven, according to the Fifties wooden clock on his mantlepiece. Five hours and four visits later, Jo stood with Cynthia looking into the window of the pet shop. They had had bitterly strong coffee and sugary marzipan things from an ancient old woman with a German accent whose body was bent almost into a right angle. She had shown them photographs of strapping blonde young women striding along with rucksacks on their backs, amidst snowcapped mountains.

"That's me, there," she stabbed a misshapen finger into the centre of the picture and Jo looked in amazement from the upright young Amazon to the twisted old body beside her.

"Ya, I was different then."

Not half, thought Jo.

"That was before."

"Before what?" Jo had asked curiously.

"Life."

They had moved on then to "Mag's place", where three under-fives had immediately converged on Cynthia, pulling at her clothes, her arms, her legs. She had responded with laughter and tickling and the kind of cornflake packet jokes that sent them all into screaming giggles and, watching them, Jo had experienced that familiar envy, that longing for family. As the four sprawled across the floor, Jo had sat stiffly on the sofa with Mags who was as thin as a stick, who smoked her cigarettes down to the filter and said she was twenty five but looked forty.

"Don't ever have kids," she had told Jo, "they eat your life away." And Jo had looked from the fleshless woman to the fat children, while Mags smoked and drank cup after cup of milky, sugary tea.

And so they had continued Cynthia's social round. Cynthia was a familiar figure in the neighbourhood. Everybody seemed to know her. And, what's more, accept her. And Jo, through Cynthia, was accepted too. "My friend, Jo," Cynthia had said possessively and it was almost as if, in belonging to Cynthia she had belonged to that community. There had been the time when they had gone into the sweet shop for Cynthia's favourite bar of Toblerone and the people there had been agog with some story about a monster baby in a wood and some Jekyll and Hyde scientists who'd created it.

"They shouldn't be allowed to do those sorts of experiments," one had said.

"No one knows what goes on in there," said another.

"I know," Cynthia had piped up. "I been in there. I seen those experiments!". And everybody had laughed. That was Cynthia for you.

"I have! I seen them wicked experiments!"

"I believe you, thousands wouldn't," said the tobac-

21

conist with a wink at Jo.

Now the two of them stood with their faces pressed against the glass of the pet shop window as they stared at a cageful of fluffy white kittens.

"I want a little kitten or a little puppy or budgie or a hamster …"

"Make up your mind," said Jo, amused.

"I don't care, I just want a little pet to cuddle."

"Why don't you ask your mum if you can have one?"

"No", Cynthia put her arms across her chest and hugged herself, bent inwards, as though nursing a pain.

"She won't let me. Not after Tommy."

"Who's Tommy?"

A tear started down Cynthia's cheek. "My baby mouse, I was stroking him and he kept trying to wriggle out of my hand. I didn't mean to hurt him. He was my baby. I loved him."

The tears fell thick and fast now.

"Then he stopped wriggling and went all cold and mummy took him away and I didn't see him again."

Jo led her away from the shop, wordlessly. What could you say?

"I gotta go now."

"No," Cynthia caught at her arm, "don't go! Come and see my mum. She's nice. She finishes work in a minute. What's the time?" Cynthia held out a chubby arm with a gold watch strapped to it.

"Four o'clock."

"She works in a bakery. She'll give us cornish pasties. Yummy."

But Jo's stomach, unused to such plentiful rations as she'd consumed today, was feeling bloated. Also, in her experience, mothers were a nosey lot. There would be questions. Who's your friend? Where's she from? What's she doing round here? No, it was easier to move on. It was always easier to move on. Besides, she had things to do.

"No, I gotta go now."

"I'll see you tomorrow."

"Maybe."

"Please. You're my friend." Cynthia held onto her hand tightly. "I live at 57 Holmes Park Crescent. Promise you'll come. Please."

"Yeah, alright. Or I'll see you in the park. One or the other."

And they left it at that. Cynthia standing smilingly waving her on her way.

"One or the other," she had repeated.

"Yeah," Jo had called back, having no intention of doing either. It was time to move on, in search of the sea, in search of that memory.

Chapter Five

"Ssshh!"

"I'm not saying anything."

"You sound like a stampeding herd of elephants, crashing through the undergrowth like that."

"I can't help .. ouch!"

"Sshh!"

"Those roses just clouted me one!"

"Do stop whining, Hugh!"

Hugh leant against a tree and dabbed gingerly at his
cheek with a handkerchief. He felt quite sure he must be
haemorrhaging fatally. He had had more than enough
already and they'd only just started. He had unravelled a
mile or so of wool from his jersey, squeezing through a
miniscule hole in the fence. His socks and trouser bot-
toms were wringing wet from wading through the dew-
soaked grass and now his face was gashed to the bone
and he would probably be scarred for life. But worst of
all was the thought of being caught hiding in the grounds
of the Hunt Laboratory! The repercussions were just too
awful to contemplate! At least a public reprimand from
the Law Society.

"Dont breathe so loudly!"

"Sarah, I can't stop breathing. I refuse to stop breathing, even for you!"

Well, he was only staying till midnight and that was
flat. He had managed to talk her out of a break-in, thank
God, but she had still insisted they case the joint, see if
there was any after-hours activity going on, that sort of
thing. Total waste of time, but there it was. Luckily the
night was mild and he had had the foresight to bring a
groundsheet and the car blanket, as well as a little snack,
in the shape of a few cold cuts and a bottle. As he spread
out the groundsheet he began to cheer up slightly.
Perhaps it wouldn't be too bad after all, cuddled up
together against the chill vagaries of a September night.
Things could get quite cosy, especially with a glass or
two of very drinkable Côtes inside them.

"Did you hear that?"

"What?"

"Sshh! Listen!"

Hugh sshhed. Hugh listened. There was a steady hum of traffic from the main trunk road a quarter of a mile away. High above them a jet was making its noisy way to or from Gatwick.

"I can only hear .."

"Sshh!" It was a hiss. Then he heard it. The snap of a twig, then another, twenty or so yards away. His heart seemed to take on the propensities of a big bass drum. Boom boom boom, the noise of it was deafening.

He had often imagined a moment like this in the fantasies he had about Sarah. She would cry out, a tiny, vulnerable sound, heard only by him. He would move close, assertively, protectively, between her and the danger. It had been very pleasant, very reassuring, but a total fantasy. For now he found himself riveted to the spot. Visions of dragons, demons and monsters rose into his consciousness from the depths of childhood nightmare. There they were again, the footsteps. And now the sound of something being dragged, something heavy, something that resisted the clutch of bush and thicket. A torch light flickered uncertainly around the edge of the building and went out. The step again. The dragging. Suddenly from a place directly above him came a high-pitched scream, a scream of pure terror. It froze his blood. It stopped his breath. Bewildered, he looked up into the trees. There was nothing there.

"Hugh! Shut up for Christ's sake!"

What was she talking about? Why was she blaming him? A heavy, smarting blow landed on his cheek. The screaming stopped. And now a silence around them, followed by the footsteps again, this time running, crashing through low bush, over gravel, away from them. Their sound died away. And now Sarah was moving away from him, around the corner of the building, Suddenly he knew he did not want to be alone. He followed her. She was crouching beside a large bundle on the gravel path.

"Sal, what is it? What .. what's in that sack?"

25

Her voice was flat and seemed to come from a long way away.

"It's not a sack, Hugh. It's a woman. Or it was."

Malcolm Beamish enjoyed keeping his family guessing. About everything. Particularly the hour and the day, often even the week of his arrival. He was always unexpected and that's how he liked to keep it. It was all so sweet — the half-moment of surprise and puzzlement on his father's face, followed by the expression of pleasure that began in the eyes and travelled via wrinkle and line through the heavy jowls, to a broadening smile on the lips. His father would stretch out his arm in a gesture of benediction. It should have been painted. It probably was, had Malcolm been more au fait with the arts. The elder son, returning home, receives his father's blessing. His mother's face? Now that was a different matter. It registered an immediate and profound dismay before the voluntary processes began their efforts to wrestle it into something resembling a travesty of maternal affection. As for his brother, there was no ambivalence there, no attempt to hide the true feelings. Yes, the old alliances. Some things never changed.

"Did you fly in this afternoon?"

"Yes," Malcolm lied with ease, handing his father the inevitable bottle of duty-free Scotch and his mother the perfume she never wore. His brother's present he would save till later. They had eaten, the dishes shared mainly between him and his father, his mother and brother scarcely touching the food before them. He had lingered over a third helping of apple charlotte, keeping his mother hovering, his brother pinned to the chair. No one was allowed to depart till all had finished eating, that was the rule of their childhood.

"And how is it out there?" his father lit his pipe at last, the table cleared. Malcolm watched his brother skittle from the room like a timid doe.

"It's beginning to wake up, at long last."

"How so?" His father puffed a dense cloud into the air and his countenance was serious. He always gravely

26

heeded the views of his eldest son and Malcolm was flattered by the rapt attention of a man whom everyone else
listened to.

"All this liberalism of the last few years. That's disap-
pearing, and not before time. If they'd left it much longer
they'd have been overrun. They'd end up strangers in
their own country."

"Amidst the alien corn?" The man of God nodded and
tapped his pipe.

Ian climbed feverishly into his pyjamas. In bed, with
his light out, he could feign sleep. His fingers slipped
over the cord around his belly, pulling roughly on the
cotton tie, fumbling the knot. Never mind. Hold them up
till he got into bed. He snapped off the light. Darkness.
One knee in the bed, the covers drawn back, he halted.
The door. Had he bolted the door? He felt for the switch
of the bedside lamp. Blinking in the light, he made
towards the door. It opened.

"Hello, little brother."

"I'm going to bed."

"Good idea," Malcolm's hand reached out lazily
towards his chest and, as if by accident, the fingers slid
over his nipple.

"Very good idea."

Quickly Ian turned and dived towards the bed but the
hand was quicker still, stronger. It pushed him forward
against the dressing table. Looking up wildly, he saw his
brother's face in the mirror. That terrible grinning face.

"I've got you a present, baby. Look."

His brother held out a bright red lipstick, unsheathed it
and slashed the red wax twice across his lips. The top lip,
the bottom lip. Gashed blood red.

He wanted to be sick, to vomit out this moment and
the moments upon moments to come.

"Please don't!"

But his pyjama trousers were pulled away. The awful
pause, and then the pain, driving up him through his
bowels, his belly. In the mirror the two red gashes swam
into one terrible wound as the tears filled his eyes.

Chapter Six

"Come on, Cynthia!" Jo sat huddled on the park bench, shivering in a thin, misty drizzle. Last night she had set her course for the sea but, for some reason, although only those last few miles remained between her and her goal, she had been unable to continue. She was tired, she had told herself. All that unaccustomed socialising. People took away your energy more completely than anything else. She needed rest. But it wasn't that really. She had scarcely slept all night. No, when it had actuallly come to it, she had found in herself a marked reluctance to leave this place. Not that it was anywhere special. It was pretty dreary really. Looking at it from the outside. But that's not the way she had looked at it. For once she had been on the inside. And it was sweet. With Cynthia, trailing all day in the other girl's wake, she had, by proxy, experienced what it was like to be in a community, surrounded by people who knew you, who had known you for many days and weeks and years and who would go on knowing and accepting you through many more. All day, around her, had been laughter and companionship. Come evening, when she should have been moving on, the thought of her solitary journey to the sea had aroused not yearning but a sense of desolation. She didn't know what was happening to her. And so she had decided to stay another day.

Now she was impatient, wanted Cynthia to come immediately. If she didn't show, should Jo go to her house? 57 Holmes Park Crescent, the address had lodged itself in her brain. Yes, why not? Of course, Cynthia was waiting for her there. She should go straight away. But doubts began to creep in, cold companions of the chill wind that poked through the holes of her thin parka. Suppose Cynthia had forgotten her already? She wasn't normal, was she? Who knows what goes on in the minds of people like that? Suppose Jo did go to her house, who was to say Cynthia would even recognise her? Jo suddenly felt an anger flare inside her. To be taken up and dropped as soon as hope was kindled, it was the story of her life. Serve her right for falling for it all over again. She got up. Fuck 'em all. Who needs them? It was time to move on.

Suddenly a figure appeared through the park gate. Cynthia. At last! But no, it was a man with a dog. She recognised him from the day before. He had been in the sweet shop, buying an evening paper, had exchanged a joke with her and Cynthia. She waved and called a greeting to him now. That's what you did if you were local, didn't you? The man stopped, open-mouthed, and stared at her. It wasn't that odd, was it? To be sitting in a park in the rain? Didn't normal people do that sort of thing? The man began to back off, toward the gate, pulling at his dog, still staring at her. She stood still, not knowing what to do. Frightened suddenly. Was she such a freak after all? What was the matter, for God's sake?

At the gate the man shouted, "I don't know how you dare, after what you done. I'm getting the police!", and with that he was gone. The police? Jo turned on her heel and ran. Ran faster than she'd ever run in her life.

Chapter Seven

It was above a grocery store. The kind with unhappy piles of wrinkled peppers and withered grapes outside, untouched and unwanted because a new supermarket has just happened half a mile away. The street sign for Windsor Avenue had been broken off just after the 'Ave' and a 'Gr' graffitied in front of it. Vanessa Hunt decided she would not quarrel with the correction. The street had that air of neglect, of a recent abandonment because something better, or worse, had turned up. Recession, she supposed. The holiday letting agencies had moved on, the first-timers been repossessed, leaving empty houses boarded up, with the occasional squat triumphing in between. It was a place where people routinely lost their daily skirmish with poverty.

Bob's Newsagent was a dim, joyless cave that smelt of damp and sour milk and Bob himself had scarcely been able to summon the energy to reply to her question.

"Down the road. Hundred yards," he'd eventually muttered.

She had driven the short distance and opened the door of her Volvo estate onto a welcome mat of broken glass and an old car tyre.

Number 33b sported a weather-stained plaque announcing "Sam Carter Enquiry Agent – Private and Commercial". She stared at the door. It cried out for a coat of paint. A cry that she guessed would go unheeded. She reminded herself that this was the kind of joint she'd been after. Up-market firms asked too many questions. For a seedy business you needed a seedy set-up. And she'd certainly found one here. She pressed the buzzer.

The woman was at least five eleven and overweight. She had a haircut that badly needed a shape, any shape. Light grey chinos were topped by a black silk shirt. The gear was alright, but twenty pounds of redundant flesh strained at the seams. Vanessa winced. She spent a lot of time and money eradicating her own extra flesh.

"I've come to see Sam Carter," Vanessa tried to sound crisp and businesslike.

"Come up," a grunt. No smile. No social skills at all. None of the little niceties that protected you from the unbearable impact of others. She wanted to turn and run. Instead she followed the woman up the carpetless stairs, stilling her fears as she did so by wondering what role she had in the firm. It was either that or trying to guess the original colour and design of the wallpaper. She didn't look like a secretary and it seemed unlikely that Carter, judging by the state of his decor, could even run to one. Wife, maybe? Though, once again, she didn't look the type. Green, she estimated, with an unbelievably awful rose pattern! She steadfastly turned her mind away from both woman and wallpaper and entered the room at the top of the stairs.

It was unexpectedly rather pleasant, though in need of a good clean. Vanessa, who had 'a woman' in twice a week, was quite fastidious about things like that. The dove grey walls held a series of maps of Britain and a bookcase complete with a set of bound law books. So far so good. A large wooden desk in front of the window gave an air of professionalism that was immediately offset by the mess on top of it. Folders, papers, news cuttings, used envelopes and a few cans of soft drinks littered the surface. Following Vanessa's gaze, the woman simply scooped the contents off the desk and into the top drawer of a filing cabinet.

"Gives a whole new meaning to the word 'filing'," Vanessa joked. The woman grinned. It was a wide, attractive grin and gave a sparkle to her eyes.

"Milk and sugar?"

Vanessa became aware of a pleasurable sensation in her nostrils and looked in the direction of its cause. A steaming pot of fresh coffee.

"Neither, thanks."

The woman brought the cups and lowered her bulk into the big swivel chair behind the desk. There was a pause.

"You're going to tell me I should have made an

31

appointment, aren't you?"

"Uh-uh," the woman sipped her coffee.

"But I can see he's out," reasoned Vanessa, beginning to feel irritated.

"Who?"

"The man .. your boss, whoever. Sam Carter."

The woman made a noise like drains in trouble. The brown eyes gazed thoughtfully at Vanessa as she leant back in her chair and swivelled slowly from side to side.

"I'm Sam Carter," she said at last.

Chapter Eight

Sam had lain in bed that morning, watching the early sun rounding the corner of the big bay window. Each morning it came a little later now, signalling the approach of autumn, the dying of the year. Autumn – season of alcoholic mists and fruitlessness! Or had been for her these last few years. But this autumn was going to be different. This autumn her first waking thoughts had not been of Julia. Not quite, anyway. Perhaps, after all, there were still pleasures to be had in this life and she would rediscover them one day. Meanwhile, she was going to have to get her life into some semblance of order. The weight thing for starters. Well, knocking off the booze would help that one. But exercise, too, was called for she suspected. She groaned and snuggled a little deeper into the duvet.

And then there was the work. Oh, she was getting enough of it, but did she really want to deliver writs for the rest of her life? Be screamed at? Called "fucking bitch" and "cunt" and the rest? But writs had been all she could get this last eighteen months. You could lose a reputation fast in this business and after Julia had decamped, she'd lost it. Fast. She'd discovered downward mobility. It was swift and bottomless. Or almost. She had gone down almost as far as Australia and wouldn't recommend it. But coming back up, that was another matter. She was going to need help. Plenty people owed her and maybe now was the time to collect.

Yes, work. That's what she'd concentrate on. Yesterday she'd had her first proper client in a long time. The writs didn't count. They never looked at the walls, weren't interested in the state of your office, only in your ability to get past a slammed door and half a ton of Rottweiler. But Vanessa Hunt – she was different. The perfume preceded her by a good twenty yards and the rest, when it came, made quite an impact too. Her coat was the kind you saw in shop windows without a price. Presumably to save you a cardiac arrest. Her hair was auburn, with the kind of healthy sheen that cost a lot.

"I want a man followed," she had begun. Nice opening. Dramatic. "By car or on foot?"

"Whichever he's using at the time of course."

"It's possible to tail someone for two miles in a car and that's the limit."

"They do it in the movies."

"Then go see a film director not a detective."

"And on foot?"

"People do a lot of things on foot. They go to the bank. They do their shopping. They walk the dog, but mostly they sit at home or in their office for hours at a time."

"I know that."

"What I'm trying to say is that it can come very expensive, with very little result."

"I need to know who this man is, so anything he does, anywhere he goes will be of interest to me. OK?"

OK, thought Sam, it's your money, as she scrabbled for a pen that worked.

"Got a photograph?"

"No, but I can describe him from head to foot. In every detail."

"So you know him?" Sam tried three broken biros and rummaged in the drawer for a spare. What had happened to all the stationery? Had the mice eaten it?

"Oh, I know him intimately ... do you want to borrow this?" Vanessa drew a heavy platinum Parker from her bag and held it out.

"No, no," Sam triumphantly seized a green biro from its cunning hiding place under the desk.

"... But I don't know him at all."

"Sure, I know the feeling. OK, fire away."

"He's about twenty five, a little over six foot, muscular build, broad-shouldered, short blonde hair, blue eyes, clean-shaven, though sometimes he has a five o'clock shadow"

"Like at five o'clock?" Sam grinned. The woman ignored her.

"Just incredibly attractive really. People notice him in a crowd. Women, anyway. He's the sort of real man every woman wants, if you know what I mean?" Sam, who had

34

never wanted a man in her life, real or otherwise, merely nodded.

"His name?"

"Richard." Sam looked up expectantly. Vanessa shrugged. "Just Richard."

"You never asked his surname?"

"It never came up."

"And no address, I presume?"

"No," she lit a cigarette.

"You meet at your place?"

"Good God, no! An hotel." So some people really did say 'an' before hotel. You lived and learned.

"How long have you known him?"

"About six months."

"And you don't know anything about him?" Sam tried to keep the incredulity out of her voice. So this is what heterosexuality's like?

"Anonymity gives sex a certain frisson, don't you think?"

"The first couple of times it could, but maybe I'm just curious by nature."

Vanessa Hunt blew smoke rings thoughtfully in the air.

"Mm. You see, he's away a lot."

"On business?"

"Who knows?"

Sam studied her notes and swallowed a mouthful of coffee. This could end up being more trouble than it was worth.

"When will you see him again?"

"He'll leave the hotel around five thirty tomorrow afternoon. I want to know where he goes from there. It's ... it's not another woman." Incredibly the sang froid slipped momentarily and she seemed embarrassed.

"It's none of my business what ... "

"It's just that he may have ... borrowed some keys from me. Keys to my husband's laboratory. I lost them for a day or so."

"When Richard was around?"

"Yes. My husband's anxious because he suspects someone was in the lab, someone unauthorised."

35

"And you think it was young Richard?"

"I'd say there was a possibility, at least," Vanessa Hunt arched an elegant pair of eyebrows quizzically at Sam, opened her bag and drew out a Coutts cheque book.

"What are you worth?" Well, put like that ...

Sam had quoted twice her usual fee and been handed it without a murmur. Fingering the cheque after Vanessa's departure, she had felt a slight pang of conscience. But that had been quickly stilled by the smell of perfume that lingered in the air twenty minutes later. It was the kind that came in treble figures an ounce. In which case, Sam's fee was but a dab behind the ear. She would use it to re-decorate the office. It would be a first, symbolic, step to getting proper work again. To getting back to the way things used to be, with the phone ringing all the time ... clients, friends. The phone rang.

She couldn't place the voice at first. It had been a long time. Jenny? Of course, she'd been a colleague of Julia's from the Help Line days. She had an adopted daughter with learning difficulties. Nice kid. What was her name? Celia, or something. Jenny had been desperate to adopt. The authorities weren't having any of it. Lesbian adoption was definitely not on their agenda. If there was a child in need of a home it would have to wait for a real family to come along, not a pretend one. But then they discovered they had a quantity of disabled children on their hands and not enough families, of the real variety, who wanted them, so the goalposts shifted and Jenny got her child. Suddenly it seemed a good idea to pair lesbians with disabled kids, as though the two deserved one another. Julia had had bitter rows with her about this. Didn't Jenny see that she was acquiescing in a social policy that was, by definition, oppressive to both parties? Jenny did not and Sam had had to agree with her. She was giving the kid a home, wasn't she? That's what mattered. Julia and Jenny had stopped communicating then. That must be over six years ago.

"Hi, how are you? And ... Cynthia?" That was her name.

"Sam, Cynthia's dead. Somebody killed her. Last night."

36

The voice had been drowned in sobs after that. It had been impossible to get the whole story. Yes, of course Sam would come. She would do anything she could. That's what old friends were for. No, not as a friend, Jenny insisted. She wanted Sam's professional help. Murder was a little bit out of her class, Sam reasoned gently. The police would be dealing with it. Yes, the police were there now, but Jenny wanted someone she knew, someone she could trust. Another dyke, for God's sake! So Sam promised she would go round that afternoon, as soon as the police had finished. She put the phone down.

It rang again. This time it was Vanessa Hunt. There was more than a hint of anxiety in her voice, but it still managed to ripple down the wires like golden syrup.

"Sam, there's been a development."

"Richard?"

"No-oh," but doubt treacled it's way into the receiver.

"There's been a murder in the grounds of my husband's laboratory." Two murders in the space of as many minutes. This wasn't quite what Sam had had in mind when she had wished for a better quality of work.

"Uh-huh?"

"But I'm sure there's no connection." Sam was way behind.

"Connection?"

"It's just a coincidence, that's all." Sam heard her take a long breath, accompanied, she guessed, by a lungful of tobacco smoke. "You think there's a connection between the murder and the break-in?"

"No. I'm sure there isn't." But she said it too hurriedly. There was a pause.

"It'a just that ... look, I want a guarantee that whatever you find out you don't tell the police. I want to be kept right out of it, you understand?"

"I understand."

"Good."

"But I can't oblige, I'm afraid. If I find out Richard's involved in a murder I have to report it to the police."

"In that case the contract's cancelled."

"I'll send back the cheque."

"Forget it. Buy yourself an exercise bike." And the phone went dead.

Chapter Nine

"Thank God that's over!" Hugh flung himself into the passenger seat of Sarah's Triumph, wrapped in ignominy and a badly crumpled mackintosh.

"It was the very worst night of my life! Seat belt, Sal."

Sarah ignored him and turned the key savagely in the ignition. To Hugh's infinite relief the engine roared instantly to life. With a clash of gears and to the accompaniment of a chorus of horns, the car leapt from the kerbside and into a steady stream of traffic. Hugh shut his eyes. The scenes of the night before blazed across his closed lids with all the vivid clarity of detail the mind bestows on unwelcome memories. If only life had a magic marker to erase those scenes and his own, yes, he had to admit it, utterly ignominious part in them.

There had been the screaming, brought on by an hysteria that had grabbed him by the throat at the merest whiff of danger. Humiliating enough. Then that appalling discovery of the body. He had never seen death before, least of all violent death and there it was, like a broken doll on the path. Then there had been the old man, the caretaker, clutching at him, at his collar, choking him, dragging him, shouting about the police as though he, Hugh, had been the perpetrator of that awful crime. And all the time the tears rolling down the old man's cheeks, into his mouth, onto his neck till his pyjamas were sodden with them.

Then had come the police. With all the commotion there had been no time to collect up their belongings, stow them in the car. Yes, officer, he realised he had been breaking the law, trespassing on private property. The reason? It was quite simple, he had been helping do a spot of investigative journalism. And how did he explain the presence of the car rug and the picnic hamper? Oh, it was all so unutterably embarassing. He felt like a silly schoolboy discovered in the middle of a midnight feast that had gone terribly wrong. Until, that is, he had caught the look that had passed between his interrogator and the man in the abominable blue suit. With a jolting, double-somersaulting swallow dive of his insides, Hugh realised that, unbelievable as it may seem, he was actually under suspicion. He, Hugh Manders, junior partner of Manders, Cape and Manders of Hove.

"Look here ..." he had begun. At least he thought it was him. Only his voice had risen an octave or two and had all the solidity and authority of a babbling brook.

The questioning had continued intermittently throughout the night. In the intervals between he had been locked in a tiny cell, with only a thin blanket, (not his own), for warmth. He had been unable to sleep but had paced up and down the narrow concrete square between bed and wall in his stockinged feet. For, the laces having been removed from them, his shoes slid irrevocably from their occupant's possession. Fear ate at his bowels and he had constantly to relieve himself into the foul-smelling latrine in the corner of his cell. In keeping with his class and his aspirations, he had, until now, always considered the police his natural allies, the necessary buffer between him and that vaguely-perceived but dangerous world where lurked the delinquent, the dispossessed and the damned. He had never, save for the occasional incidence of speeding, been on the wrong side of the law before and he found the experience terrifying.

Eventually, somewhere through that interminable night, the questioning became a shade less persistent, the approach more open, the looks a little friendlier, if still downright puzzled. At 10am the blue suit, looking somewhat the worse for wear, faced him across the desk. This time the tape recorder was not switched on.

"Well, Mr Manders, we're satisfied that neither you nor Miss Ginsberg had anything to do with the murder of Cynthia Fenton last night," the voice was heavy with weariness, but the eyes, though bloodshot, were still alert.

"And you'll be pleased to hear we won't be prosecuting you for trespassing."

"Oh thank you. Thank you very much. I ..."

The voice continued as if he had said nothing.

".. But what you did was very very silly." Hugh felt ten years old.

"You've wasted valuable police time checking your stories that could have been spent looking for the murderer."

Well, that was hardly his fault if they got the wrong man. Hadn't he spent half the night telling them just that very thing. Hugh stared at the desk in silence. If he kept very very still he might yet escape a caning.

"You can go now, but don't get under our feet again, you understand?"

"Yes. I won't. Thank you."

And they had let him go. Ignominy. That was the only word for it. But it was not just the fear and the humiliation, excruciating though both were. His whole sense of self, of his stature and position, of his place in the world, had suffered a blow, a fracture of such seismological proportion that the shock of it continued to reverberate through his entire being. For the first time in his life Hugh Manders had felt the shifting of tectonic plates and the sensation was not a comfortable one.

"What did they do to you, Sal?" he asked gently. "Did you get the third degree too?"

She did not answer. He looked across at the pale, grim face, the whitened knuckles around the steering wheel. Loyally he pushed back a wee small voice that whispered it had all been her fault. The undignified arrest, the frightening imprisonment, the none-too-polite interrogation, the whole awful night of helplessness and sleeplessness had been entirely due to the pig-headed vendetta she waged against her mother. Oh, but she looked so young and vulnerable. Had they broken that proud spirit? A very small and utterly detestable part of him wished terribly that they had, that he were not the only one to have crawled and pleaded. He quickly squashed the renegade thought before it could see the light of day. Had he not been hampered by his seat belt and were she not negotiating, (if so inoffensive a word could be applied to so violent an activity), a bend at that very moment, he would have taken her small frame into his arms and hugged away the horror they had both been through.

41

With a scream of brake lining and some irate hooting from behind them, the Triumph swung into the kerb and lurched to an abrupt halt. Sarah jumped out.

"Where are you ...?," but she was gone, to emerge a minute later from a tobacconist shop, a copy of the Brighton Herald in her hand.

"Shit!," she delivered a kick to the front tyre.

"Sodding shit!," she dashed a patent leather toe against the chrome of the hub cap.

"Sal, what's the matter?"

"That dickhead Don's got the story. It's not fair. I found the body. It's mine by rights. What am I going to say to my editor?"

"Tell him you're sorry, but there wasn't a fax machine in your cell."

"It's not funny. Stop laughing at me." Incredibly, her eyes were bright with what looked horribly like tears. Sal, crying?

The test-driven in Death Valley, toughened tungsten radial received another clout from Sarah's boot and, with a deprecatory sigh of decompression, expelled a long column of air.

"Oh, that's all we need! That's bloody typical! That's just ... just ..," and this time the tears flowed, long, glistening rivulets of them. She crumpled over the bonnet.

Hugh clambered out of the car and rushed to her side.

"Oh Sal! Oh love," and in the midst of the clamour and confusion and car fumes of downtown Brighton, he held her in his arms, safe. His heart had wings.

"You poor old thing! It's been a terrible strain and you haven't slept a wink I bet. Your nerves are shot. It's alright, we're out now."

He stroked the soft brown hair tenderly.

"We're free. Because we told the truth and stuck to it and they believed us at last."

"Oh, don't be a dipstick, Hugh!" She pulled roughly away from him and rubbed a hand across her eyes.

"We're free because my mother got us out. It's her we have to thank. My bloody bloody mother!"

Chapter Ten

Jo leant on the iron railings of a church. Her breath came in long, painful, sawing gasps. Her chest ached. Sweat slid between her skin and the thin cotton of her shirt and jeans. She must have run for at least two miles. Fleeing the park, she had navigated a way through the bleak suburban landscape, instinct finding her the less-frequented walkways, the shortcuts via wasteland, playing fields and factory outbuildings. She had kept the main trunk road some two to three hundred yards to her left, hearing the rumble of fast lorries, the occasional siren. Police.

What had the man meant? He said he was getting the police, "after what you done." What had she done? If only she could remember. Lodging it in memory would be a safeguard against her inadvertently doing it again. For to have committed a crime of such enormity and not to know about it meant that at any time and in any place, she would be capable ... of what? What unspeakable transgression? Her head pounded. In spite of her sweat and the warm September sunshine she shivered, her teeth chattering uncontrollably. A passerby, an elderly woman with a tartan shopping trolley in tow, gave her a curious look. She felt conspicuous. She would walk, as others did. She looked about her at the passersby. Some walked quickly, their heads pushed forward, already anticipating their destination, some pulled impatiently at dogs or dawdling children, while others ambled by, staring into shop windows or eying their fellow pedestrians as though seeking something, anything at which to direct their restless attention. So, there was no one way to walk, no one pace or stride or attitude that was normal. That was good. Or was it? Did it, perhaps, simply leave more scope for error.

Ahead was a main street, cafes, shops, on one side a garage and a giant new Sainsbury, on the other a cemetery that seemed to stretch the length of the hillside. So this was Brighton. Still no sign of the sea. She walked unsteadily down the street. Nobody spared her a glance.

She pulled her parka closer about her. Through a tear by the bottom of the zip some stuffing was leaking out.

The smell of greasy food hit her, causing a rush of saliva to her mouth and a spasm of longing to her stomach. It seemed a long time since the last of their snacks yesterday afternoon, when she and Cynthia had divided the Toblerone scrupulously into two, one chunk at a time, each waiting for the other to finish a portion before going onto the next. Cynthia. She seemed a million miles away. She, Jo, had done something wrong, something unforgiveable, she did not know what. But Cynthia knew, as did all her friends. And they had banished her, would get the police should she ever return. Well, she didn't need them. Didn't need anybody.

"Sausages, bacon, egg, two fried slice and tea – £2.00," read the sign in the window. It might as well have said two hundred pounds. She put her nose to the steaming pane. A man got up from the table by the window, leaving a barely-touched plate. In a pool of bright red tomato ketchup lay a half-submerged sausage, the yellow sphere of congealed egg yolk, a whole rasher of bacon, its flesh already greying. Jo salivated. It was but two tantalising, unreachable feet through the glass. Her eye caught the front page of a tabloid that lay tossed on the formica beside the abandoned plate. Ice skewered her brain. She was going round the twist. She must be. For there was Cynthia's face on the front page. Beside the photograph, in thick, black, accusatory letters a mile high was the single word, "Murdered".

The police had finally departed Jenny Fenton's squat council bungalow, taking with them some photographs of Cynthia and her leather shoulder bag "for fingerprints". It was scratched and spattered with mud and Jenny had given it over thankfully, having no wish to see it again. The officers had been gentle, kind, a little awkward. She had found herself trying to put them at their ease. There had been a woman pc "on call" just outside the door, in case she should break down, she supposed. Then presumably, they would have retired tactfully, leaving the woman officer to cope with her grief, waiting till the embarassing scenario was over before continuing their quiet questioning. But she had not cried, had not even been close to it. The tears were locked up in a cold, dark, silent place, accessible to no one. Least of all herself.

Next had come Reverend Beamish. God was by her side in her hour of need. Funny, in the eighteen or so hours since the police had broken the news, she had not once thought of God, not once sought the succour of the Divine Presence, nor of his ambassador for that matter. No, it had been an old connection from her long-abandoned lesbian past that she had called upon, almost without thinking. Had she paused to consider in the misery and confusion of that morning, she would surely have been surprised. For it was a world she had left behind over eight years ago for a new and dedicated life within the Christian church. But the thought had not overshadowed the action and she had merely picked up the phone.

"... and an evil place." the reverend growled.

"What is?" her mind must have subsided into the numb vacuity that was becoming a part of this terrible day.

"That accursed laboratory."

Yes, it had had to happen there, the attack, (she could not yet bring herself to say the word, "murder"), as though the place itself was exacting an exquisitely cruel revenge.

Harold Beamish swallowed another mouthful of over-sweet sherry. It hit the raw beginnings of an ulcer and inflamed his ire.

"It's the Devil's work!" he winced, fortified wine or his metaphysical adversary sending a sharp burning sensation to the vicinity of his solar plexus.

"First that pathetic monster foetus and now your poor innocent child." And if Jenny's face paled a shade further and her eyes slid away from his, the good man did not notice, so intent were his thoughts on iniquity and his stomach on acid.

"But there's no connection between the two." There couldn't be. Dear God, there just mustn't be.

"Then what was she doing at the Hunt that time of night?"

"She probably went to see the caretaker, Maurice. I was out, at a meeting."

"A meeting?"

"At the church hall."

"Why wasn't I told there was a meeting? About what?"

Once more Jenny's eyes slid away from the vicar's and once more he failed to notice.

"Just the jumble sale next month."

"Ah."

"She often used to pop in on Maurice when I was out. He was very kind to her."

The reverend's face registered incredulity that an agent of the Devil, albeit a minor one, was capable of such Christian behaviour. But, seeing the misery on the woman's face he drained his glass and, reaching out, took her hand in his.

"Let's pray together, shall we?" he murmured.

Several prayers and two schooners later, Jenny thankfully closed the door behind him. For once prayer had left her unmoved. She had hastily declined his offer to send one of the women from the Mothers' Union. She needed to be alone. To face that awful unbroken silence of the empty house without Cynthia. Besides, Sam would be coming soon and she had no wish for past and present worlds to collide. How explain the tall, streetwise, rather butch-looking Sam to grandmotherly-at-thirty Mrs Dimshaw? Or she to Sam, for that matter? No, the two worlds definitely must not blunder into each other's orbit.

Thinking about it now, she should never have asked Sam to come. It was an aberration, a throwback from the past. She should phone now and tell her not to bother, that she had no need of her. Too late, the front doorbell rang. And suddenly she was glad. She did want to see Sam. To re-connect, to talk, for the first time in all these years, with another soulmate, from a time before her soul had become otherwise engaged. She opened the door.

"Hello, I'm Sarah Ginsberg from the Brighton Herald."

Judith Ginsberg sat in an armchair by the french window and watched a dying wasp propel itself further towards oblivion against the glass. She had not opened it, feeling the first autumn chill in the air. She could not get up and open it now. She could not move. She was dead tired, with the fatigue that comes from a period of intensive and unrewarding exertion, followed by a sleepless night. She and Roger had been called to the lab at 9.30 the previous evening because some imbecile had got herself stabbed to death in the grounds. A local girl. It was unfortunate. It was very sad for the immediate family, but why the hell choose their property? As if they had not had enough unwelcome publicity to last them the rest of their lives. And if that had not been bad enough, to top it all she had had to spend half the night trying to explain to plainly baffled and sceptical detectives why her own daughter had also been prowling round the lab under cover of darkness.

"But why," the older and more thoughtful-looking of the two men had asked her, "was she spying on her mother's laboratory?"

"Because she has a supreme gift for melodrama. Because she is desperate to connect the lab in some way, in any way, with this cock and bull monster foetus story." Comprehension flashed perfunctorily across the officer's eyes.

"Because she wants to get at me, basically."

"And why would that be?"

"God only knows. Some grievance, real or imagined. I'm sure Freud had a theory for it."

"He did. The Electra Complex. A girl gets fixated on her father, with resultant jealousy and hostility towards the mother."

"Her father did a moonlight when she was two. Haven't seen him since. So that lets him out."

"I'm sure you can have half a complex. Now, to your knowledge, did your daughter know the dead girl?"

And so it had gone on. She had no idea who Sarah did and did not know, she had wanted to scream, not since she was ten years old or thereabouts. She was not her daughter's keeper. But, to her mind, it was patently unlikely, if not almost totally improbable, that Sarah, whose preferred friends appeared on television chat shows and talked of picking up Italian villas for a song, that Sarah should have ever claimed acquaintance with a retarded girl from the very unchichi neighbourhood of Moulston. She had done her best for Sarah and, eventually, the police had abandoned their incredulity, or found a more suitable target. But only after she, herself, had had a thorough grilling, almost as if she had been the suspect. And she wouldn't be thanked for it. Far from it. Even more resented, probably. For two pins she would have let Sarah get on with it. Get herself out of trouble this time. Perhaps it would have taught her a lesson. But the anger failed to ignite somehow. Where it should have been, had every right to be, was a treacherous bog of bewilderment and hurt. Judith, as was her habit, turned resolutely away from it, unable and unwilling to venture beyond its shallows.

The wasp lay stunned on the carpet. She should pick it up, throw it out into the garden. She did not, still could not, move.

This morning she had felt unable to work. A first, surely. Her mind had felt utterly incapable of closing and clenching around anything. She had stood irresolutely by as Roger had stalked around the lab, the ginger hairs of his eyebrows bristling like hundreds of antennae. He was "determined to get to the bottom of this." Of course he had had to be told about Sarah's childish antics in the Herald. And, of a mind with the police, had made thinly-veiled allegations, suggesting that if Sarah had been involved in two incidents concerning the lab that there was every possibility she knew something about the third, the damned break-in. Especially as it had been an inside job. Again Judith felt accused, but with more reason this time. If Sarah had come into possession of the keys to the lab, there was only one conceivable place where she could have got them. Oh yes, Sarah was perfectly capable of such an escapade, but the opportunity had definitely never presented itself. Yes, for the nth time, she was quite sure. Still, the whole incident had wrong-footed her.

She felt unable to clear Sarah's name and, by implication, her own. It was most irritating. She had gone prematurely, and thankfully, home, leaving Roger supervising the changing of every lock in the building.

Now, unaccustomed to this unwanted free time in the middle of the day and too tired to sleep it away, she sat staring out of the french window, a little knot of panic tightening in the pit of her stomach. Her mind, the mind that had wrestled for so long with the complex conundrum of Hewitts Disease was now suddenly, temporarily and terrifyingly empty. Could not deal with the problem of a dying wasp. She felt a vacuum at the centre of her being that threatened to suck her inwards. All these years of frantic endeavour to push back the frontiers of knowledge, to find the cure, all seemed fruitless. She had never once questioned the task, never looked for an escape route from what others considered to be an endless maze of paths to be gone down, explored and rejected. After David, her son, Sarah's brother, had died she had kept the faith, no matter at what cost to herself. Or others. For that was surely the epicentre of Sarah's resentment, that she had committed everything to that quest, had sacrificed, yes it was true, her own daughter. But it had had to be done and to question it now was not only apostasy, it was madness. Too much pain had been poured into that crucible, her own included. Too many years of her own life. There was no going back. Motherhood lay behind her in ruins. She had tried. Had tried very very hard after David's death but, somehow, the heart had gone out of her. With no resources left and already pregnant with Sarah, she had found herself fighting a losing battle. And this new baby, with its shock of black hair and its wide, wailing mouth, had been so demanding. Give me! Give me! it had screamed, but she had had nothing to give. It will come, the nurse had assured her. The closeness would come eventually. It was natural. She was just in shock, from grief, from the amputation of her first-born from her. It's a natural process, she had been told. Let Nature take her course. But Nature had not. The process had failed to happen this time, the bonding did not take place. So she had turned her back on Nature, fickle and ill-regulated and cruel as it was, tearing from you a child you loved and presenting you, willynilly, with one you simply could not, however hard you tried. And she had chosen the path of Science, particularly that brand of science that sought to control the course of errant nature, to re-construct the very building blocks of life itself. She had thrown herself into this work, out of desperation and exhaustion and bitter disappointment at the limitations of human relationships, even, and particularly, the most primary one.

Now, if only she could turn this monstrously heavy blunt instrument that was presently her mind into the gleaming razor-edged steel of its familar self. With a magnificent effort of will she rose slowly from the chair, picked the wasp up carefully in her handkerchief, opened the french window and threw the insect out onto the lawn. At the expensive feet of Vanessa Hunt. "Is that a novel way of telling me to buzz off?" Plucked eyebrows were raised ironically, the smile was taunting. Vanessa Hunt was a vain, indolent, self-absorbed, unscrupled, oversexed, (Judith consulted her mental thesaurus for an ultimate insult and settled for a biological one), parasite!

"Oh hello, Vanessa. I wasn't expecting anyone. Is Roger with you?"

"No, I left him at the lab, telling the locksmith how to put in a double barrel, or whatever you call it." With a flick of scarlet fingernail, Vanessa relegated the mystery of mortice and yale to mere mundanities.

Judith gazed at the silken coil of auburn hair insinuating itself into the long elegance of Vanessa's neck and, feeling a cloud pass over the garden, poked irresolutely at her own directionless bob. The younger woman always made her feel like this. Her own not inexpensive bottle green pleated skirt had seemed perfectly adequate till viewed in the light of that teasingly-severe, iron-grey, slit-sided pencil-line tightening around Vanessa's loins. In the simple contours of her own crisp, white cotton blouse had lain the virtues of intelligence, composure and self-reliance, until its very validity was called into question by that exuberance of satin that clung to the other woman's generous bosom like … aghast, Rachel reined in thoughts that had, through tiredness, begun to bolt. She looked up. Vanessa was staring at her. Arranging her face into a tight, serviceable, all-purpose smile, Judith said, "Do come in."

Chapter Eleven

Ian made his way over to the far side of the church hall, the side furthest from the road and hidden from neighbouring properties by spreading chestnut and overgrown blackberry. From this side you could forget you were just thirty yards from the main road of a large connurbation and imagine you were in some quiet country churchyard, far from the mad and the maddening.

He stepped up onto a pile of rubble beneath one of the tiny casement windows that ran along the side of the building and pressed a palm of one hand to the pane of glass. It gave easily, providing an opening just big enough for a small body like his to wriggle through. Once in, he closed the window carefully after him. It would never do to have his escape hatch discovered and sealed off.

He looked around him with satisfaction at the shabby hall, with its drab coating of green gloss, its uncompromising concrete floor and the musty piles of discarded jumble that had not sold at the last sale, or the one before that, and would most probably be there still after the next. He took a deep breath, relishing the familiar and comforting smell of damp and sweat and old shoes. Here was the antechamber of his sovereign domain, the entrance to his hideout. He strode to the end of the hall and into a small, tidy kitchen. It had a cupboard beside a scrubbed wooden table topped by a tea urn in one corner, and in the other, beneath a window was a spotless sink. Ian climbed onto the table and stretched up towards the handle of a trapdoor in the ceiling. After a couple of tugs, the little door slanted inwards and a ladder slid down. Ian swung himself onto the middle rung and began to climb. Almost at once there was a flurry of sound in the attic above his head, followed by a loud and heavy thump.

"Who's that?" Silence. Ian remained perched midway up the ladder, unable to move. His throat was dry as a bone, his eyes tight shut. Soon the blow would come. It did not. He opened one eye and saw nothing. He opened the other and looked into the face of a girl. But she was not coiled and poised to strike. She swung gently two and fro, her thin canvas shoes dangling a foot or two above the attic floor. Around her neck was one end of a cotton sheet, the other was knotted round a beam in the rafters.

"I'm from the Brighton Herald," the small, smartly-dressed young woman repeated more slowly. Still, Jenny stared at her uncomprehendingly.

"No thank you. I don't take a paper," she said at last, her mind stupid, fumbling, unable to find a reference point.

"I found your daughter last night."

Cynthia. It was about Cynthia.

"You found her?"

"Yes," the voice was gentle, "in the grounds of the Hunt lab." The Hunt. Always it came back to the Hunt. She didn't understand. What did this woman want? Gratitude? Was that it?

"Look, can I come in? Just for a few minutes?" The woman moved forward, but Jenny's survival instincts had reawakened. "No! What do you want?"

"I just want to ask you a few questions, that's all."

"I've nothing to say."

"Look, I can see you're upset." Could she? How? Jenny felt nothing. A vast empty nothing.

"But it won't take long. And it might help to find the murderer."

"I don't want to talk to anyone, let alone the Press."

"The paper's prepared to pay. I can't tell you exactly how much right now but .."

"I don't want your money," the door began to close. Sarah inserted a foot in the opening.

"Look, you're going to have all the nationals round here any minute. They're vultures. They're much worse than me. If you give us the exclusive, they won't bother you."

"Go away! I'll call the police!"

Sarah winced as the door was pulled back several inches and then rammed against her foot. She did not budge, however.

"Look, all I need is ten minutes. And a couple of snapshots. You won't regret it."

The rage and grief that had lain like a slab of granite across Jenny's ribs suddenly dislodged itself and smashed its way through her chest.

"Fuck off, will you!"

"I know it must be difficult .."

"You don't know a thing. What do you know about any human feeling? I've just lost my daughter! Don't you understand? She's dead! My little girl," and the tears, gentle harbingers of healing, came at last.

Sarah backed away and the door slammed shut. She had expected that, of course, expected to be met with animosity, indignation, and had come prepared to reason. She had anticipated some pathetic outpourings of grief and had ready-coined words of sympathy about her person. One had to deal daily in this business with the jagged and jaded emotions of others and go prepared to deal with them. But she had not come prepared to deal with her own. For, against that look in the other woman's face when she had said, "My daughter," Sarah had no defence. No defence against the recoiling force of this emotion that threatened to choke the breath from her body. Her lungs hurt as though she had been running hard or had not inhaled air for a full minute.

"My daughter," the two words sliced through the tempered steel of Sarah's journalistic heart like a blade through butter.

She slouched down low into the red leather of her convertible. For once the car gave her no buzz of excitement, no immunity against the world.

"My daughter." A hard, many-pronged spike twisted and turned in her breast. It was poison-tipped and hurt like hell. The spike, she realised with disconcerting clarity, was jealousy and she could not pluck it out.

Chapter Twelve

"I want her eggs! They belong to me! You have no right to keep them!"

Dr Shilpa's long, thin hands fluttered over the desk in front of her, as they always did in moments of stress or anxiety. Just now she felt plenty of both.

"No, of course we can't keep them. The problem is we can't legally give them to you."

"Fucking hell!" the woman facing her was in even more distress, "They are mine by right. Morally, emotionally, every which way."

"But not legally," appended the doctor gently, gazing at the other woman over a fathomless sea of compassion that she could not ethically bridge.

"I have to remain within the law, Jean, or risk losing our licence."

"If I'd been her husband I'd have a right to those eggs, wouldn't I?" Jean flung herself out of her chair and began pacing the room, as though treading the narrow cell of her own anguish. The doctor's hands moved involuntarily, like the wings of butterflies.

"We were lovers for ten years. Ten years! We would have been for the rest of our lives. We wanted to bring up her child together. Don't you understand what that feels like?"

Yes, Sunita understood very well, She had lost her husband three years ago. They had had no children. In a year or so they had always said. There was plenty of time. But there hadn't been. He had died quite suddenly. A heart attack at forty one. Something unforseeable, unthinkable. And she, who spent her days bringing to others the gift of children, herself remained childless.

"Please," Jean had ceased her restless progress and was leaning over the desk.

"Please," the eyes were taut with urgency, "inseminate her eggs and let me carry the baby."

Sunita looked down at her hands and, with a great effort of will, placed them firmly on the desk. Since all the hooha of the so-called "virgin births," she had had to close the doors, (on the fertility side, anyway), of her clinic to all but heterosexual married women. Parliament, prompted and advised by the Baroness Warnock, had deemed that children remain the reward for heterosexual activity and that any woman wrong-headed and immature enough not to indulge in it was undeserving of maternity. And, indeed, if, as was almost universally accepted, you learnt the template of child care through the nurturing of men, you could not, and should not, have one with without the other.

Dr Shilpa had done her best to get around the foolishness of the law by putting it on the grapevine that if a woman were to come to her clinic with a man claiming to be her sexual partner, no questions would be asked. In this way a number of lesbians got their babies, who might, otherwise, have gone without. So it was going to be with Jean and her lover, before the latter had been killed in a car crash.

"Jean, if you want a child, why don't you come here with a male friend and we can inseminate you with his sperm."

"I want Cal's child. Our child! All that remains of her, for Christ's sake!" Jean crumpled into the chair, half slumped over the desk.

There was silence. Neither moved. Even the doctor's hands were temporarily still. From outside the window came rhythmic chanting. Demonstrators. Born again interferers in other people's lives. From inside the building, on the other side of the door, the telephone seemed to be ringing almost continually. At last the doctor spoke.

"Jean, I can't do what you ask. Our funding, our legal position, they are all so precarious. There are too many people who would like to see us close. I can't put all this at risk. Women need our services. Have a right to them."

"Except lesbians. We have fuck all rights of any sorts."

"But," Sunita continued, phrasing her words with deliberate care, "we obviously don't keep eggs any longer than is necessary and, when they are no longer required, we get rid of them. We shall be dealing in this way with

Cal's this morning. I believe they may, in transit, be left for a short time on my secretary's desk."

Jean looked up, her eyes alive with the hope she had been given.

"There are clinics in Holland. I'll go there."

The doctor did not answer. It was possible. It was worth a try. Although in her experience the miracle of birth was a perverse phenomenon, an unwelcome guest in some bodies, whilst not deigning to enter many who longed for a visitation. To this woman who wanted so badly to host her dead lover's child, she hoped Nature, with a hefty bit of assistance from Science, would be merciful.

After Jean had gone, Sunita sat for a long time staring out of the window. The customary Wednesday demonstration was fuller than usual and there were new placards. Ones she had never seen before. The blown-up foetus picture was the usual currency of their argument, charging an increased interest of guilt to the already precarious emotional balance of the clinic's abortion clients. Yes, these placards had a new theme, a new image, but, peering through short-sighted eyes, (she must make another appointment at the optician), she could not make it out. If it were a foetus, it seemed scarcely human. Were not those animal hooves? There was a knock at her door.

"Yes?"

The portly figure of Doreen, the receptionist, a vision in ripe peach polyester, wedged itself in the doorway.

"Doctor, I must talk to you. It's serious." Since Doreen was capable of and, indeed, accustomed to dealing with emergencies of many kinds, Sunita took "serious" to mean exactly that.

"Come in, Doreen."

Doreen came in and closed the door carefully behind her. "Have you seen the Herald today?". No, Sunita had not. It was rare for her to see the Herald any day. Doreen's prim mouth, (surely that shade of pearly pink went out with the Sixties), was tightly pursed.

"I think you should read this." She plumped the paper down on the desk. "Son of Frankenstein," announced the headline, an inch high. In increased wonderment, for, astonishingly enough, she had not heard of the story before that moment, Sunita read out loud, "Three days have passed since the Frankenstein foetus appeared and then mysteriously disappeared in Hannerley Woods and no progress has been made to find it. The police have officially declared the case closed, yet little Emma Gatwood swears she saw it. Worrying questions remain. If the story is true, what has happened to the pathetic remains of this half-human, half-animal creature? Are there any others like it still enduring a pitiful existence?" The doctor looked indignantly over her spectacles, "What a load of unadulterated poppycock!" she said with feeling. "Is this how they sell newspapers these days?" She thrust the paper across the desk. Doreen pushed it back.

"Go on reading. There's worse to come."

Dr Shilpa sighed deeply. The world was full of unnecessary silliness. She read on, catching her breath as she did so.

"Who created this terrible creature to start with? And where did they get the human half from?" To answer the first question we need to look no further than the genetic experimentation lab on our very doorstep, itself the home to a brutal murder last night. As for the last question, what better place to get the genetic material than the fertility clinic not two miles away."

"What!"

"So irresponsible!," fumed Doreen, her large peach bosom throbbing palpably.

"And dangerous," the doctor's hands traced strange peregrinations in the air.

"The telephone ...?" the memory of insistent ringing surfaced from her unconscious.

"It hasn't stopped ringing all morning."

So that was it.

"All the media, plus a few dozen crackpots into the bargain. I told them the whole thing was a stupid hoax and they ought to have better things to do."

"Well done, Doreen," said the doctor mechanically.

58

"The last caller was Lady Fortescue. I think that means it's serious."

Yes, for their patron, who never communicated from one annual general meeting to the next, to have rung, the situation could correctly be adjudged as serious.

"What did you tell her?"

"I said you were in consultation and could not be disturbed."

"Get me a number, will you Doreen?" The doctor's rebellious hands, uncontrollable till now, were strangely calm.

"Lady Fortescue?"

"No, someone called Carter."

"Initial?," Doreen hoiked a pen from a salmon-coloured cardigan and stood poised.

"Alex? Chris? It's an androgynous name."

The doctor rifled sequentially through the vast filing cabinet of her mind.

"Jo? Robin? What was the name of that detective in that film about the bird?" Doreen, who in the face of such monumental vagary, could scarcely be expected to contribute an answer of any kind, promptly said, "You mean Sam Spade?"

"Sam. That's it. Sam Carter. I wonder if she's still around."

59

Chapter Thirteen

Before meeting Jenny, Sam had prepared herself for what she knew would be an awkward and painful encounter. Jenny had never been a close friend, being more on the fringes of their group and, after all these years, it would not be easy to pick up the threads of their relationship. The ending had not been so much bitter as unresolved, allowed to trail off without either side prepared to acknowledge it. Sam could no longer recall the exact sequence of events but it had been around the time Jenny had adopted the ten year old Cynthia. Having a disabled child had introduced her to a world none of them had previously known much about. Jenny had thrown herself into that world with the same totality she had allotted to all her undertakings. She had called upon the rest of them to do the same. In empathy, in solidarity, to make her cause theirs too and she had felt angry and let down when they had not.

A year or so later they had begun to take seriously the issue of disability, ensuring meetings were accessible, providing lifts to discos, sign language interpreters for plays and concerts but, by then, it was too late, for Jenny at least. She had drifted away, sensing betrayal, suspecting a false communion, anticipating by a few months the cracks that had opened in the ranks of the women's movement.

She had returned but once. She had again embarked upon a crusade, this time against the new techniques of genetic experimentation, had wanted them, too, to take up the campaign. Amniocentesis, she claimed, was not the scientific miracle it was hailed to be but the thin end of a very long and deeply Darwinian wedge that would make the eugenics of Nazi Germany look like a mild splash in a paddling pool. The quest for genetic perfection was a highly political and suspect act, for who would be deciding what constituted imperfection? How wide a category would it eventually become? And how many of us would find ourselves included? They had to do something about it. Now. They had not. Partly because their priorities were, once again, elsewhere, for it was the time when res publica was fast becoming privata and one had to look out for oneself or risk missing the gravy train altogether. But also, many of their group had arrived at an age when the ticking of the biological clock was sounding suddenly very loud and both the joys and risks of motherhood seemed to have doubled, thus techniques like amniocentesis appeared to be more of a reassurance than a threat. So Jenny had gone, for good this time. And to people who shared her concerns, to the Church of St Saviours, the very hub of evangelical, Born Again Christianity in Brighton.

In the event, her meeting with Jenny turned out both better and worse than she had expected. She could not altogether have prepared herself for the signs of grief and devastation on the other's face. But Jenny had not seemed to want to talk about the emotions of loss and bereavement. It was on purely practical measures her mind was bent, with an urgency that took Sam aback at first.

"They're looking for some girl."

"Who?"

"Her name was Jo. Cyn talked about her at tea last night," Jenny's voice cracked momentarily at the memory of that last supper.

"They spent the day together. I don't know much else. Nobody had seen her round here before. Cyn said she didn't have a home. I suppose she's a runaway. Cyn was like that. She'd just go up and talk to people. I tried to drum it into her. People are dangerous. Strangers are not to be trusted. She got the message about men, but she never saw it with women. She'd say, but why? No one had ever been horrible to her. And now this."

There was a pause. Around Jenny was that invisible but vast waste of desolation that separates those in pain from the helpless onlooker. Sam wanted to reach out, to touch this woman in her agony. But she was a stranger now. And strangers were not to be trusted.

"Sam, you've got to find her. This girl. She's probably not gone far."

61

"The police will do that, if only to eliminate her from their enquiries."

"The police!" her voice held contempt.

"They've got the resources."

"It could be ages before they find her. It could be never. People drift in and out of Brighton all the time. It'd be like finding a needle in a haystack. You know where a girl like that would hang out."

Sam stared at her. Yes, she knew.

"If it was her who … who did that to Cyn I want her inside, for life."

Sam nodded. Revenge was not a pretty thing, but it was perfectly understandable under the circumstances.

"And if it wasn't?"

There was a pause. Jenny seemed to be struggling hard, and losing. When she spoke her voice was bleak, like a lost child's.

"Sam, I need to know who killed her. And why. If .."

"If?"

"If it's anything to do with the Hunt."

Vanessa Hunt pulled shut the door of her Volvo and looked back through smokey glass at Judith's house. Yes, she was well satisfied. She had achieved her objective. In a half hour or so of guarded pleasantries she had elicited the information she had been after. She could rest assured now, neither Judith nor Roger harboured the remotest suspicion that she had provided, albeit inadvertently, the means of entry to the laboratory.

It had not been an easy interview. No encounter with Judith ever was. Judith didn't like her. That was alright. She returned the compliment. It was the same with all her husband's female colleagues. They were either hostile or patronising. They thought her stupid. There was the, by now, stale old joke that were she to be confronted by the map of the human genome she would, mistaking it for a car atlas, try to find the M23. It was trotted out at every dinner party, along with the Courvoisier and gave the same amount of enjoyment. She didn't care. She would smile her slow, liquid smile that would bring looks of

tense, hungry sexuality from the husbands. And, sometimes from the wives, for that matter. Oh how they all
bored her! She had heard it all before. The dreary intellectual one-upmanship amongst themselves, that insulting
mixture of desire and contempt towards her.

For had she not come from a large family of intellectu-
als and been dubbed at an early age "the pretty one"?
Whilst Beth, Rose and Olivia were referred to, respective-
ly, as "brainy", "artistic" and "musical", as though each
category were mutually exclusive of the other, as though
it were as impossible for one person to incorporate two
different virtues as it was for two people to share a single
one. Oh well, she didn't care. She could never have toler-
ated the rigorous regime of daily piano practice that
Olivia had submissively undergone. Even less to her taste
would have been the extra maths and science tuition that
were the bane of Beth's life.

Still, she would have liked to paint, like Rose. Like
Rose, to have skin, hair, clothes permanently covered in
flakes of colour, like the petals of a dozen flowers. One
time, she had stolen secretly into Rose's attic room, had
squeezed little globules of umber, magenta, crimson and
vermilion onto the wooden palette and, standing amidst
the easels and canvases, the pots and brushes, the sickly-
sweet smell of turpentine in her nostrils, she had painted
her picture. Oh how they had teased her when they had
discovered it! Mocked the clumsy amateurishness of her
efforts. And she had cried, in disappointment, in humiliation. In a family full of genius it was hard to be mediocre.

"But you're a genius with your smile and your dimples,
Nessa," her father had laughed. "Your art lies in wielding
a hairbrush not a paintbrush. In giving pleasure to us
poor men."

And, in following the life so obviously ordained for
her, she had been, by any standards, successful.
Attracting, with those selfsame arts, the attentions of the
most promising and ambitious of her father's students,
she had succeeded in marrying him within a year of their
acquaintance. And if, at a sister's exhibition, or recital or
book launch, she felt, at times, a twinge of envy or regret,

and if, some nights, she had that recurring dream wherein she savagely tortured her father to death with her curling tongs, well, it was a price that had to be paid for a life that had been easy, comfortable, luxurious ... and deadly dull. And if, after the first three months of marriage, she had found herself asking, "Is this it? Is this all there is? All there is going to be?" and if the relationship with Roger left her acutely conscious of an emptiness at the heart of things, well, she had taken care of that too. There were compensations to be had. Men. Many men. She was on her way to meet one now. A man who was definitely not dull but who might turn out to be deadly. She felt a tiny thrill of fear and found it to have aphrodisiac properties. She turned the ignition and the heavy engine throbbed to life. Oh, yes, there were compensations.

Chapter Fourteen

Malcolm tilted his chair back from the kitchen table, blew a cloud of smoke from his cigarette and, through it, watched his mother knead the dough. The vicar liked his bread fresh-baked. She had big, square hands, with thick, swollen fingers and red knuckles. He had been fascinated by them as a child. They were forever in motion, making and mending. Dry, they plied a darning needle in and out of the fraying strands of his father's woollen socks. Wet, they plunged his shirts down again and again into warm, soapy water, rubbing and plunging till the dirt was forced mercilessly from its hiding places. Spotlessly clean, they drove the big kitchen knife through the bread and spread the butter. Mud-covered, they pulled the stubborn leeks from their anchorage in the soil. How he despised them! They were work hands. Hands of a work horse. That's all his mother was, had ever been.

He watched her and she knew it. He despised her and she knew that too. Yet she never tackled him about it, never complained, never shouted to him to stop this constant, unnerving observation of her, however intolerable she found it. Malcolm tried to remember at what age he had realised that his mother was afraid of him. Nine? Ten? Still at primary school, he was sure of that. He had wanted something very badly. A pocket knife, a toy gun, he could not recall. Now it was so unimportant, then it had meant everything. Life could not, would not proceed without it. That's how he had felt about everything, always in those same extremes.

"But we don't have the money," she had told him patiently and he had stamped his feet, kicked the sofa, punched his fists into the wall, had advanced on her with arm raised. Instead of delivering him a sharp slap across the face as his father would have done, she had backed away, into the corner. They had stood staring at each other for a long minute. Then she had gone to the old money box on the dresser, had unlocked it and, wordlessly, handed him the coins. He had triumphed. He had bullied and threatened and vanquished his own mother. And he never forgave her for it. Which is why he watched her now, knowing she hated it. Hated him.

"How long are you staying this time, Malcolm?" she had asked him earlier.

"I don't know," which was a lie, of course. He knew very well when he would return to Dusseldorf, had his seat booked, the ticket in his pocket. But he preferred to keep her in an agony of unknowing. She and Ian both. His mother and Ian. They were a couple. Like a husband and wife. Far more so than she and his father were. They communicated silently across the table, across the room, over your head, when they thought you were not looking. His father did not notice, or chose to ignore it. But he was conscious of every pulse of brainwave, of every unspoken, yet clearly understood thought that passed between them. It was the most perfect telegraphic accord he had ever seen. Deliberately he would try to sabotage it, block it through the sheer weight and density of his body between them. Then the air would crackle with the friction, with the voltage of their combined transmission pitched against the force of his resistance. That he was an effective barrier to their superconductivity gave him a tainted kind of pleasure.

"Where's Ian?"

"I don't know," but she said it too quickly, too casually. She was a rotten liar."

"I think I'll go and look for him."

She turned now, her big, rough hands, sticky with dough, held up as though in a gesture of protection of self and child. A gesture she had never used for him.

"What do you want him for?". She was stalling, playing for time, a stupid, dumb cow safeguarding, as long as she could, her wounded calf against the advancing lion.

"Just want to have a chat with him, that's all."

"He might be doing his homework."

"Then I'll give him a hand with it. Like a big brother should."

Defeated, she returned to the mixing bowl, her hands pulling and thumping the dough. Malcolm rose, kicking the chair aside behind him.

"See you later."
She did not answer.

Sarah had sat for a good half hour in her parked car, outside Jenny's front gate. What is more, she had sat quite still, a thing almost unheard of for her. In the entire thirty minutes her right arm, resting on the steering wheel, was not once raised in the habitual act of putting pen to paper. Her eyes, ever bent on the snapping up of unconsidered trifles to turn into succulent news bites, seemed unaware of the comings and goings around her and were, instead, focussed on a point in middle distance. Her friends may have passed her by without a glance of recognition, so unlike her usual self did she appear. She whose life was spent in the immediacy of a perpetual present, for whom the past stretched as far back as a day-old newspaper and the forseeable future embraced only the next edition, she had been jerked back to a time of warm and milky infancy, when her mouth, straining towards a mountain of soft and yielding flesh, had closed on empty air and, opening wide this time, had howled alone in the darkness.

After about thirty minutes or so of this total immersion in mammary, the articulate, twenty-two-year-old, absolutely un-oral Sarah took control and leant with all her weight against the door of her memory, whilst plump, gurgling six-month-old Sarah leant with equal weight against the other side. For several minutes there ensued a struggle of such Olympian proportion that no clear odds-on favourite was seen to emerge, until the combined forces of intellect, grit and twenty or so years of guerilla practice allowed adult Sarah to wrest control of the door from the podgy, clinging hands of her child self.

As chance would have it, the slamming shut of Sarah's mental door coincided with the closing of Jenny's garden gate. Sarah looked up to find Sam walking away from it along the pavement. She looked for the first time upon Sam with the eyes of one who had just escaped annihilation by a hair's breadth and, consequently, the surge of gratitude she felt was explicable if not entirely rational. It was

Sarah the Journalist, however, who rapidly took over and any stray, misspent emotion quickly gave way to professional interest. Who was this woman? And what had she been doing in Fenton's house? Too butch for a policewoman. Even if a dyke or a gay did occasionally slip through the fag filter, they moved heaven and earth to pass for straight, either that or get eaten alive in the canteen. She watched Sam get into her car. Too disreputable, and too intelligent-looking to be another bible basher. Nor was she a Moulston resident, looking more at home in cosmoplitan, downtown Brighton than this dull and respectable suburb. Sam pulled out of her parking place and headed in the direction of town. Sarah, without knowing why, but telling herself that, her star interview having failed, she had sod-all else to do at that very moment, turned her Spitfire in the same direction and followed her.

It was only after the third time of looking in her rear view mirror and seeing the white sports car still behind her that Sam began to take notice. She had been driving relatively slowly, taking her time at lights, using exaggerated care as she did when her mind was elsewhere than on the job. But this part of the road to town was a dual carriageway and anyone in a hurry could overtake her. Many had, but not the Triumph. She observed it more closely. You didn't go to the expense of buying a twin-cylinder engine with a souped-up carburettor if you were of a mind to dawdle behind irritatingly slow and distracted motorists. Could it be that she was being followed?

Watching the detectives? The idea amused her and she chortled none too quietly to herself. She checked the mirror again. Still there, fifteen to twenty metres behind. Obviously not a professional, it was a god-awful tail job. She hit the brake suddenly, held it a moment, then accelerated hard. The car behind had shot alarmingly close before the brakes had been applied, nearly sending it skewing onto the grass verge. It had recovered and had now resumed its previous distance behind.

Very interesting. Sam screwed up her eyes, squinting

into the mirror. It was a woman, of that she was pretty sure. Even more interesting. They were entering the downtown section of Lewes Road. Sam entered the right turn stream by the big Sainsbury and indicated a left. The Triumph did likewise. Sam began to ease into the bend, then, at the last moment, pulled the car out of the turn and carried on round to the next left. Her shadow followed effortlessly.

"Not bad," Sam grinned. "Not bad at all."

She had intended making a pit-stop at Preston Park. The twenty five acres or so of playing fields, cycle track and tennis courts on the London Road out of Brighton had seemed a good enough spot to start a new training regime. Vanessa's suggestion, that she should spend her cheque on an exercise bike, had hit Sam at her most vulnerable point, her vanity, and she had gone out that morning and bought a pair of running shoes. They now lay reproachfully pristine and white on the back seat and were likely to stay that way for a while longer. She was certainly not about to heave her eleven and three quarter stone around the park under the eyes of her pursuer. That was something she wanted to do anonymously. At least until her muscles were in better shape.

Waiting at the T junction at the top of the hill she heard a familiar strain.

"Oh my darling, Oh my darling, oh my darling Clementine You are lost and gone forever ..," the music snapped off mid-bar. Sam's taste buds salivated in a Pavlovian fashion. Yes, on this warm, windless September afternoon, Marco's double cone with all the trimmings was infinitely preferable to what she had had in mind. She was no masochist by nature. Why go for pain when there was pleasure to be had? As she joined the queue beside the ice cream van she reminded herself that that was what she'd said about the booze. A couple of months of drying out had been pain enough to cancel out any pleasure she'd ever had from the stuff. "You can't go on abusing your body," the clinic doctor had said before she'd left there. "Get yourself an exercise bike," Vanessa had told her.

"Yes, my love," said Marco, "what can I get you today?" She hesitated.

"A double with everything." Looking back down the road she saw the Triumph parked twenty yards behind, the driver's head hidden behind a newspaper.

"No, wait a minute. Make that two."

Chapter Fifteen

What on earth had Vanessa wanted? She backtracked over their conversation. It had meandered, as was usual with Vanessa, up and down corridors of intrigue, onto which doors would be opened and Judith would be invited to peep through, to glimpse the illicit and sordid doings of their mutual acquaintances. A little extra-marital affair here, a professional betrayal there, a scientific argument that had swollen and deformed into personal jealousy and spite. Judith would be left, after these sessions, feeling rather shabby, but feeling also, and this is what so unnerved her, quite definitely aroused.

Damn Vanessa! What had she wanted? She would hardly have driven all the way from her own exclusive, over-priced village at the foot of the Downs just to indulge in a bit of grimey muckspreading. Surely the woman had friends who would have enjoyed it far more, with whom she could sit and chew, with relish, over those tainted tit-bits. Instead, she had folded her opulent self into the corner of Judith's sofa and proceeded to "blow the gaffe", (what a ridiculous expression!), on their various friends and colleagues. Vigorously Judith shook and slapped cushions, but Vanessa's perfume clung stubbornly to the fibres, had, somehow, woven itself into the upholstery, so that the delicately cerebral blue-grey fabric seemed shot with threads of heavy, scarlet sensuality. Damn! Damn! Damn! What had the woman wanted?

There had been some silly tale of a professor friend of theirs who was having it off with a student in his office, of all the stupid places! He had locked the door but forgotten the cleaning lady also had a key. With predictable and farcical results. That story had somehow sprawled into another of similar vein wherein another, like-minded, couple had foolishly contrived to lock themselves on the outside of a car whilst, at the same time, locking their clothing securely within. Feeling called upon to make comment, Judith had merely said that, in her opinion, adultery, like any other experiment, needed careful planning and

detailed preliminary preparation if it were to obtain satis-
factory results. To which eminently sensible statement
Vanessa had stared in surprise and then burst out laughing.

"Remind me not to do it with you," she had said. And
Judith had blushed. Which was something she had not
planned for. Damn Vanessa!

She beat the cushion savagely and hurled it onto the
sofa. The stories were irritating her now. They and the
memory of Vanessa's languid laughter. What was so
funny about saying how she would have double-checked
the cleaning rota or installed a mortice lock on the office
door. Or that, should she have been thrashing about
naked in the grass, (here Vanessa's very blue eyes had
twinkled, "fucking al fresco?," she had suggested), she
would have had the foresight to take a full set of car keys
with her.

Locks? Keys? Perhaps there had been a recurring theme
throughout the length and breadth of Vanessa's discursive
ramblings after all. Each story had revolved around the
crucial appearance or disappearance of a key. Having just
come from the lab, where a fundamental shake-up of
security was in progress, Vanessa may well have
absorbed these preoccupations into her subconscious
and, co-mingling with her own obsessions, they had syn-
thesised into a fugue on a theme of locked doors and
unleashed passion. It was a possibility. Or had Vanessa
had a more subtle intent than Judith gave her credit for?

The problem had revived her. Its clean, clear parameters were refreshing after the sully and muddle of the
visit. It was something to get to grips with. Her curiosity
had been aroused and once her mind began ferreting
after a thing it would not let go until that curiosity was
satisfied. Was she not, in her own way, one hell of a
detective? She whose life's work it was to help uncover
the most extraordinary and complex secrets in plant and
animal biology, had now, with an unoccupied mind, set
herself the task of probing an infinitely lesser and more
banal mystery – that of Vanessa Hunt's convoluted intentions.

The phone rang. It was Roger.

"I've been bombarded with phone calls all afternoon. Press, radio, telly. Is it true we have a monster baby factory in a shed at the back? That sort of thing."

"Oh Christ, that's all we need – more negative publicity!"

"That's what I thought," his voice sounded remarkably cheerful under the circumstances. From his next sentence she understood why.

"So I thought I'd do a bit of positive proselytising for us. I'm going on telly." So that was it. If there was one thing Roger loved more than getting DNA under a microscope, it was getting himself in front of a spotlight. "When?"

"Tonight. Southern TV. I'm on a panel with a hellfire vicar and that woman from the AI clinic. Coming?"

"Not on your nelly, mate!" Roger laughed and put down the phone.

Ian touched the girl's foreheard. It was damp and very hot. The sheet had cushioned her neck, preventing it from snapping with the impact of the drop. She must have hung there only a minute or so. Long enough for the blood vessels to burst in her eyes. He had lifted one of the lids, searching for any sign of movement in the pupil, but it had been motionless, a black pinpoint surrounded by the red rawness of the eyeball.

He had seen them do it on telly. His mouth to hers, he had pushed firmly, rhythmically down on the almost flat chest, pushing out the air to open the bellows. His arm and shoulder muscles ached with the effort of it. And now the ribs moved up and down of their own volition, though still the eyes remained closed. Anxiously he studied the thin, flushed face. It was dirty and the curly hair was tangled and matted. She smelt. Her anorak was ripped and stained. Lying there on the old blanket he had spread over the dusty chipboard flooring, she was at his mercy. She was the baby thrush, the scrawny, inert bag of almost featherless flesh that his father had found and thrown in the bin but which he had rescued and nursed,

73

gently forcing open the beak and dropping in tiny globules of warm milk. For weeks he had tended it, here, in
his den, weaning it gradually from milk to small grubs
and worms. He had watched it beating its wings against
the air, testing its strength, had seen, reluctantly, its first
clumsy attempts at flight and knew that the time had
almost come. Whenever he visited now it would be flying
from rafter to rafter, crossing and re-crossing the narrow
bounds of its captivity. It would no longer come to his
hand for food, feeling now the call of an instinct stronger
even than hunger. It was so unfair, after all his love and
tenderness, that it should want to leave him. He felt a
fury at the ingratitude of the bird. He had got his mother's
secateurs from the garden shed. In some parks they
would clip the wings of ducks and swans, wouldn't they?
It was to stop them straying into a world too dangerous
for them. It was a kindness, to keep them safe. He had
caught the young fledgling, held it in his hand, tracing
with his fingers the curve of the wing, where the muscle
connected to the body. It was here one must cut. Only a
little snip and the bird would never leave him. But,
instead, he had taken it out into the yard, held it close to
him for a moment, then, with a gesture of benediction he
had thrown open his hands and the bird had flown away.
He had watched it till it became a small dot in the sky.
Come back and see me, please, he had whispered. But,
to his knowledge, it had never returned.

   He studied the face of the girl now and felt a growing
excitement riding on the rhythm of her breath. If she
lived he would have a companion again. Like the thrush,
she was unwanted. You could tell that. But not any more.
Here, she'd be safe. He'd make sure of that. Sensing the
slightest of alterations in the atmosphere, he looked
down at her. The eyes were open. They were hazel and
very bright. He was suddenly nervous.

   "How you feeling?". The eyes closed for a moment,
then opened again wide.

   "I'm starving," she said.

Chapter Sixteen

"Double cone, flake and ripple do you?" Sam leant over the side of the Triumph convertible and held out one of the ices. Sarah lowered the copy of the Herald she had not been reading.

"No nuts?"

"Fresh out of nuts." Sarah took the icecream and Sam leant against the white car bonnet. They licked their ices in silence, eyeballing each other, sizing each other up, taking in every detail and making a thousand rapid calculations a minute. Sarah spoke first.

"When did you realise?"

"Half a mile or so," Sam said through flake.

"Oh," Sarah was pleased, "only half a mile back."

"No, half a mile from Moulston."

"Oh," Sarah was not pleased.

"That's not bad."

"It is," Sarah was disappointed, but it was hard to feel too crushed when demolishing double whipped vanilla icecream.

"She's just a kid," thought Sam and said, "To do it properly you need half a dozen cars and two years advanced driving. So I've heard," she added.

"I suppose my car doesn't help," Sarah stroked the Spitfire's sleek side tenderly.

"It does sort of catch the eye," Sam leant in and there followed the sort of conversation that is fairly standard between a besotted car owner and an admiring stranger, in which the words, "chassis" and "carburettor" and "nought to sixty in ..." are most often heard and during which Sam ran an appreciative eye and hand over dashboard, leather, chrome and paintwork.

At last Sam straightened up. "So what did you want to know anyway?"

"Who are you? What are you? What were you doing over at the Fenton place? Was it anything to do with the murder of her daughter?"

"Any reason? Or just plain old curiosity?"

Sarah flipped open a press card.

"National?" Sam asked affably. Sarah scowled back.

"Not yet. I'm with the Herald. But not for much longer. They're too narrow-minded, too cautious."

"Not in the last few days. There was a front page article on Monday …"

"That was mine!" her eyes sparkling, her mouth full of chocolate, Sarah looked all of a happy nine years old.

"And then the piece on the murder this morning …"

"That was Dickhead Don," Sarah's face settled into a six year old scowl. "But I found the body! At the Hunt last night."

"Did you now? What, you just happened to be there?"

"No," Sarah gave a proud flick of her head and bit into her cone.

"I wanted to do a follow-up on my monster story so I was doing a spot of detective work last night, trying to find out what goes on there at night."

"All on your own? That was brave," Sam noted the blush that crept up the cheek and the slight look of discomfiture in the eye, but Sarah answered lightly enough, "All part of the job."

"And did you see anyone, apart from the body I mean?"

"Yes," halfway to taking a large mouthful of icecream, Sarah stopped and shivered. Strangely enough, it was the first time since it happened that the thought had hit home – she had been but several yards from a murderer!

"Man or woman?"

"It was too dark to see."

"Tall? Short? Fat? Thin?"

"I don't know," Sarah did not seem to think the questions unusual, "Medium, I think. I can't be sure. It all happened so quickly." Sarah stared ahead, her eyes fixed on a dark, indistinct shape that had, eighteen hours earlier, emerged round the bulk of the Hunt's outbuildings …

"A silhouette, bent over," her voice broke, became small, husky.

"I thought at first it was a sack of coal or something …

76

this thing he .. she was dragging," icecream, stained red with raspberry sauce, dripped from her fingers.

In silence Sam took the unfinished cone from the other woman's hand and pitched it into a bin. Sarah stared down at the gooey mess on fingers that did not seem to belong to her.

"I feel sick," she said. Sam handed her a tissue.

"Why don't you call it a day and go home to bed," she suggested gently. In an instant, sharp investigative journalist that she was, Sarah realised that not only had she discovered exactly nothing about this woman, but also she, herself, had been supplying an awful lot of answers.

"Who are you anyway? How do you fit into all this?" but Sam, with a cheery wave, was already heading for her car. A sudden, unspeakable thought occurred to Sarah.

"Hey, you're not Press too, are you?" If this woman were from one of the nationals, not only would she have Fenton's story but her own first-hand account. Horror upon horror! That she could have been so stupid! She saw Sam get into her car and start the engine.

"O.K. lady," thought Sarah grimly, "I'm going to sit on your tail till I find out who you are and what you're up to." As Sam's car slid decorously from the kerb and started down the hill to town, Sarah reached for the ignition key and encountered empty air. She stared uncomprehendingly at the vacant keyhole. She had not taken it out. She searched her pockets. No, it had been there all the time she had been talking to that woman. And now it was gone. Hugh, her mother, any one of a number of Sarah's friends might, with justification, have steeled themselves at this point for one of Sarah's famous outbursts. They would have been astonished, then, at what they saw. Like Ratty who, thrown roughly into a hedge by the first motorised vehicle he has ever seen, stares after it not in fury but admiration and, in a wistful little voice, imitates the car horn. "Poop poop," he says. Thus did Sarah, a smile beginning at the corners of her mouth and spreading from ear to ear, gaze after the rear fender of Sam's car as it disappeared around the bend of the road. The smile stayed in place long after she had reached under the dashboard and begun to hotwire the engine.

As Sam drove off, she experienced a pang or two of guilt, but that was all. She was a nice kid, but a reporter, nonetheless, and reporters were awkward, inconvenient people to have around at the best of times. Right now, asked, begged to investigate the murder of an old friend's daughter, the one thing she did not need was an inquisitive bloodhound puppy breathing down her neck. She dropped Sarah's car keys into the Herald office and parked her car. She needed to walk and think, to cover a lot of ground mentally and geographically. Strictly speaking she should never have agreed to Jenny's demands. Murder was a police matter and they didn't take kindly to interference from outsiders. That was one thing. Another was that she was out of practice. In the old days she had taken on all sorts of bizarre and dodgy cases with a recklessness that Julia had deplored. Many times when Sam had been off for days on a case and turned up in the middle of the night looking as though she had gone ten rounds with a gorilla, Julia had been literally sick with worry, pale and shaking with fright. Then, some time later, she would shake with fury. Why had Sam not phoned at least? Could she not have just let her know she was alright? The answer was no, most times she couldn't. Phones were never conveniently there when you wanted them or else your attention was taken up entirely on the business in hand. If your eye left the ball you lost it. But Julia had never wanted to understand that. Such single-mindedness, such absorption in one thing, to the detriment of all else, was foreign to her nature. And, basically, humanly, she was jealous. And so Julia had gone and Sam, discovering too late that there were other things, beside her work, that needed to be accorded energy, passion, commitment, found she could no longer concentrate on her work. Of all the ironies, when she most needed her work to take away the pain, she was no longer capable of doing it. And so for the last eighteen months or so she had drifted, by day delivering writs to the bonded and the bankrupt, repossessing and dispossessing and feeling she was only a little way short of that herself. And at night drinking herself to sleep. Yes, she was out of practice for a case like this. There had once been a quick-thinking, fast-talking Sam, who had lived on her wits and lived well. She was gone. Never to return again? Maybe not, that was the terror. She had really screwed up this time.

And so she pounded the pavement, past the Pavilion, that outrageous, minaretted pleasure dome a long-dead monarch had bequeathed to the town. Up St James Street, into Kemp Town, she turned into Marine Parade, with the wide, iron-grey bowl of sea on her right and the grand terraces of four-storey, Edwardian mansions on her left. Once occupied by a single family and its complement of domestic servants, most were now divided and sub-divided into shoebox size apartments, still too up-market for the likes of her. As she tramped, she indulged in the kind of pitiless barrage of criticism one saves exclusively for one-self, never dreaming of letting it loose on any one else. By the time she reached the Marina she had exacted an uneasy truce with herself or, at least, regained her sense of humour. She snarled up at the concrete mass of this monstrosity, relic of an earlier Town Council's tribute to the yachting classes, a gesture they had acknowledged by navigating well clear of Brighton.

"I could be even more of a failure," she grinned to herself, "I could have designed you."

The idea of investigating a murder was daunting in the extreme. The thing to do, she reasoned, was to see it as a missing person case. She had done plenty of those. And that's all Jenny had asked her to do – find the girl Cynthia had been with yesterday. The fact that it would not nec-essarily stop there, that if she found her and the girl hap-pened to have nothing to do with it Jenny would insist she go on and find the real killer, was something she would gloss over now. She would deal with that when and if she came to it. O.K., so that was manageable. She would put it out on the grapevine. If the girl was a run-away she would eventually make contact with the street population, that growing underworld of the unhoused, unloved and outlawed that subsisted and co-existed on the edges of respectable Brighton society. If she was there Sam had a good chance of finding her. And turning her in. That's what Sam did not relish. But if the girl was violent then Sam had no choice. Most likely she was some frightened, confused eject from a mental hospital, an outrider of the government's new policies, another casualty of Community Care. Well, she would find her anyway. Go from there. At least she had made some decisions, formulated a plan. By the time she reached Norfolk Square, her mind was clear and she was experiencing once more that thrill of the chase, an exhilaration like no other she had ever known.

The bus shelter in Norfolk Square was a haven for the down and outs of Brighton, to the annoyance and disgust of many of the bus travellers. Here the dispossessed were in possession of every seat and the comfortably-off hovered, transient, pulling their warm coats tightly round them, scant protection against the blasts of icy wind off the sea and the fumes of Tennants Extra off the lips of the shelter's occupants.

"Jerry, I'm looking for a woman."

"Good, you must be feeling better. I'll drink to that," he said, hopefully. But she had steered them in the direction of MacDonalds and coffee. Biting into a Big Mac, he remarked sadly that food was no substitite for alcohol. She pretended to ignore it. He "wintered" in a hostel and slept rough during the summer months. His face was red and puffy from years of exposure to wind, sun and drink. He had done her a good turn on a number of occasions, knowing the underbelly of Brighton like the back of his hand. He would boast that he was her undercover agent, her plainclothes man.

"Well, you can't get plainer clothes than these, can you?" he would joke. The police had asked him to do the same thing, be their eyes and ears in a world that was not theirs.

"But they can kiss my arse," he'd say, "I'm not working for those bastards." He had had experience of the police, on the picket line, back on the docks of Dundee. Nineteen great ocean liners he'd helped build, bound for destinations as distant as China, Canada and the Cape of Good Hope. Now the hand that had riveted steel shook as though with the palsy.

They had rituals. He always said, "Come and have a drink," and she always replied, "No thanks, Jerry, I never drink while I'm on duty." Which was true, though not honest. That was not the reason she did not accept his hospitality. It was one thing to sit with this group of dirty, dishevelled men and women in the middle of Brighton's main thoroughfare, but quite another to share a convivial bottle with them. To the eyes of the respectable world there was, in all probability, no difference for, in briefly joining this disreputable encampment, she had already sunk beneath their field of vision. But, for her sake, the distinction had to be made. Not because she felt herself so far above them, but because, having lived at least part of her early twenties on the streets, she felt too close for comfort. And so she kept a distance and if Jerry noticed he did not comment. But it bothered her.

"Where you been hiding yourself all this time?"

"Haven't been hiding," she countered defensively. "I've just had no cases. Only writs. Business has been bad." Which was all true, of course. Still, she could have come to visit. They both knew that. It lay unsaid between them. Why hadn't she? She knew very well why she hadn't. It would have been like staring into the face of her own alcoholic self. There would have been no possibility of making a nice distinction between her and them. What had previously been comfortable distance would have turned into excruciatingly close proximity. During that time, in her last conscious minutes at night, before she had fallen into a drunken sleep, she would think, "At least I'm not as bad as them." For this ultimate betrayal she could not forgive herself.

Chapter Seventeen

The boy called Ian had gone away and returned some minutes later with a hunk of hot fresh bread and a pint of milk. She drank the milk hungrily but the bread she could not eat, her throat hurt too much. She rolled the soft dough into pellets between her fingers and tried to swallow them in vain, as he sat cross-legged watching her. She did not resent this attention on her, for he asked no questions, offered no comment. Having been, in her life, alternately badgered or ignored, pestered or neglected, she found this concern at a distance immensely soothing. Suddenly he got up, held out his hand for the bread and disappeared down through the hole in the floor. She heard the clatter of saucepans and crockery from below and wondered what he was doing. He was strange, this boy. Not like any other she had met before. Not that she had known many, having no brothers, nor sisters for that matter. And, at the home where they had sent her at twelve, the boys of her own age had seemed unbelievably childish whilst the older ones had looked straight through her, as if she were not there, her thin, boyish body holding no interest for them.

Ian came back up the ladder and held out a steaming cup to her.

"'Pops,' my mum calls it. She used to make it for me as a kid, when I was sick." And, as she simply stared at it, "It's hot milk and sugar and bread. It's delicious. Try some."

She tried some. It was delicious, warming her stomach and easing her throat. The comfort and homeliness of it made her want to cry. Her body relaxed and a great weariness came over it. Her eyelids grew unbearably heavy. Her head dropped forward. Sleep. She yearned for it. To drift and sink into warm, milky gooiness. Her head jerked upright. The drink had been drugged. The boy had tricked her. She would sleep, and then what? What would he do? But what could he do to her that had not already been done? And perhaps she would not wake up, ever. So much the better. And resistance was impossible now.

She was just too tired. He took a blanket from a pile and laid it over her.

"Sleep now," he said. And she slept.

In her dreams she felt, through her bones, a deep, thrumming reverberation, as though she were in a ship, its bows slicing through the darkness of the silent seas. She felt safe and contained in its great throbbing interior for, behind her, as though it were itself adrift, lay in ruins the abandoned continent of her former life. When she awoke, the oblong of blue through the skylight had darkened to black. There was a small circle of yellow light from a bare bulb dangled over one corner of the attic. Here Ian was sitting bent over a table, his back to her. The regular thud thud continued. She felt it through the floorboards now, bringing with it the memory of her grandmother at the treadle machine.

She watched him working for a few minutes, his absorption giving her an unaccustomed feeling of security. They were there, together, in his den, but neither intruding on the other. She looked about her and saw for the first time the drawings pinned to the beams. They were like the patterns her grandmother had cut out of magazines – skirts, blouses, trousers. Only these were for children and they were more colourful, more adventurous. Had he drawn them? But boys didn't make clothes.

"What are you making?"

The vibration stopped and he turned round to face her, holding up a pair of jeans.

"I'm altering these for you. I couldn't find any your size in the jumble. Mine would fit you but my mum would notice they were missing." Yes, his would fit. They were as tall and as skinny as each other. They could have been brother and sister. But still she did not understand. Why was he giving her clothes? What did he want?

"I found you a shirt and jersey and a jacket," he indicated a neat little pile beside her. There were also two things in brand new polythene bags. She reached out and touched them.

"Um," he coloured pink, "there obviously weren't any

83

underwear downstairs, so I gave you a pair of my socks and pants. They're new," he added unnecessarily.

"I get them from my Aunt Sylvia every birthday."

She went on staring at him and this time he saw that she did not comprehend.

"You can't stay in those. For a start they're filthy and they've got rips in."

She looked down at herself. Yes, she must look like one of those scarecrows she had passed in the fields on her journey cross country. She half-expected to see straw poking out of her belly.

"And anyway, they've put out a description of you in those clothes on the radio. The telly too, probably."

"A description? Of me?"

"They're looking for you in connection with the dead woman." He was bent over the garment, his face hidden.

So that was it. There was no doubt then. She had not imagined that newspaper. Cynthia was dead. He was saying something more.

"What?"

"I said, did you? Do it?", still not looking at her. The question was almost casual, as if he had been asking her had she slept well.

"No." Pause. "I don't know."

"Don't you remember?"

"No."

"Do you remember going to the Hunt?"

"Where?"

"The Hunt laboratory." Her mind fumbled through the itinerary of that day. Had it only been yesterday?

"Yeah, we did."

"Oh." He was silent a moment, thinking.

"Is that where she ... where they ..," but her mind boggled at it, refused to see any picture of the scene.

"Yeah. That's where she was killed. In the grounds last night. Don't you remember?"

Last night she had walked to keep warm, passing rows of houses, peering into brightly-lit interiors where people sat together, eating, talking, watching television. Had she gone then to Cynthia's house? 57 Holmes Park Crescent –

there it was, lodged in her brain.

"No."

"The police are always getting things wrong. Look at the Guildford Four." But Jo had never heard of the Guildford Four, could think only of Cynthia's round, plump face, her hand held out as she said, "be my friend?" Some friend Jo had been.

Cynthia's hand. She looked down at her own hand. The image of a baby mouse. She could feel the frightened beat of its heart against her palm. It must not get away, this mouse. She held it tight. Tighter. If only it would stay still. Presently the wriggling stopped. She looked down at her clenched fist as tears dripped down her nose and onto the knuckles.

"I strangled her."

Ian looked at her in silence.

Sam left Jerry with a promise from him to start enquiries about the girl "this very hour." Walking away from Norfolk Square she felt at a loose end. What to do now? She could look for the girl herself, she knew quite a few places to start off, but Jerry would do it that much faster and draw less attention. She phoned up her answer machine. Her accountant's smooth voice asked her whether his fee was already in the post, if not he was sure it was just an oversight. No, it was an overdraft, which he knew all about, but obviously didn't mind adding to. A used car firm in Shoreham would like her to chase up a headmaster who had defaulted on his H.P. payments, which said a lot for the state of British education. Then a woman's voice, warm, comfortable, with a slight Asian accent – would Sam phone her immediately, there was rather an urgent matter on which she needed advice. Sam phoned immediately.

"Hello, the Glenning Clinic," came a brisk voice. "Can I help you?" After only a few seconds' hold Sam was put through. The same easy, affable voice that made Sam feel an immediate intimacy with its owner. Of course, the first sentence helped a lot too.

"Sam, I've heard so many wonderful things about you."

Go on, stroke me, thought Sam.

"Everyone I've talked to has spoken highly of you."

"O.K. you've won me over. What would you like me to do?"

The voice gave an attractive chuckle.

"I need to talk to you rather urgently."

"I'm free right now as it happens."

"I've got a holding operation to do with our patron in ten minutes, then after that I've agreed to sit on some dreadful TV panel on the ethics of genetics."

"Why do it if you don't want to?"

"Have you read today's Herald?"

"Only the front page. The murder."

"Look on page two. There's an accusation linking us with the Hunt in creating this mythical monster foetus. Look, will you meet me after this panel thing? Or would it adversely affect your social life?" Sam refrained from saying that it would be hard to adversely affect a social life that was practically non-existent, arranged to meet the doctor in the Paris, Texas Cafe at 9.30 and hung up.

The Hunt. Everywhere she turned it cropped up, one way or another. That kid reporter had found the body in the grounds of the Hunt. And what had Jenny said? – "I need to know who killed Cynthia, if it was anything to do with the Hunt?". Why? Why should the Hunt have any more importance than that it was the murder location? What else? For there was something else. Something that nagged on the fringes of her memory. There had been another lab mentioned recently. A lab where a key had been stolen, an incident which she had been temporarily engaged to investigate. By Vanessa Hunt! Now there was a coincidence. Sam was a firm believer in coincidences. Synchronicity Julia had called it, but then Julia always had given long names to simple things. To Sam it was the same thing coming up again and again and begging not to be ignored. The way the Hunt was doing. When that happened you had to respond. And sometimes it led you all the way up a dead end and sometimes, not always, but just sometimes it led you to the jackpot. She felt that familiar charge of electricity again, as in the old days. She had a feeling about the Hunt, just a feeling but, like the tracker for whom the spoor is merely a confirmation of what she knows already – the presence of the beast – she knew she was on to something. But where to start? The Hunt itself? It would have battened down all hatches by now and have sentries on every corner if they had any sense. The reporter? But she was no fool and wouldn't be so easily milked next time round. She might also be more difficult to shake off. Best keep her at a distance. Vanessa Hunt would clam up if approached, understandably so. Which left Jenny … no, to go back now and question Jenny would be like prodding flesh already flayed and skinless. Whatever was eating Jenny about the Hunt would have to wait till she was ready to tell. So, that left .. who? Only the highly-mysterious, all-male Richard. She looked at her watch. It was 5.05. At 5.30, (how the hell could sex be so perfectly timed?), Richard would be walking away from his assignation with Vanessa.

Chapter Eighteen

The Gresham was fairly typical of its kind, with a dozen or so rooms, some en suite, some within walking distance of the bathroom, a bar and a nondescript restaurant that offered a limited menu to guests who were either too tired or too undiscriminating to go in search of one of Brighton's innumerable eating places. In the six months of their acquaintance, they had always rendezvoused there. Not that they liked it particularly. It served its purpose, being no better and no worse probably than any other of the seafront hotels punctuating the Regency facade of Marine Parade. It had all they needed – a bed, a locked door and complete anonymity. And if, sometimes, the shower had been tepid or the room smelt too strongly of that cocktail of air freshener and stale tobacco smoke peculiar to rooms rented for an hour or a night, then they would agree to meet somewhere else next time. But when the time came, one or other of them would renew their booking at the Gresham, being overcome by – what was it in her case, Vanessa asked herself – the instinctual return of animals to their old mating ground? A desire for continuity in their very uncontiguous relationship? Or just plain inertia? Whatever, it had now attained the value of ritual. They would enter separately and from different entrances. The one coming in by the main door and signing the register, the other entering by way of a small service entrance by the bins in the mews behind. They had been offered this facility when they had booked in that first time, (for the Gresham prided itself on fifty years discreet service to its customers) and they had availed themselves of it more as a joke. Now it had become habit. She preferred the back entrance. It gave her the thrill of the illicit, set up a tingle of excitement for the encounter that was to follow. Whereas, if she used the main foyer, the bald, bored desk clerk would nod in her general direction, push the book towards her and hand her the key. And that was it. As though she had been purchasing a theatre ticket. She supposed a brothel must be like that.

The protocol would have to be scrupulously exact and impersonal, because one was dealing with an activity so intimate.

It was always the same room, even at the height of the season. Perhaps they kept it for that purpose. The thought did not disconcert her, for the sheets were always freshly laundered. It rather intrigued her to imagine how many couples regularly slewed across this bed in an excess of passion and possession. It made her feel less alone, somehow. As though part of a secret society, whose members never met but who left occult signs, bearing witness of their presence – a hair grip in the corner of a wardrobe, the faintest smudge of lipstick on the bathroom mirror. At times she had felt a crazy desire to carve her initials on the underside of the little wooden table in recognition of this strange bond of fraternity for, in spite of all the flagrant intimacy that took place within these four walls, the room remained utterly impersonal.

She had tried, during the two to three hours of their occupancy, to hide that aspect of the room, change it, drive away that imhuman, uncompromising blankness. But however much she would scatter bits of her make-up on the surfaces, strew articles of her clothing across the pale blue of the carpet, fill the air with perfume and sweat and come, the room remained as remote and impersonal as when they arrived. It was as though the very anonymity of the room was a personality in itself, powerful, overwhelming her own feeble, human presence. And was not their own intimacy just as impersonal? Oh yes, there was arousal, a quickening of the pulse, body heat, the mingling of odours and juices that supposedly characterised a successful sexual interchange. No, Vanessa could have no complaints in that direction. It was just … she was not used to thinking in these terms. She was not used to thinking, full stop. It only confused her. But she had come this far now. Go on, what was it? It was just that the greater the proximity to the body of another person, it seemed the greater the distance from … what? Their soul? One did not use that word in respectable company. To be in possession of such an object was thought to be a definite liability, like having chronic asthma or a stammer and to bring the subject up in public was now considered "inappropriate behaviour," unless of course you were a christian, in which case, Vanessa supposed, you were capable of anything. No, for soul, best substitute mind. That was more acceptable. The distance, then, between two minds.

There had been men with whom her mind had seemed to come within nodding distance, but not Richard. Richard did not talk. Not only was he silent on the subject of himself, (many men would deftly deflect the conversation onto sport or current affairs whenever you strayed too near the core of them), but he simply did not talk. The onus would be on her and so she would go babbling on, about the people she knew, the things she had done, Roger. He would ask questions about Roger, about his work, his connections. At first she had taken his interest to be a sort of male competitiveness, had been rather flattered, as though by vying, if only in imagination, against her husband he had been indirectly complimenting her. But, after the break-in at the lab, she had begun to suspect other, less comforting, motives. That the security of the lab should have been violated did not matter to her in the least. That she should have been used was also of little consequence. She had done much the same with all her lovers. Was not this sexual grappling a form of masturbation with another present, rather than any kind of lovemaking in the real sense of the word? No, what piqued her pride most of all was his lack of pretence. He displayed no affection. Perhaps he disliked her or, what was worse, was wholly indifferent. She had no idea. He was impenetrable.

Still, after six months she knew only the outward details of him – his hair close-cropped blonde, his clothes good quality, carefully casual and conservative, no scent or jewellery to give the game away, no clue to the personality. Only once had he shown her, unwittingly, an Achilles Heel. She had discovered a small vanity of his – his body. It was a superb body, lean, straight, well-muscled, an athlete's body, covered in fine red-gold hair.

She had surprised him once in the act of loving it, discovered him, as it were, in flagrante delicto, absorbed by his image in the mirror, the tips of his fingers moving slowly down his chest to the hard flatness of his stomach, moving with a delicacy and a sensuality he had never shown towards her. She had watched fascinated, an intruder, a gooseberry, a peeping Tom on what should never be seen. And she had felt a thrill of jealousy. Which had later given way to loneliness.

No, she knew nothing about him – work, home, friends, relations, interests even. This afternoon as she lay in bed smoking a cigarette, listening to the steady drumming of his shower against the steamy glass of the door, she wished she had not warned off that detective. Suddenly, she wanted to know. She wanted to know very badly who this man was. Oh, the mystery had been fine, had been fun for a while. She had told herself that this was a rare old game. That she could be fucking a junior minister or an international terrorist for all she knew. That there was excitement in not knowing the petty banalities of someone's daily life. But suddenly, lying here in this dingy hotel room, with Richard scrubbing off any remnant of her that clung to him, she felt it for the bitter insult that it was. Anger surged in her, the like of which she had rarely felt, (well, perhaps towards her father). She got up quickly, crushing out her cigarette. Her body felt alive with rage, in a way it never usually did. Her mind was utterly lucid. It raced with an urgency she was not accustomed to feeling. She had to know about him or risk feeling totally degraded. With a glance over her shoulder at the still-closed door, she moved to the chair by the window and slid her hand into his trouser pocket. Small change, the keys to his VW. Next the jacket pocket. She drew out a worn, dark leather wallet. Her hands were trembling now as she fumbled the press stud. The shower door was still shut. Impatiently she pushed fingers into the outer pouch. Paper money, £80–£100 and a few hundred deutschmark. That was all. Hardly an insight into his character. There must be something else. There was an inner pocket. Empty. No driving licence, credit card, no ID of any kind? Ah, but there was something, she felt its shape through the soft leather. Something hard and rectangular that was not a banknote.

"Looking for something?" He stood in the doorway, a towel knotted around his hips. She had not noticed the rhythmic tatoo of water had ceased.

"Just a fiver for a taxi," she hoped her voice sounded casual, for she was suddenly afraid, "you don't mind, do you? Only I'm broke till I get to a cash point."

"Of course not," he came towards her, the drops of water still clinging to the tiny blades of hair on his neck and chest. Taking the wallet, he pulled out a note and handed it to her. His eyes were as blue and empty as a rain-washed sky.

"You have only to ask," he said.

As was usual he had left before her. Once the door had closed behind him she felt a terrific outpouring of relief that seemed to shake her whole body. She had no idea she had been feeling so tense. She would not see him again. In all the months of their relationship he had offered nothing of himself, had scrupulously engineered that supreme act of giving and receiving so as to exchange exactly nothing except a little bodily fluid. She felt robbed, cheated, furious with him, with herself. From the window, she watched him run lightly down the hotel steps, not pausing to look back, for she was already forgotten. His receding back told her that more plainly than any words could. He turned left now, westward, toward the town centre and she wished again she had not cancelled the tail on him. She wanted to know more than anything, no matter at what cost, who this man was that had dare pass through her life and leave no trace of himself, as if they had never met or as if she, herself, did not exist. He was walking quickly now, had gone twenty yards along the road, when a figure emerged from the phone booth outside the hotel and began striding in the same direction. A man was it? Tall, leather-jacketed, with an abominable haircut! She craned her neck, pressing her forehead against the glass in a effort to make out. Then she began to laugh her deep velvety laugh as the two disappeared into the distance.

He was surprisingly easy to follow. He didn't amble or hesitate or gaze into shop fronts, things that would have necessitated a frequent change of pace or direction, a pretence to be, herself, entranced by a window display. He was the perfect subject, maintaining a steady speed and with, presumably, a single purpose in mind. He went straight to the Easterner, a pub down one of the many lanes that honeycombed their way up from the seafront. She knew it well. It was mainly frequented by gay men, with a sprinkling of straights and dykes. Perhaps he just wanted a drink, but they had passed several pubs on the way. Perhaps he had only just acquired his thirst. Perhaps.

She hung about outside for a couple of minutes, giving him time to buy a drink, get settled, then she, too, went in. He was sat at a small table near the door to the Gents. She went up to the bar, stationing herself nearest the exit.

"Hi Fats," the barman looked up from expertly pouring a pint and smiled. No one knew his real name. He had been barman of the Easterner from time immemorial. It was rumoured he could serve an order of three pints, two bacardis, a white wine and a shandy in just under a minute. His eighteen stone spun round the tiny galley with the grace of a ballerina, churning out pint after pint, the bright-red bandanna round his bald forehead soaking up the sweat, the huge tatoos of naked men on his biceps seeming to animate and pulsate with life.

"Well, look what the cat's brought in! I'll be with you in a minute," he winked at her and deftly slid two dozen cider bottles onto the shelf with mechanical precision. Turning he said,

"I missed you. Where you been, dear, Holloway?" and grinned.

"No, worse. At home, on the booze," and wondered immediately why she had told him. As soon as he answered she knew why. The smile disappeared and the unshaven folds of his face straightened and resolved into an expression of concern.

"Solo drinking, that's bad, Sam."

"Tell me about it!"

"Well, at least you're doing it in public now. That's something to be thankful for."

"Even better, I'm not doing it at all. I'll have an orange juice."

"On the house." A tumbler of juice appeared before her as if by magic. He disappeared for a moment in response to an order for two gin and tonics and Sam took the opportunity to check on Richard. He was staring at a table of young men dressed in the paraphernalia of gay male S and M, nipple clamps and bondage bracelets, regalia of servitude and power play. One of the young men rose from their table and went over to join Richard. He was a scrawny, nervous-looking lad of no more than eighteen or nineteen, with a hundred pound a day habit she guessed. The two sat leaning forward across the table. Fats returned.

"I see this isn't just a social call." She looked at him in surprise.

"How did you know that?"

"I know that look in your eyes, Sam. You've got the heart of a hunter and you're on the scent. Right?"

"Right. Look Fats, if I haven't been in it's just because … I haven't been in. That's all. Things haven't been easy and …," how do you explain to someone that you didn't think they gave a damn when they most patently do, withour feeling crass?

"I know, Sam. You've been in the wars and out of the other side. But you don't have to do it all alone, you know. Next time, remember who your friends are."

Sam felt a lump in her throat that seemed like it meant business. He tactfully turned his back and unloaded a second crate onto shelves, his huge hands grasping six bottles at a time. When he turned back to the bar Sam was comfortably sipping her orange juice.

"So, who's the unfortunate prey this time? Anyone I know?"

"The bloke sitting to the left of the cigarette machine, the blonde one." Fats glanced up momentarily then carried on wiping the bar.

"Know him?"

"He comes in from time to time."

"How often?"

"Every four, five weeks. I've often wondered if he was a commercial traveller or something."

"That regular?"

"Pretty much."

"Who's the guy he's with? A friend?"

"No, rent boy."

"Does he often pick them up?"

"Every time."

"Always leather?"

"Yep," he scowled. "A lot of them refuse to go with him any more."

"Because he's Positive?"

"Because he's vicious."

"I thought that was the point. Get yourself beaten up, have a good time."

"Nah, none of these boys are into the hard stuff. They'd probably all be vanilla if they didn't have a habit to support. But your chap takes it seriously. He hurt one lad quite badly."

"Why didn't he go to the police?"

"Oh come on, Sam, act your age. You see, constable, my arse has been ruptured by a sadist with a beer bottle and I've had cigarettes stubbed out on my nipples. Oh, by the way, I'm a hooker."

"Jesus! Why do you let him come in here?"

"It's a free country, as the bishop said to the beggar. And," he added grimly, "it's not my pub. Look out, your bird is flying." Richard was walking past with the thin, leather-bound youth beside him. Sam could see his ribs protruding through his torn teeshirt.

"They'll be heading for the cottage. You can't go in there."

"No, I'll discreetly fade into the shadows outside. Thanks Fats."

"Whenever," and he swung a twenty litre beer barrel into position as if it were a milk jug.

"And Sam ..?"

"Yeah?", she was halfway out the door. He seemed embarrassed.

"I know you're a big girl. But that guy's mean. Watch out, eh?"

"Sure," and she was gone.

Chapter Nineteen

Hugh stood in front of his full-length looking-glass and held up a light blue angora sweater against his chest. Oh God no, it made him look like a teddy bear. Why ever had he bought it? He threw the offending garment onto the bed. He had phoned into the office on leaving Sarah that morning and pleaded a touch of flu, a twenty four hour virus or something, he was sure he'd be better tomorrow. His father, though displeased, had not been inclined to question.

And so Hugh had fallen into bed and slept most of the day away, awaking at five to a clear head and a mighty appetite. The ordeal of the night before was over. He was rested, restored, revived. He was to see Sarah that evening, (he pulled a lemon jersey polo neck from his drawer). They would have the evening and, hopefully, night to themselves. The prospect before him, (ugh no, the yellow made his face look jaundiced and the wool mixture irritated his skin he remembered now, stuffing it back in the drawer), looked quite definitely cheerful. Then why did he feel like this? So ... out of synch with himself. It was as though, after last night, somehow, something had been jolted out of focus. His normal vision, his way of looking at the world had been skewed, leaving unfamiliar and disturbing images on the retina of his mind.

There was the matter of his ... well, not to put too fine a point on it ... (for Hugh was capable of great honesty) .. his cowardice. Up till now, he would have described himself as an ordinary kind of bloke, really. Definitely not macho, but then, just as definitely not effeminate. Whilst holding to the view that men and women possessed different qualities, different but equal, he also admitted that manhood could, indeed should, display the virtues of gentleness as well as strength, vulnerability as well as protectiveness, (he had forgotten where he had read that). Thus, he had, until now, considered himself as embodying the better values of the thinking, (and feeling), man of his generation. All well and good up till now. But the Battle of the Hunt, for so would last night's events go down in the annals of Hugh's personal history, had been an unequivocal defeat, one so shameful and humiliating as to be forgotten as quickly as possible. There was the rub. Hugh could not forget. However hard he tried. his mind would keep returning to it, over and over again. It was as though some power greater than himself, some all-seeing objective eye were examining this thing called Hugh's masculinity under a microscope. And there it was, stretched spreadeagled, its helplessness magnified, its warts and pimples exaggerated and visible for all to see. He had appealed to the greater power, "but you can't judge a whole person by one act. Everyone makes a mistake, when, forced by extremity, now and again he doesn't come up to scratch. The next time …," the eye had stared down, blank, unwinking, immense. The next time? The part of Hugh that was of one with the eye had to admit that if there were a next time he would, in all probability fail again, that, were he tried and tested twice, thrice, a dozen times, the result would be the same. The discovery that you are not, as fondly imagined, the type that, seawater swirling round your ankles and steadily rising, gamely hands women and children into the lifeboat, that, on the contrary, you are the sort that, hurling all others aside, dives in first, that discovery is bound to make a chap feel out of sorts.

Irritably, he wrested a bottle green v-neck from a hanger and pulled it over his head. Awful! It emphasised his podgy tummy in a thoroughly disgusting manner! He had never, in the past, felt disaffected with his own body. It was good enough. Cuddly, rather than rugged, rounded rather than sculptured. Not that the muscles weren't defined as such, more that the definition was a little blurry in places. Now, for the first time in his life, Hugh wished for a different physique. One like that chap had in the restaurant the other night. But that would have been at the expense of hard training, something for which Hugh had great distaste. His eye strayed to the exercise bike in the corner. There was a tacit reproach in its gleaming white metal, its price tag still unbroken, as virgin as when it had left the shop. Not that he regretted buying it. It came in useful as a clothes horse.

His body. He looked at it in the glass. Tubby was the word, he presumed. But some women liked that. They felt safer with tubby men, (for so he had read). He had asked Sarah once whether she would have wished his appearance different in any way. Leaner? More muscular? She had kissed him on the forehead in the most delicious way and told him to "be yourself," which imperative had, at the time, seemed too absurdly easy to obey. He would have been quite prepared to dash into the water, (they were walking by the sea on a freezing cold February day), to retrieve her glove or something, had she requested it. Now, however, staring into the glass at his face, (too fleshy) and his chest, now encased in the heather mixture pullover his grandmother had knitted him, he began to see the sting in the tail of that "be yourself." For the first time in his life and with a growing panic inside himself he asked who exactly was this Hugh Manders? And answer came there none. Luckily, at that point the phone rang.

"Hugh, where the hell have you been all day? I called your office…"

"I phoned in sick."

"And are you?"

"No."

"So what have you been doing, for God's sake? Why didn't you answer the phone?"

"I pulled it out. I've been asleep."

"Asleep!", by the incredulity in her voice anyone would have thought he had said he'd been to Mars.

"Isn't that what you've been doing?", he ventured.

"Sleeping?" She heaped scorn on that activity and all who succumbed to it.

"I've driven sixty miles, done two interviews and written three articles," which wasn't strictly true, but Sarah, having virtuously remained awake and at her post while Hugh slumbered, was entitled to a little hyperbole.

"Anyway, look, about tonight…"

"You're not calling it off, are you?" Hugh's tone was aggrieved. That would be the last straw.

"TV South have organised this public debate ..." Hugh groaned.

"Oh, Sal! Do you have to go?!"

"Yes, it's all because of me in the first place. Well," more modestly, "partly because of my article on the Frankenstein foetus, then this murder. People are rightly concerned," this rather self-consciously.

"So it's going to be packed out," she added with glee. "Are you going to come?" Hugh, who was normally averse to most sorts of public gatherings, suddenly did not want to be alone that night.

"Of course."

"OK, got to go. Bye." Hugh began to replace the receiver, but her voice came again, calling suddenly and urgently over the line.

"Hugh, Hugh!"

"Yes?" he said eagerly grabbing at the re-connection.

"Bring your camera, will you? I want photographs of the audience." The line went dead.

Chapter Twenty

From the public toilets, Sam had followed Richard to the cab rank on East Street. He had got into a taxi at the front of the queue and she had slid into the backseat of the one behind, saying, "Follow that cab". The driver, a fresh-faced youngster in a Snoopy cap, had laughed.

"For real?" he asked. She handed him a couple of notes as reply.

"You've made my day." He swung into Upper North Street as the Escort ahead turned left.

"Don't get too close, but don't lose him."

"Teach your grandma to suck eggs," he grinned back at her in the driving mirror.

"Go easy. I don't want him to know he's got a tail, so if there's a choice between the two, lose him."

"Gotcha."

He was good, she had to admit, hanging two cars back in the flow of main traffic along the trunk road out of Brighton. When the car ahead turned off the Lewes Road into one of the side streets, he turned in also, but braked to a halt on the corner.

"Just put a bit of distance between us. It's an empty road. We can see if he turns off." But the car didn't. It stopped half-way along the street and Richard got out. As the cab drew away he crossed the road.

"O.K. cruise past and try and see which house he goes in," Sam crouched down low onto the back seat as the cab pulled off. At the top of the street he stopped again.

"Subject went into the park," he announced, with obvious enjoyment.

"Park?"

"Sort of big playing field. You know, couple of goal posts and a lot of dog shit. I used to play soccer there as a kid."

"Any other entrance?"

"No, just the one."

"OK, cruise back down and park opposite the gate."

"You're the boss."

When they reached the park he crossed to the far kerb and pulled up, then looked round questioningly.

"Would you just go and see what he's doing?"

"Sure."

He returned a few minutes later.

"There's a little local tournament going on with a Shoreham team."

"And?"

"Useless. Our side. God knows where they dug them out. I could do better blindfold."

"What about our man?"

"He's watching the game."

Which meant he could be there for at least an hour and a half. He guessed her thoughts.

"There's only ten minutes to go till time, thank God. Put them out of their misery."

"OK, we'll sit tight."

They waited, Sam with her eyes on the park gates. He took out a book and became immediately engrossed in it. Sam was amused to see it was "Zen and the Art of Motorcycle Maintenance". The Sixties hadn't quite died then and been buried in post-Eighties contempt. On the hour he turned on Radio Brighton for the News. There was another appeal for anyone to come forward who had seen the young woman wanted for questioning in connection with the Moulston murder.

"Bad that, hey?" he looked up from contemplations of spark plugs on lonely mountains, "To think a girl did it?"

"They just want her to help with enquiries."

"And we all know what that means."

There was a piercing whistle from within the park and Brighton's humiliation came to an end. Soon after people began emerging through the gates, getting into cars or setting off down the street.

"There he is," he hissed in an unnecessary whisper.

"Where?"

"Behind the bald bloke in the green track suit."

"That's not him!"

"Isn't it? You sure?" Of course she was sure. She'd stared at that slim straight back and that short-cropped, golden hair long enough to know that. It resembled him, perhaps, but the shoulders were too narrow, the joints too angular. A sudden suspicion arose in her.

"Is this the guy who you said was watching the match?"

"Yeah. I thought it was your man." In which case … She waited impatiently as more people, mainly men in football gear now, emptied out of the grounds. No Richard.

"There can't be anyone else left in there now," he said ruefully.

"I'll go and have a look." He returned with a glum face. "Only two old biddies walking a dog."

"I thought you said there was only one entrance."

"There is. He must have walked straight out again as we were driving on up the street. Looks like he knew you were after him and gave us the slip."

Yes, he'd put his finger on the sore point, on what worried her most. It was possible, maybe, to pick up the trail again, but not if her cover was blown.

She had him take her back into town to pick up her car. He refused to take the further couple of notes she offered.

"No, we wouldn't have sat waiting around if I'd have looked for him properly."

"Don't beat yourself up. It was my responsibility. I'm the detective. You're just the cab driver."

"Now we know why," he drove off determined on self-abnegation.

Well, if that's what he wanted. With her own sense of failure sitting sneering on her shoulder, she didn't have time to nurture anyone else's. Besides, she had begun to feel the nagging pangs of what she distractedly recognised as her stomach, mutinying in a bid for her attention, and so made for the nearest burger bar. Halfway over its threshold she remembered her resolution to get "the junk" out of her system and headed, instead, for Food for Friends. It was busy but she found a table and spent the next twenty minutes eating mechanically and writing up her notes – times, places, observations, things to follow up, something she had taught herself in the early days. At last she stopped, finding the page full and her plate empty. For all her palate had registered the taste it might have been a burger. She just hoped her body had noticed the difference.

She arrived at the hall where the debate was to be held just minutes before it was due to begin, not wanting to bump into old friends, preferring not to have to catch up just yet. She'd do that another day. Like the jogging. The venue was a revamped community hall in Kemp Town, chosen as much for its sparkling new paintwork as its public access. Brighton, for all its present troubles, could put on a good show. There was a crowd outside the entrance and, as she pushed her way through, an elderly man in a shiny suit grown too big for him barred her way. The caretaker pressed into service as bouncer.

"The hall's full. Fire regulations. You can't go in."

"Oh but I'm on the panel," Sam's hands flew up in agitation.

"They said there was only going to be four of them up there," the man was suspicious. He had already had a few yobs trying to sneak in through a side window.

"Don't you recognise me? From the television?" He peered at her uncertainly. His sight was not as clear as it had been.

"Go and ask them inside if you don't believe me." The man looked at her and then at the crowd pressing behind her.

"But," Sam added, "it'll mean the whole show going up late. That was enough, he had done his bit, presented his bayonet, demanded friend or foe and that was as far as his orders went.

"In you go then. Hoy, let the lady through, will you!" The Red Sea parted and the 'lady' was allowed through.

She found a vantage point, perched on top of a cupboard, from which she could survey the whole room without being, herself, too visible. The hall really was packed to capacity. In the front she spotted a large group of women, many her former friends. Why did she say former? She just had not seen them for a while that was all. After the split-up with Julia some, admittedly, had stopped calling, either siding with Julia or else finding the position midway between them too uncomfortable. But really, if she were going to be honest, it was her own over-sensitivity to exclusion as well as her instinct to hide away that was the reason for her isolation. For many had gone on calling, attempting to breach the barricade of answer machine and locked door. Ellen for one. She was there now right at the front, a tiny figure in her electric wheelchair, between her lesbian friends and a band of men and women from Disabled Power a group that espoused revolutionary disablity politics. Sam, along with other able-bodied women, had gone on some of the demonstrations, holding up the traffic in Western Road, to protest against the lack of access to public transport, things like that. Ellen had refused to take no for an answer far longer than the others, sending little notes and postcards with messages like, "Keep the faith, baby. Nothing's that bad," and "Quit hibernating, dormouse. The world still loves you." The world being Ellen, at least. But by then the drink had taken hold. After she'd dried out she had been many times on the point of picking up the phone, dialling her number, but what would Ellen, or the others for that matter, say if she came back after all this time? Probably not a lot. The world kept rolling on if you stepped aside for a while and absorbed you back into its flow again when you rejoined. It was up to you whether or not you chose to be part of its momentum.

She scanned the rest of the audience. If the Hunt really did have anything to do with Cynthia's murder, apart from merely being its location, then her killer must be here now in this bustling, chattering crowd of ordinary people. However great the fear of being found out, the fundamental human instinct of curiosity would have driven him (or her) to an event where the lab and all its doings were bound to be the focus of attention. She studied the faces of those people who were not turning to neighbours or sitting in groups. For murderers were supposed to be loners, weren't they? Or was that another cliché? She gave up the guessing game. Physiognomy told you nothing. Facial expressions told you even less.

Shiftiness could be just as likely to indicate the person was trying to avoid an unpleasant encounter with an old acquaintance, (she probably had just such a look herself right now), while the contorted features so beloved of Conan Doyle would more often be the result of constipation than guilty convulsion. No, better stick to gathering impressions and facts. Less room for fantasy there. She turned her attention to the panel.

So that was Dr Shilpa, the small Asian woman in the smart grey suit at one end of the row and next to her a sandy-coloured man in a fawn suit, cream shirt and biscuit tie. Luckily for him the wall behind was a vibrant blue or he might have faded out of sight altogether. So here was the man at the eye of this storm. Vanessa's husband. No, she couldn't see the attraction. But then she never could. Next to him, a vision in vivid orange and unapologetic purple, was the presenter. Sam had seen her on telly. And next to her, presumably, the choleric cleric. His massive, leonine head above the dog collar had gone to fat, its features coarsened, but he must once have been a handsome man. The fluorescents went out in the hall and several dozen kilowatts of studio spots lit up the stage. There was a hush as the people on the dais gathered to themselves the estrangement and power of actors in a play. The presenter looked out into the darkness and held a moment's silence, then, the distance having been achieved, the debate began.

"... been proved that unmarried mothers are one of the main factors in the rise of juvenile crime and drug addiction." That's it, blame the mother again, you boring old fart – Maggie, who was unmarried with a five year old son but also, luckily, an income in the mid five zeros to support him and his nanny, took a slug from her water glass. It was almost straight vodka. Maggie didn't go in for half measures. Not that she was a lush. When she was on the wagon she was dry as a bone. Drier. But when, as right now, she had a high-octane show to get through, (and this one tonight was being networked nationally),

106

she needed to have a head as clear as crystal, which is where the vodka came in.

"... because if you separate procreation from the sex act then the family disappears."

"And good riddance," came a woman's voice, followed by a chorus of tutting, like busy sparrows at daybreak.

Maggie did not interrupt to hush them. Let Beamish shepherd his own flock, for they were, presumably, his. The hall, filled to bursting point and spilling out onto the sidewalk, had, apart from the normal complement of your ordinary man in the street, two definite and opposing factions. Both had muscled their way into prime positions. Front right was the God bloc and front left the politicos – feminists, gays, Lefties – with an Iron Curtain in between. Neither had come prepared to listen to any idea they did not agree with, she reflected morosely, but to shout down the other. So why bother coming? Her sympathies lay with those in the middle, the ordinary Joe Schmoes Don't Knows, who came with a mind to be swayed. Here she took another swig of vodka, which tinged her thoughts with sentimentality towards them. They were her natural congregation. It was for them that she did this job. There was a slight commotion from the floor. A young woman had got to her feet. Maggie stared irritably at her. She had not yet opened up the discussion.

"I agree with the reverend about unmarried mothers," the voice was soft with an Irish lilt.

"The floor isn't opened to questions yet," Maggie was peremptory, but the reverend waved a dismissive hand towards her and she got a whiff of sour armpit.

"Let the child speak her mind," he glowed benevolently at 'the child'. "For out of the mouths of babes and suckling ...," he left the quotation suspended. "Comes a lot of goop," she mentally added.

"What I don't understand is," the young woman gazed up at him, as if to catch the pearls.

"Yes?", he prompted encouragingly.

"If unmarried women are such bad mothers, why do you try and stop them having abortions every Wednesday?"

Maggie joined in the laughter. It had been nicely done, she had to admit. She glanced across at Beamish. The veins in his nose had turned a particularly disagreeable shade of purple. A more intelligent man would have seen the trap, a more generous one admitted he was caught in it and made the best of it, but the reverend was sadly lacking in both qualities.

"If they get themselves pregnant they should have to pay the consequences!" he roared.

"There seems to be a slight confusion in your argument, Reverend Beamish," put in Dr Shilpa, gently, from the other end of the table, "On the one hand you say that children are a reward for good behaviour in getting married, and on the other that they should be a punishment for a woman having sex."

The good man, interrupted full-flow, was painstakingly polite.

"Because marriage is the natural and Godly place to have children."

"If marriage is so natural why do we need a system of rewards and punishments to compel women into it?"

"I think we're getting off the point here," Maggie felt the need to take back the reins.

"I think not," replied Dr Shilpa smoothly. "The whole debate about reproductive technology and genetic engineering is about whether we let Nature take its course or whether we intervene. Reverend Beamish insists on confusing the issue by attempting to conflate the course of Nature with the will of God. Nature, in one shape or another chugged along on this earth for two billion years before the human race appeared and came up with this notion of God." There was an intake of breath from Beamish's side of the hall, but his reply was pre-empted by Roger.

"You can, in some respects, consider God an accident of history, arising out of a certain configuration of cell life at a certain time."

The reverend opened his mouth and the cell life within prepared to emit thunder. His face was like a map, Maggie thought, the tiny capillaries navigating around the bumps and crevices like rivers about the eruption of hill and dale. She flung a dazzling smile at Roger and asked,

"Can you explain that for us, Dr Hunt?"

"Surely," he replied in kind.

"If, as some geneticists claim, we can isolate the gene resposible for ageing, we will, theoretically anyway, be able to do away with death itself. At least with natural, if not violent, death."

"To live forever? What a terrible prospect!" murmured Dr Shilpa. Maggie, who had only that morning discovered two new wrinkles under her right eye, pricked up her ears at these intimations of immortality and gazed with respect at their guru. "So you can see," Roger continued, "if the notion of God is premised on the fact that we are mortal, that some day we all must die, well then, we won't have any more use for Him. We'll all be Gods ourselves."

There was a stir of disbelief from the audience in general and some heavy-duty heckles from the God corner. Their representative turned on his fellow panel members with a snarl, "Scientists playing God are turning the human race into their own laboratory guinea pigs. Not content with taking an egg from a woman and joining it with the sperm of a stranger, they co-mingle it with the seed of a beast!" His supporters stamped their feet and called encouragement. Other members of the audience, Maggie's Joes, looked uncomfortable, hesitant, as though with half a mind to join in. This, after all, was what they had come for. To find out if they were, really, living in a Sci Fi novel. The horror of the Frankenstein Foetus had drawn them in fascination and revulsion. Maggie used the power of her mike to get control.

"Come on, we've got no proof about this. Only the word of a child that she saw a tiny dead thing, half animal, half human. And I mean tiny. From her description it could have been only two, three months old."

"Old enough to suffer," came a cry from the audience and a round of applause from the front right.

"But," Maggie was undeterred, "It was never found. She could have made the whole thing up as a joke."

"My little girl is no liar!", came an indignant male voice. Heads turned, a few cameras clicked.

"Dr Shilpa," Maggie's tone was firm, business-like, "can you talk about the kind of experiments you do?"

"No."

"I think, then, the audience may draw their own … "

"We don't."

"Pardon?"

"We don't do any experiments," Dr Shilpa explained as if to a child. "Reproductive technology is nothing to do with genetic engineering."

"But surely," Maggie was beginning to feel out of her depth and searched desperately for land, any land.

"You must have something in common?"

"Well," Sunita smiled, "we both use test tubes, I suppose."

"But surely, all that playing about with eggs and … sperms," she had been about to say, "spoons" and, draining her glass, hid a giggle in a cough. She ploughed on. She knew from experience that she had the gift of seeming knowledgeable on topics she knew nothing about. It was something you needed to cultivate in her line of work and involved being able to find exactly the right question that would set off that chain of information from the other and to which she would merely have to return the occasional "mm" and the fascinated frown.

"I mean," her smile included the audience in their commonality of disbelief, "you're not going to tell us your work involves no experiments at all, are you?"

"Yes. Didn't you know that?"

No, she did not. Research should have told her. It was their fault. True, they'd given her a bloody ten page thesis but how in the hell was she supposed to wade through that before she came on air?

"Artificial insemination involves the implanting of sperm at the neck of the womb, fertility treatment can very often be just a question of counselling or passing on relaxation techniques and abortion is .."

"Genocide!" contributed Beamish from Maggie's elbow, so suddenly that she jumped almost out of her chair. Too

110

nervous. Have some vodka. Her glass was empty. She reached for her own personal water jug.

"Genocide on a level with the holocaust happens in clinics like hers every day," Beamish jabbed an accusatory finger in the direction of the doctor. There were angry shouts of "anti-semitic" from some corners of the audience.

"The foetus has a human soul but no human rights," Beamish was immune to criticism.

"At what point do you think the soul enters the body?" Maggie slightly overstressed 'soul', to denote incredulity. Pouring the colourless liquid from her water jug, she watched the bubbles crowding around the rim and her mouth watered. Or should she say, vodkad?

"At the moment of conception."

"When egg meets sperm? Then an embryo in a test tube ..?"

"Has a soul. Of course."

Dr Shilpa laughed, "Why should an event that has only biological significance invoke this divine intervention you talk about? What did the egg and sperm have previously? Half a soul each? We're talking about something microscopic at this stage."

"The soul knows no size or shape."

"What about this allegation, doctor, that the egg or sperm for this foetus, if it ever existed, came from your clinic?" Maggie, at that very moment in close-up on several million television sets throughout the nation, looked sharp, intelligent and deeply humane. Her thoughts were actually entirely on vodka, teasing out the seconds in anticipation of that exquisite first swallow of the glass.

"The sperm could have come from roughly half the adult male population. With the egg, that's more difficult, but it certainly didn't come from us."

"And Dr Hunt," Maggie swung round to Roger. His eyes were inviting. She felt a bond between them, a conduit through which gushed a much-needed injection of sexual confidence. The bond would last the duration of the show. For as long as she needed it and no longer.

"This merging of human and animal genetic material,"

(that was a good phrase) – "is it really possible?"

"Gosh yes. Animal genes have been used for a long time in the treatment of some diseases, to alter human chromosomes." At this there was an audible gasp from the audience. A tiny thrill of horror and excitement. Here, at last, was the spine-chilling proof, that science and fiction had met, coupled, mingled their mysteries and produced their hybrid offspring.

"But you're not talking about any joining together of animal and human sex genes. She hesitated ever so slightly over the word "sex". He smiled. It was as if, watched by an audience of five million, they were having an intimate conversation that would lead inevitably to the bedroom. It was this gift for polymorphous intimacy that had made her twice the centrefold of TV gossip magazines and that gave viewers the vivid impression she was talking to them and them alone.

"No no," Roger went on, "I'm talking about an animal gene responsible for, let's say the thyroid gland, being zapped into a human thyroid gene, where the glands are dysfunctioning."

"So there are people walking about, at this very moment, with animal genes in their bodies?"

"Oh yes, quite a few. There might even be some in this hall right now." There was a general shocked whisper and an uncomfortable shuffling as people looked about them, peering sideways at their neighbours for any recognisable signs of bestiality.

"But, combining human sperm with an animal egg – how possible is that?"

"Well, it's possible to do, but impossible to conceive of anyone wanting to do it." They both smiled at his joke. His eyes spoke volumes that she read with pleasure.

"Why is that?"

"Because there's no money in it." Dr Shilpa's voice cut in and broke the spell utterly. Maggie scowled and reached for her glass. Raising it to her lips, she took a mighty swig. And nearly choked. It was full of straight water. Which of those bastards had done that to her? She skewered each of the camera crew in turn with a mental dagger. Or was it the P.A.? Had that bitch spiked her drink? No, she herself had poured the first measure and it was the real McCoy. So someone must have her carafe and she theirs. The two doctors shared one and it was still untouched. That left the bloody vicar, God burn his goolies in hell. He'd somehow got hold of it and now the old fool had it beside his left elbow, just out of her grasp. Too far to lean over and get it, an action that would, anyway, look ridiculous, seeing as she had a half-full carafe in front of her. Roger was talking.

"Yes, the economics of it is one reason, but, also, the scientific community as a whole is a responsible bunch of people. We think deeply about what we do. I'd say you can trust us, wouldn't you, doctor?"

"About as far as I could throw us," Sunita's comment brought a round of applause from her fans in the audience.

"That is the first and last time I'll ever agree with you," Beamish fixed Sunita with a sardonic half-smile.

"And what would be the spiritual status of such a chimera, Reverend Beamish? Let's be clear on this, shall we? Would it have a soul? Or half a soul, perhaps?" Maggie, furious at the annexation of her water jug, denied her liquor, would now settle only for blood.

"A tormented one."

"And would you then welcome this 'tormented soul' into your congregation?", Maggie's eyebrows arched in delicate disbelief.

"I would baptise it myself." In the pin-drop silence the reverend's congregation looked at each other uncertainly.

"Let's get this absolutely straight, Reverend Beamish. Are you saying you would actually confer membership of the Church of England, indeed, the 'fellowship of the Holy Ghost', (where on earth had she dredged up that phrase?), upon this thing with ... ass's ears?"

"I would!"

Maggie's smile, for her six million viewers, was bemused but benign as she, like them, gazed pityingly at the clergyman. She well knew that the people who got pleasure from watching a public flogging would draw the line at seeing anyone actually gloat over it. That would be obscene. So she crowed to herself alone, imagining in glorious technicolour the phone calls that would be coming in right this minute from members of the synod, denouncing his words, perhaps even calling for his defrocking or whatever kinky things they got up to between them. She winked at Roger but his precise, scientific brain was rebelling against this excess of fantasy.

"Look here, we're talking about the *possibility*, only the possibility of a half-formed foetus that someone *may* have seen and that, if it existed at all, would not have lived to attain consciousness, whether animal or human."

Maggie swung round to face him, pushing her chair back towards Beamish, crowding him, manoeuvring her body so that she could get within arm's reach of her carafe. She was frankly desperate. Her mouth was dusty dry and tasted of rank old bedclothes. She needed a drink. Badly. But, as with Tantalus, the grape, or the potato in this case, was just out of reach. Roger was going on.

"Such a creature as you're suggesting would not live longer than ...," he looked towards Dr Shilpa for inspiration. She shrugged and shook her head, it was not her line of work.

"About two to three months," he concluded.

" Which is exactly the estimated age," here Maggie's voice slowed perceptibly, heavy with portent, "of the foetus that was found."

There was a hush in the hall, as if eveyone had stopped breathing together. Outside, in some anthropomorphic transference, there seemed a similar cessation of sound. Birdsong, cars, buses all momentarily halted.

At first sight the battle lines had seemed clear. Of Sam's own friends, many had come in support of Dr Shilpa and the clinic and to register a protest against a religious Right they deemed anti-feminist and homophobic. To the Hunt man, however, they maintained, at first, a puzzled ambivalence. He had not, as yet, given them any reason for opposition. Science was Science after all, and went about its own obscure and baffling business in faraway laboratories where people in starched white overalls made smells and did unpleasant things to white mice. Some, indeed, even took it as read that any enemy of the Born Agains was a friend of theirs. Others had looked more closely at the issues and were there in solidarity with Disabled Power. But, even here alliances were not as assured as they looked. For many of Ellen's disabled friends were anti-abortion. It could have been me, they said. If it had, I would not be here today. Many, too, were pro-family. Understandably so, when you are denied the possibility of a relationship and family of your own. To denounce the family outright was a luxury of the able-bodied. But what sort of family are we talking about? Many women were impatient with them, hearing the adjective, "pretend" tacitly and tactlessly applied to the families they themselves had painstakingly built up. That Disabled Power should occupy a place in between two camps, or that they had not been allowed a position within the bounds of the warring factions was something that many of the able-bodied women preferred to ignore, Sam noticed. Again, this urge for unity, this attempt to obscure difference. Would we never learn, she thought?

And so the battle waged that night, with no point going unscored. At one point an elderly woman in an impeccably atrocious peach two-piece stood up and announced: that A – she was a life-long Christian, to which there were murmurs of approval from predictable sources, that B – she was a life-long lesbian, at which she was immediately clutched to another, different bosom and that C – she worked at the abortion clinic and D – she had a sister with cerebral palsy. It was possible, she continued, without trying to be all things to all people, to have a foot in many camps and she concluded by reminding her audience that the building of bridges was generally a more profitable exercise than the mining of them. Having exhibited her coat of many colours and confounded all possible critics, she sat down with an embarassed grunt. Then suddenly, in one of those volte faces that only happen in war, far Right and far Left, pro-Family and

115

pro-Feminist, found themselves encamped on the same spit of land, uncomfortably and embarrassingly cheek by jowl, opposed to a common foe, though for very different reasons. It happened like this.

Asked earnestly whether he could categorically state that he had never in the past nor ever would contemplate creating a hybrid of the kind described, Hunt had replied that, on the contrary, he, like other scientists, was engaged in the search for human perfection. For, would they not all, he asked the assembled people, if they had the choice, choose to have a child without defects? It was then that Ellen took the floor. Wheeling herself to the front, (her frequently raised hand having been continuously ignored), she proceeded to make the kind of speech which those hearing it would remember for the rest of their lives. It is the kind if speech whose power remains in the memory long after the details have blurred, because it has managed to gather together all the several and separate, the scattered and wayward fragments of unease and confusion, to bind them into a single whole and offer them again to their owners, as though returning lost property gift-wrapped.

The gist of it was this. The quest for perfection? Had she not heard that somewhere before? Fifty years ago, when the jackboot had marched across the face of Europe (and the face of many Europeans, she added in parenthesis). A world fit for the fittest, free from imperfection, that had been their rallying cry then. The message had, (to the eternal shame of the Church), been echoed from the pulpit. The imperfections then were Jewishness, disability, homosexuality and communism. The "solution" was from the pages of a horror story, and should have remained there. It had been called, among other things, "social engineering," a nice, innocuous-sounding word. Now, fifty years on, they called that same process "cleansing". What Dr Hunt (she was meticulously polite) envisaged was genetic cleansing. All future generations would be subject to strict quality control. But what was the new standard for perfection? Which of those here tonight would it exclude?

116

Sam, joining in the applause afterwards, looked around her at the hotch-potch of humanity crammed together in that hall, the different shapes, sizes, ages, races and religions in that two hundred or so square metres and she felt a sudden warmth and affection for her fellow creatures, a fierce joy in their infinite variety. It was crucial, she decided, that that diversity be preserved, that no nation or government or interest group be allowed to stamp it out.

After Ellen, others stood up to speak. A young black man who spoke of the genetic cleansing in progress right now when black women in Britain were sterilised under anaesthetic, without their permission. Then a woman in a chador got up. In her country the perfect baby was male and thousands of girl foetuses were being aborted regularly. Others followed. There was a passion rising in the hall, a tide of frustration and pain and anger. Hunt remained impassive, smoothly answering any questions put to him, smiling as darts from Right and Left aimed at his straw-coloured flanks bounced off unnoticed. At last he framed a question to Beamish. Had he not earlier described homosexuality as a sin and a wickedness? Beamish agreed, he most certainly had. Well, unimpeachable, empirical evidence now existed to prove that it was not so at all, that it was, in fact, a genetic defect and that sufferers from it, as from other defects like spasticity or blindness, were deserving not of blame but pity. He was, at this minute, involved in research to find the gene responsible in order to eradicate it. The uproar that followed brought the meeting to a stormy and abrupt close. Sam slipped away.

Chapter Twenty One

Detective Sergeant Walsh was almost dead on his feet. He had been up all night interviewing two suspects who had turned out to have been just larking where they shouldn't have been, and all day talking to pathologists, Moulston residents and the victim's poor mother. He had been honourably discharged by Chief Inspector Sparrow at six with the admonition to have a hot bath, a square meal and a sleep. But he could not. There was one thing he knew he had to do first, before drawing the curtains on this day, (or two days, it had been) and which, left undone, would cause him to worry all night. The public meeting about that stupid monster baby could have been adequately covered by one of the eager, pushy young detective constables, but as far as he was concerned they saw everything and noticed nothing. The whole damn thing should have been officially closed, would have been had there not been the murder in the lab grounds and then all that hooha about a link between the two, even talk of witchcraft. That always came up whenever there was a crime a bit out of the ordinary, a bit inexplicable. Witchcraft explained everything and could be relied upon to get everyone worked up. If people really believed it was the devil, why did they blame the police? Did they expect bobbies to go around with stakes instead of truncheons hanging from their belts. No, this whole thing was a typical response to a community threatened by something it couldn't put its finger on. This monster foetus had become a sort of symbol and before it the collective unconscious reared up like a frightened horse. (Walsh's dad had been a bookie and his own major hobby was psychology which, perhaps, explained his imagery).

But psychology wasn't just a hobby, it was a way of life for Walsh. In his job you had to understand what made people tick. When he had first joined the CID he had been sent on a psychology course and that's where the bug had bit him. He had been on many courses since that first, each one opening a gateway to a new and exciting discovery. He was considered quite an expert now on things of the mind and it had ensured he kept a fresh approach. While other men of his age and length of service had developed that hard, bitter knot of cynicism inside well before that long last run-up to retirement, he had kept his enthusiasm. Twenty years of daily contact with people you wouldn't wipe your arse with, that's how they described their life's work. But he still saw something of interest in everyone. He still liked people, whereas in his mates he could see all around him that contempt, for the villain and for the victim alike. The one was as bog stupid as the other, he'd hear them say. The whole rotten world was locked in an eternal embrace of the shafters and the shafted. It was understandable. They met no other category of human being, preferring to associate in their free time only with their families or other cops.

He had never had time to marry and here he was, coming up forty eight, which was alright, with no family but with a lively, enquiring mind and plenty of interests to fill it, which was also alright, and very little time left if he was going to make it to Inspector, which was not alright. He needed to do well on this Fenton case or else there were lads, younger than him, coming up fast behind. So he was following every angle, even the least likely ones. His own view was that the murder was a quite separate affair, nothing to do with all this hue and cry about the foetus. That it was a sex crime, a case of necrophilia, (stabbings often were, one penetration being the precursor to another), but the man hadn't had time to get that far before he was interrupted. Well, that was his theory, but still the link had to be chased up. Which is why he was here tonight and wondering, as the hall erupted into angry revolt, whether he should take charge of the situation as official representative of East Sussex Constabulary. No, let the uniform boys do that. They had bouncers anyway, surely. Serve them right if they didn't. He slipped out, unnoticed.

Sliding gratefully behind the wheel of his Polo he picked over his memories of the meeting. He had had no plan in mind beforehand, just a general brief to himself to be "on the look out". He couldn't really explain what that meant to anyone else, but he knew. Something, someone might catch your eye. You might not even register it at the time, but then, days, weeks later it would slide into your brain, impose itself, till you recognised its significance. What had there been like that tonight? He was very tired, but it was best to go over these things immediately, while they were still fresh. There was more chance then, that anything important would push itself into view earlier. Bill Gatwood had been there, he had noticed. But that was hardly surprising, seeing as his little girl "saw" the foetus. What was worth noting was that he was part of that noisy bunch from St Saviours. Anything there? Perhaps, but he could not, at the moment, make any coherent pattern of what he had seen and heard tonight. He was just too dead beat. Tomorrow. Tomorrow he would try and sort out this foetus nonsense once and for all.

Chapter Twenty Two

As they drove to Al Forno's for a late lasagne and a bottle of house red, (it was Sarah's turn to pay), Sarah had been jubilant, had talked non-stop. What had she told him? The hall packed, everyone roused to a fervour of revolt against the hated Hunt and all its doings, (which was something of an exaggeration, although feelings were running high by the end, Hugh had to admit). And all because of her. She had single-handedly exposed the Hunt, alerted the good citizens of East Sussex (of the nation in fact, for had not that meeting tonight been seen by at least twenty million people?) to a horror in their midst, by her superb piece of investigative journalism (would Reuters be interested in her in-depth article on the debate?). Hugh was silent, listening to his beloved, for once in his life, with but half an ear. He was engaged in something extraordinarily difficult and which was absorbing most of his energy. He was attempting to piece together thoughts and feelings that were as yet inchoate, unformed and, as this was a far from habitual task for him, it was consuming a large part of the attention he normally dedicated to Sarah. Dredged from the hitherto unplumbed depths of that subterranean pool that was Hugh's unconscious, creatures of an indeterminate and largely amphibious origin, (judging from the state of their evolution), flippered their way to the surface, hovered motionless an instant and then plunged back down again before they could be adequately grasped. It was most frustrating. Particularly as he would rather not be attempting such a futile exercise at all. Having stayed so long deep within caverns measureless to Hugh, they had much better not emerge at all. But emerge they would, inviting arrest and eluding capture. And if this were not bad enough, these vague stirrings carried with them the bubblings of discontent, of disaffection and, worst of all, doubt. Doubt was something Hugh was unfamiliar with.

It was not until they were comfortably ensconsed with garlic bread and bottle that Hugh ventured to give form

to the formless, to attempt to give coherent and compre-
hensible utterance to something he could not, himself,
comprehend. In doing this he cut her off mid-flight, a
thing unheard of for him. Astonished, she heard him out,
aware, even before him, of the significance of his words.

"Sal, I ... oh hell!" he began inauspiciously, and
stopped.

"Sal ..," he groped for a vocabulary for things nameless.

"Am I ..? I mean, do you think ... the thing is, I don't
know .. what's inside me," he finished up with a rush.

"Two hunks of garlic bread," but her flippancy was to
hide her awkwardness at things to come.

"Seriously. Do you think there is anything underneath
all this?" it came flooding out now.

"I mean, who is Hugh Manders when he's at home? I'm
fairly intelligent," she was about to make a joke but
thought better of it.

"I'm quite good at my job, generous to my friends, tol-
erant to my family, (even Deirdre's ghastly sprogs), I
mean, I'm an alright sort of a bloke, aren't I?"

"Can't complain," Sarah stared fixedly into her wine.

"But those .. evangelist people tonight ..."

"Awful," Sarah shivered.

"And the feminists and other politicos ..."

"Just as tedious,"

"Yes, but Sal, whatever you think of what they said, the
thing is ... the main thing is ... they believe in something," he had reached the heart of the matter.

"And I don't. I don't believe in anything much."

"I hope you believe in me."

"Yes, of course I do. But you know what I mean, don't
you?" Yes, she did.

"The thing is ...," here the lasagne arrived and Hugh's
crisis of faith was momentarily interrupted by the distribu-
tion of pepper and parmesan.

"The thing is, Sal, there's nothing outside of us, nothing
... greater ..."

"No, there isn't," her mouth full of food she was brief.

"But watching those people there tonight, however
ridiculous they sounded, and I agree, most of them did

122

sound pretty silly, with all their talk of souls and …
visions for humanity," he was expertly forestalling Sal's
predictable cynicism on the subject, "I felt … well, jealous." There, he had said it. He looked up, shyly, but she
was busy eating. He twirled mozarella round his fork and
dove it into the steaming dish. Even the pasta had layers
he could not aspire to and suddenly he felt miserable.

"I suppose, deep down I'm scared that really I'm a
pretty shallow sort of person." His eyes pleaded, but she
was silent. Having nothing to say to reassure him, (for
had she not only that afternoon had her own lonely night
of the soul?) and being wise enough to know that pat
responses were no earthly good. Also, she did not want
to get bogged down in this. It was vital to keep her own
momentum going. She had a lot to do that night. They
ate more or less in silence till after profiteroles had been
proffered, accepted and washed down with coffee. It was
then that Sarah, finer feelings having been duly respected,
deemed it admissible to carry on the real business in
hand.

"Those photographs, Hugh?"

"Mm?"

"I need them by 6.30 tomorrow morning."

"What!" he slopped the remains of his coffee onto the
table.

"Or before if possible."

"But I'd be up all night doing that."

"That's alright, you've slept all day."

"Yes, but I'll be useless for work again."

"Flu. Takes a while to get over."

"Yes, I know but …," but he was doomed from the
outset and he shouldn't have tried, for in the ensuing
conversation in which it was gently pointed out to him
how fortunate he was to be able to bathe in the refracted
glory of so bright a talent as hers, he quite forgot that
Sarah was paying and automatically presented his own
credit card to the waiter.

Chapter Twenty Three

Sam got to Paris, Texas ten minutes ahead of schedule. The cafe was pretty full, it being a place where you could sit over a coffee, a drink or a meal any time of day or evening, with a crowd of friends, with a lover or alone, with a book. Mostly, this last year, Sam had sat alone. Her favourite table was just that minute being vacated.

"Impeccable timing, Sam," Vin, the waiter grinned at her. She ordered a capuccino and pulled out her notebook, into which she doodled a hawk, a tree and a whirligig before finally closing it with a snap. She could not assemble her thoughts. Not just yet. There was too much to assimilate, too many faces, voices, impressions, snatches of this and that all jostling in her brain for recognition. She would wait for them all to settle before she began the job of sifting through the sediment to see what should be retained and what thrown away. But the truth of the matter was that she was restless. Tonight the warmth and cosmopolitan cosiness of the cafe did not gather her into itself as usual. The couple beside her were chewing a succulent steak au poivre as though it were a pair of old sandals, their jaws rigid with tension and unspoken thoughts.

"Gives me indigestion just to look at them," thought Sam, "and I'm not even eating."

She turned away from them. In the far corner a large group of women were recalling an adventure holiday they had had together in the Pyrenees. Howls of laughter accompanied each reminiscence. The mirth was fast becoming uncontrollable and they were still on the first day. Sam wished she had suggested another rendezvous, but it was too late now. And talking of late, where the hell was she? Sam glanced irritably at her watch. Shilpa was already twelve minutes …

"Sorry I'm late," came a voice at Sam's elbow. It had the effect of cool soft fingers on a feverish cheek and Sam, looking up, suddenly felt very, very good. The phrase, "the pleasure of your company" flashed into her mind and she said, "No problem. How did you know it was me?" Sunita looked amused. Sliding into a seat opposite she said,

"You look the part. Come on, you must know that." They grinned at each other over the table.

"That capuccino looks nice but right now I could murder a drink." The doctor threw her hand into the air, "That was an ill-conceived phrase," the other hand flew too, "Oh God, I must control my unconscious before it runs away with me. Conception and death – the twin pole stars of existence. That's why people are so fascinated, of course. It's like some sort of Greek Tragedy."

"Don't those have a habit of getting out of hand?"

"Yes," said the doctor grimly, "in spite of all human efforts to the contrary."

"Do you think the two things are connected?"

"Are we talking metaphysically now? No, you mean the murder and the alleged foetus. Well, both have been dumped well and truly on the Hunt's doorstep. And I don't envy them that.

"After tonight I don't pity them either."

"I agree. Yes, a pint of lager and a piece of that divine toffee and banana thing you do ...," and her hands took flight as though in search of the divinity. Throughout the evening Sam had occasion to notice those hands. Long, delicate, tapered, they worked constantly in concert with the brain to which they were attached and both were delightfully active.

"But why?" She turned her attention back to Sam, whose own attention had wandered considerably.

"Uh, why what?"

"Why," Sunita demanded, "tell everyone about your research when it's bound to cause a furore?"

"Only in some quarters. If you're talking about his last statement, you'll find a lot of people agreeing with him, that homosexuality is a disease to be eradicated at all costs. He's probably made himself a folk hero overnight."

"Don't you think that's slightly paranoid?"

"No, I do not!" Sam's answer came fast and furious.

"Like Ellen said, they've done it before to the Jews, to

125

us, to disabled people. They're doing it now to minorities all over the world." She had not realised just how angry she felt until that moment. The other woman looked distressed.

"I am in no way trying to minimise the threat. I think it is there, though many years off. They are nowhere near being able to do anything like that yet ... thank you, that looks wonderful," to the waiter as he set pie and drink before her, and then back to Sam, "but also, there is such a thing as public pressure to stop genetic science being used for social control."

"Like I said, we're not a well-loved minority."

"Perhaps not, but there are enough of us out there who are against what Roger Hunt has in mind."

Sam noted with interest her use of "us". Was that just a term of liberal consensus or was this woman coming out to her?

"There were a lot of those people around in Germany in the Thirties. It didn't stop the death camps."

"Psychologists have been trying to pathologise homosexuality for years. So now scientists are trying to get a look in. What's the difference?"

"The difference is that we're talking about something even more fundamental than the mind. We're talking about the body. The first base."

The doctor gazed at her with great seriousness.

"In my philosophy it is the mind that is first base. The mind that makes the body."

"You try telling someone in a wheelchair that."

"No, you misunderstand. I mean it is the mind that determines the significance. Bodies are bodies. It is we who give meaning to them." Sam felt out of her depth here. Both Philosophy and Science were two worlds unfamiliar to her and she stood, somewhat overawed, at their portals.

"But now you're saying that genes aren't important at all."

"No, as a doctor I couldn't say that. But there's a gene fever going on at the moment. A reductionism that wants to ignore all social, political and spiritual considerations. I

126

think it will pass, but not before a lot of damaging things have been done."

"Like trying to make lesbians and gays extinct?" The doctor stared at her.

"So you believe there is a genetic basis to lesbianism and homosexuality?" she asked.

"Of course not!" was Sam's hot rejoinder.

"Then why are you so worried? About that, anyway. I mean I can understand far more the fears of the disabled community. They've got a lot more to be anxious about."

To which Sam was brought up short. There was a silence.

At last Sunita said, "Why do you think you are? Lesbian, I mean?"

Here we go again, thought Sam. Now who's pathologising. And she felt a deep sense of disappointment. And betrayal.

"Why don't you ask why people are heterosexual?"

"Oh, because I know why," Sunita responded promptly. "Because that's all that's drummed into them from the word go. It's everywhere, writ large in tablets of stone. I just wanted to know how you felt you had managed to avoid it where others had failed."

"I guess I just stopped taking the tablets," Sam grinned. The doctor laughed long and loud, bringing even the noisy mountaineers at the next table to a momentary halt. The atmosphere between them, which Sam now realised had been getting extremely tense, suddenly relaxed palpably.

"Have some pie. It's gorgeous." Sam had some. It was.

"Have some more. I'll never eat it all by myself."

They ate in comfortable silence, as though, Sam reflected, they had known each other years. At last the doctor put down her fork.

"I'd been longing for that for weeks. The desire for it comes over and whelms me every six months or so," she explained. "Anyway, we'd better get down to business. Having got you here at an unsociable hour and come late in the bargain, I mustn't keep you any longer than necessary."

Sam, who suddenly didn't care how long she was kept, nevertheless pulled her notebook towards her, drew a pen from the inside pocket of her jacket and said brusquely, "Care to tell me about it?"

"Well ...," but the doctor seemed to be having a problem beginning. Sam looked up in amusement, believing the source of the problem to be a residual mouthful of toffee and cream, but she found the other was staring into middle distance, a look of embarrassment in her eyes.

"Now that it's come to telling you I find it ... you see, I feel it's all my fault. If only I had done something about it at the time. We're very possibly in big trouble. This allegation in the Press that we, somehow, supplied the sperm for this thing ..."

"This thing that probably never existed."

"Oh, but that doesn't matter any more. It exists in people's minds. And what's more powerful, that or reality?"

"I might be a bit tired at this point in the evening, but if that's the case, I'd say you needed a P.R. firm not a private detective." Dr Shilpa was silent. The same area of wall seemed to be engaging a lot of her attention as her hands folded and unfolded in front of her.

"Or is there something else?" Sam probed gently, feeling like a therapist. The woman who had talked with such ease and loquacity earlier about the most complex of issues had suddenly great difficulty in producing a few simple facts.

"Yes, there is something else," Sunita replied reluctantly, "we had a burglary." Another one, thought Sam, scientific establishments were obviously a new crime growth area.

"I see. And you notified the police, of course?"

"No." Sam did not ask why. She thought she already knew.

"And what was stolen?" Sunita's hands sought for the escape her brain could not and, failing to find it, came down to rest.

"Sperm," she said, briefly. Sam, scribbling in her notebook, did not look up.

128

"Date?"

"June 21st," she had had to drag the words kicking if not screaming from her lips. Sam wrote down the date – exactly three months ago. Finally she looked up.

"Who else knows about this?"

"Besides the thief and any beneficiaries, just you and I. I found the broken window on a Saturday morning when no one else was around. I cleared up the mess and reglazed it myself. It was a toilet window. I never thought anyone could get through such a small gap."

"They use kids sometimes."

"I've had a security lock put on since but …"

"Was it obvious? I mean, was it in a box labelled, "Sperm in here" or something?"

"God no. You'd have to know what you were looking for."

Sam chewed the end of her pen and stared at her notes. At last she said, "I don't understand why."

"Why I didn't report it at the time, you mean? Well, it was a small quantity and, to be honest, I thought I knew who it might be. We'd had a girl working for us, very unhappy young woman, always being abandoned by one boyfriend after another and desperate to be married. I thought she might have taken them. I thought maybe she wanted a baby so badly."

"Why didn't you tackle her about it?"

"Oh she would have been mortified. We weren't sup- posed to know all her blokes left her. It was she who left them, that was the story. Good time girl, onto the next one. Anyway, she would have denied it." There was a pause.

"You see, Sam, if it gets out we lost the sperm, there's a lot of explaining to do about lax security at the time. But …"

"But if it gets out you failed to report it," Sam con- tinued, "That would be the end of the clinic?"

"You've got it."

"So you want me to do a damage limitation number and cover for you? Say, if anyone asks, that you called me in and I investigated the matter and found nothing?" The doctor looked shame-faced.

"I'm afraid that is exactly what I am asking. You see, I still believe it was that silly girl who took the sperm so I don't want a proper investigation ..."

"It would be too late now anyway."

"Exactly. We'll pay you, of course."

"No, don't worry about it."

"And maybe this will just all blow over and we'll hear nothing more about it," she was trying to convince herself.

"So really all you need to do is sit tight and I'll call you if it's necessary."

"I'd better come round and take a look anyway. So that if anyone does ask at least I know the layout. And I might be able to give you some tips on security."

"That would be very kind of you. Thank you." The doctor's eyes shone with relief and gratitude.

"It'll be a pleasure," Sam said. And meant it. Utterly.

Chapter Twenty Four

At eight fifteen the following morning, Jenny Fenton made a phone call. The recipient answered with a cautious, "hello" and when he heard, for it was a man, who the caller was, became anxious and whispered hurriedly that he could not talk now as he had a visitor. As to who his early morning visitor was he did not or could not elucidate and Jenny found the receiver dead in her hand.

"Now, Sandra, your evidence has caused a lot of people, a lot of very important people to get very hot under the collar already. And if everything is as you say it is then … well, they're going to get even hotter," Detective Sergeant Walsh finished lamely. He had been trying to instil into Sandra Gatwood a sense of the seriousness of her allegations and to inspire in her the correct mixture of awe and respect for authority that was only proper in a girl of thirteen. But Sandra merely nodded her head in vehement agreement with his words, her eyes sparkling with excitement.

"I know. There was all these reporters and telly people trying to get into our school yesterday – through the windows, up the drain pipes, everywhere. Our headmaster said it was driving him to an early grave." She smiled happily. She had never had so much attention in her whole life and she was thriving on it, so that reminding her of the power of her words on the nation's media as well as the nation's susceptibilities was not a promising path to follow. He would try another tack.

He always preferred interviewing at the station. For a start it was your own territory and that gave you a distinct advantage. Also, you had privacy. Seated now in the Gatwood's cramped, drab living room, with its lumpy, mock-leather three-piece and stained brown carpet he felt spied upon, by the tortured eyes of the crucified Christ in gold-painted plastic above the telly, by the saccharin gaze of Christ the Shepherd in dayglo pink and blue on the wall in front of him and by the haloed complacency of

Christ resurrecting over the mantlepiece, beside a pile of Reader's Digest and a battered Bible. He shuffled his notes in a professional manner and returned to his favourite theory.

"Any boyfriends, Sandra?" he began conversationally and smiled in what he hoped was an avuncular fashion, but she stared back at him, instantly on her guard. He realised his mistake immediately. He should have brought a WPC along. With her father out the room and the door closed such a question was open to misinterpretation. He now had the task of regaining her confidence, which might prove long and arduous. But she was replying to his question now, slowly and deliberately, her voice raised, as though to communicate beyond the closed door.

"No, my dad don't let me have no boyfriends, so I don't have none. I do what my dad says." So that was it. She thought he was spying on her dad's behalf. That all this continued questioning was an elaborate trick to induce her to confess her romantic and sexual liaisons. Walsh almost laughed out loud. That the adolescent mind was egotistical enough to believe its concerns would command this amount of police time and attention was amazing, even to someone who had done a course on teenage psychology. However, the fact that she should believe her father to be within earshot was a warning not to be ignored. He rose soundlessly, walked swiftly to the door and opened it.

"Yes, Mr Gatwood? Did you want something?"

Bill Gatwood's face scowled back at him, stiff with resentment and, was that fear? Or was he imagining things?

"Just coming to ask if you was wanting a cup of tea."

"Lovely idea, if you're making it. Two sugars, please," he closed the door and gave Sandra a wink. She giggled suddenly and unexpectedly. This was better. Feeling a little like a circus entertainer, he winked again. This time she broke into an unnerving spasm of high-pitched giggles that threatened to choke her. However, when these eventually subsided he felt that he had broken the ice. He began again.

"Now, Sandra, let's just run over the events of last Sunday evening, shall we?" he smiled encouragingly, but the jocularity had gone, to be replaced by a bored, sulky expression.

"I already told you everything I know".

"Yes, but just in case you left anything out. A little detail that might turn out to be a big clue." He had stressed the word "clue", conjuring up in the popular imagination those detective story visions of magnifying glasses and dusting powder. But it did not have the required effect on Sandra, whose permitted literary diet was obviously confined to the contents of their mantelpiece.

"I was walking through the woods on Sunday about quarter to seven at night …," she intoned, like a rebellious actor rehearsing a speech for the umpteenth time. Walsh almost knew it off by heart himself.

"But why?" he interposed suddenly. She was caught off-balance.

"Why what?"

"Why were you walking through the woods then?" at a time of a, by now, darkening and frosty September evening, he added to himself, when most people in Lower Hannerley were settling down to sherry or dinner and a bit of telly. Or in church. Yes, in fact …

"Don't you usually go to church on Sunday evening?"

"Yeah," she was looking at the floor now.

"So why weren't you there last Sunday?"

"I didn't feel well."

"Oh, I see. And what was it? Cold? Headache?" She hunched her shoulders. A red spot on her cheek was growing, spreading slowly outwards to her neck and forehead. She mumbled something and he caught the words, "Women's troubles."

"I see. You didn't go to church because you had a pain in your tummy?"

"Yeah."

"A bad pain?"

"Yeah."

133

"So, instead of going to church because of this bad pain, you went for a walk in the woods?" There was silence, except for the regular tap tap of her heel kicking against the leg of the armchair.

"Is that right, Sandra," he repeated sternly and could have sworn he heard a board creak outside the door.

"Yeah, that's what I told you, didn't I?"

"Fair enough. Let's go on, then, shall we?"

"I'm going to be late for school," it was a last-ditch attempt that he thrust aside peremptorily.

"I'll explain things to your headmaster, don't worry. Now, you walked up the path to the bit where it bends round and starts to descend down to the Mills," he had an Ordinance Survey map open in front of him.

"Then, for some reason, you dodged off the main path and onto a narrow one that was barely passable. Why would that be, Sandra?"

"I heard a woodpecker," she said through chewed fingernails.

"You heard a woodpecker? I see. And you wanted to have a look for it?"

"Yeah."

"An ornithologist, are you, Sandra?"

"You what?"

"Interested in birds?"

"Yeah."

"And what colour is a woodpecker, Sandra?" There was a slight pause and he leant back, pleased with his ingenuity.

"Which one? The Greater Spotted or the Lesser Spotted?" Touché, thought Walsh.

"So," he continued, "you were looking up at the trees for this woodpecker and then, all of a sudden, you looked down and saw the foetus. Describe it to me, will you, Sandra?"

"It was about four or five inches long," the bored, mechanical tone had come back. She was on firm ground now. It was all in his notes.

".. with the head of a goat and the body of a human child." Alarm bells rang in Walsh's head.

"Say that again," he made as if to be writing it down,

134

like a secretary getting behind with dictation. She sighed and repeated slowly, almost patronisingly, "with the head of a goat and the body of a child." Walsh flicked back through his book to last Sunday's notes, no longer pretending.

"That's not what you said the first time. In your original statement you said the opposite – child's head, goat's bottom half."

"That's what I said just then."

"No, you didn't."

"Yes, I did."

"No, you didn't." The door burst open, saving them both from any repetition of the pantomime refrain.

"Why don't you leave my girl alone? You're driving her to distraction with all your questions, questions. Making out she's a liar. No wonder she's getting confused. She don't sleep at night for thinking about what she seen, poor kid. I'm going to speak to my solicitor about this. What you're doing is nothing less than police harrassment of my little girl."

She's not your little girl any longer, Walsh wanted to say. She's at least half way to becoming a woman and you don't want to see it, and that's the problem. But it wasn't any business of his. He had the picture now and it was pretty much as he had supposed at first, with some minor variations. That reaction earlier of hers, to his question about boyfriends, had given him the clue. He reconstructed that Sunday evening as follows:- she had not gone to church, as usual, with her father, pleading menstrual pains and had, instead, gone out for a walk in the woods with some local boy or other. Presumably they had taken a diversion off the path and into some bushes with the intention of doing something they ought not (Walsh was immensely glad he had no children, especially girls). She had got back home in plenty of time to be still doubled up with pain when her father got back from church, but had, presumably, not taken the precaution of removing the bits of grass and leaves from her clothes beforehand. A big mistake. That she was afraid of her father was obvious. His life was dominated by an unforgiving God and hers by a similarly censorious father. So she had had to extemporise fast, distract his attention. And he, not wanting to believe his little girl capable of anything as adult or ungodly as a grope in the bushes, had preferred to be taken in by her incredible story. How she had discovered the monster thing, had rushed back down the path, stumbling over tree roots and falling flat on her face in her panic. Why a story so improbable? Well, it had been her subconscious at work here and as she had been involved, to some extent or other, in mimicking the act of procreation, that is what popped out of it. As to the added twist of a half-human, half-animal foetus, that probably indicated the extent of her guilt about the animal nature of her passions. Yes. He felt he had satisfactorily solved the mystery of the Frankenstein Foetus. Not that it wouldn't rumble on in the Press for days, perhaps weeks to come, but he could conveniently now draw a line under it as far as he was concerned. And, as for any connection with the Hunt lab murder they could, once and for all, he would tell his boss, rule that out.

Sam had woken at seven that morning in a bad temper. Looking around the bedroom she had noticed for the first time in weeks the layers of dust on the dresser and the multi-coloured flecks of thread and fluff that had sewn themselves into the carpet, making the plain grey into a riotous tweed. The kitchen had been even worse. Every plate and pan she possessed was piled high on the draining board awaiting the ministrations of soap and scouring pad. Some hope today! The larder was woebegone, with a can of sardines and a tin of cat food (she had started feeding a mangy stray with one ear and the appealing look of a vagabond). The fridge was doleful in its emptiness and stank of sour milk and things unnamable. She couldn't bring anyone back here, she thought as she slammed the door. She caught herself. Just who was she proposing to bring back, anyway? There were no prospective candidates for that. But she knew very well whose face sprang to mind. She had dreamt about her that night. "Put that right out of your mind, Sam Carter," she admonished herself sternly, "there's no future in it." But nevertheless, a pair of dark brown eyes, shining with intelligence and humour, accompanied her as she stomped irritably down the stairs and into a bright September morning. A full fried breakfast at the steamy 24 hour cafe in the market restored her spirits but also drove away any lingering wisps of enchantment. Down to business. Her running shoes sat still immaculate on the back seat of her car.

"Not today, Josephine," she addressed them, as she started the engine.

When she arrived at her office at 8.15 Vanessa Hunt was already waiting for her. She flowed effortlessly out of her Volvo, the thin silk of her dress moving like a second skin.

"Why did you tail Richard for me, when I told you not to?"

Sam led the way up the stairs.

"I didn't do it for you. It's in connection with another case I'm working on."

"Why? What's he done?"

"I don't know yet. Maybe nothing. I'm just examining all angles at the moment. Coffee?" Sam filled the machine.

"So what did you find out?" Sam told her. Minutes after she had finished Vanessa remained silent, puffing on her cigarette, squashing it out, lighting another.

"And then you lost him?"

"I'm afraid so."

"Or did he give you the slip?"

"That's what I don't know."

"But you've found out he likes football. How interesting!" Yeah, thought Sam, lay it on. I deserve it.

"So, he swings both ways," Vanessa was saying, "not unusual." Her voice stayed light, but the bright red fingernails were dug into her palms. It wasn't possible to tell yet whether she was dealing with hurt pride or a deeper emotion. Sam handed her a cup of coffee in silence.

"So, most of my men have been bastards. So what's the difference?" But Vanessa's drawl had an abrasive edge this time, its coating cracking a little in places.

"The difference is," Sam leant back in her chair, "that

137

he has a predisposition for the kind of sex that's pretty dangerous this day and age."

"Fuck it, I'd better have an AIDs test!" She got to her feet and started towards the door, then paused, her hand on the knob.

"The keys? What's all that about? If he did take them ... why?"

"I don't know yet. There's a lot of people who have got it in for the lab at the moment. And," she could not keep the anger out of her voice, "after what I heard last night, I don't blame them."

Vanessa looked at her thoughtfully. "I thought private investigators weren't allowed personal feelings. I thought they got in the way."

Sam said nothing for a moment. For the second time in twelve hours she had directly or indirectly been accused of bias. Was it clouding her judgement? What was evident was that she could not, any longer, sit on the fence.

"Anyway," she continued, "he could have been going to try some guerrilla tactics against the lab."

"Then why didn't he torch it there and then?"

"I don't know."

"There's a lot you don't know, detective. Is there anything you do know?" she blew a thin column of smoke that curled in an ironic question mark around Sam's head.

"You're sure there was nothing missing?" Sam chose to ignore the jibe. What could she say, anyway? She agreed wholeheartedly with Vanessa – she had screwed up.

"Something small, maybe? You can't keep track of everything in a big place like that?"

"Oh, you can if you're Roger. He inventories each paper clip."

Sam wondered how a man with such an eye for detail could possibly be so unaware of his wife's infidelities, but it was, after all, what you prioritised. Look at her own life. On her most successful case, while she had been busy preventing the removal of five hundred grand's worth of computer equipment from a warehouse in Worthing, her own lover had been spirited away from under her very nose.

138

"Does your husband own the lab?"

"No, it's a partnership. But Roger gets most of the research funding."

"From the government?"

"Research money from this government? You must be joking. No, drug companies mainly."

"Does he tell you about his work?"

"No. But then I never ask."

Dynamic marriage, thought Sam, and said, "This Frankenstein Foetus ..."

"Load of shit," she had come back into the room now and was lighting another cigarette.

"As the woman said, there's no money in it and it's money that motivates Roger. Especially now. The lab's in schtuck."

"Broke?"

"Oh, I don't know the details."

"You never ask?"

"No, figures don't interest me. Only what they stand for," she slid her pack of cigarettes and a solid gold lighter into her bag and snapped it shut. There was a taut silence as the two women looked at each other, a gulf of experience between them.

"You think I'm a parasite, don't you? That he makes the money and I spend it? Well, it's not quite as simple as that. There are dinner parties, intimate little evenings at our home with some backer or other. The caterers lay on the nouveau cuisine, the wine merchants deliver the best wine and Roger provides me. I'm not exactly offered on a plate, nothing quite so crude. But if Roger suddenly has to leave for half an hour to see to an emergency at the lab, well, there I am, with the brandy and After Eights. Help yourself, Roger has said. Being deliberately vague as to what exactly. And on the understanding, of course, that something will be signed later. It's a gentleman's agreement, nothing said, just ... understood."

So that's why Roger chose to ignore his wife's other extra-marital activities. You could hardly pull a jealous husband number if you were poncing her off to the highest bidder.

139

"And that snotty cow. Judith," she had taken out her cigarettes again and was drawing smoke in hard through her lungs, "has the gall to look down on me, treating me like some half-witted bimbo who can't keep her legs shut for more than five minutes. When all the time it's me who's bringing in the dosh to keep her precious research going. Roger hives off a percentage of everything he gets to her. She wouldn't get a penny otherwise. No one's interested in Hewitts Disease. She's just obsessed with it because her darling little son died of it. So she thinks nothing else matters in the world, not even her own daughter. No wonder she's turned out a right little fucker. So what if Judith finds the cure? Big deal? That's really going to set the world alight, isn't it?" Vanessa's carefully-designed face looked suddenly naked, at the mercy of emotions seldom permitted within its parameters. And there was a hell of a lot more where they came from, Sam guessed. But, even as she looked, the ironic mask was being slipped neatly back into place.

"If the research is such a dodo why does Roger keep giving her the money for it?"

"Because she owns over half the capital."

Vanessa stood irresolutely in the centre of the room, chewing her lip.

"I'm going," but she did not move.

"Have you arranged to see Richard again?"

"He said he'd phone, but I'll tell him to get stuffed. I'm not seeing that cock-sucking little turd again. God knows what I've caught already."

"Don't you meet for anything else?"

"Besides a screw, you mean? Yes, we have dinner together, or a drink sometimes."

"Why don't you suggest that when he calls?"

"Why? To help you with this other little case of yours? So you can lose him again? You know where to look for him now, in a urinal." She crushed another red-stained cigarette stump into the ashtray.

"Roger's got enough to worry about now, apart from the break-in. We've had non-stop fruit and nuts calling ever since that programme last night and there was a crowd outside the lab when I went past this morning. Roger seems to think it was Judith's daughter, Sarah, anyway. That she pinched her mother's keys. She started the whole Frankenstein rumour with her article in the Herald. Silly little bitch." Cogs whirred and clicked in Sam's brain as she swung her chair in a semi-circle and looked out of the window.

"Does her daughter drive a white Triumph Spitfire, registration number SAL 1?" Vanessa stared at her in astonishment.

"Does a brain full of useless information come of being a detective so long?"

"No, it comes of looking out the window. She's just parking her car on the other side of the road."

"What's she doing here? Has she come to see you?"

"I have absolutely no idea."

"Is there another way out of here?"

Sam led her down the hallway and through a door marked "toilet", that gave directly onto a rusty fire escape and down into an evil-smelling yard. Vanessa applied a square inch of the finest Belgian lace to her nostrils.

"Abattoir," explained Sam briefly, "Won't she recognise your car?"

"No," Vanessa seemed surprised. "Why should she? I get a new one every August of course."

"Of course," said Sam, reflecting that "broke" for some people meant no supper for the kids and for others the repossession of your third Porsche. She let Vanessa out of a wooden gate and into a mews.

"Just turn right and you'll be back at your car. And if you have second thoughts, about another meeting with Richard ..."

"I probably won't tell you." Vanessa picked her way delicately over dog shit.

"But then again," she flashed a pair of grey eyes back at Sam,

"You never know with me."

"Oh, just one thing. Why Hunt?"

"Hm?" Vanessa turned, puzzled.

"If Judith owns the lion's share of the lab, why is it

called Hunt?"

"Oh that. It was Roger's idea. The big hunt," it was Sam's turn to look perplexed now.

"You know, to solve the mystery of the human genome and all that. It should appeal to you, detective." And with that she was gone.

Sam got to the front door and opened it just as Sarah's hand was raised to the bell.

"What kept you?" Sarah demanded as she waltzed in. She didn't think much of the state of the stairwell or the noxious smells emanating from somewhere in its depths, and said so. The office fared a little better beneath her critical gaze.

"Had a client already?", she glanced at the coffee cups.

"A brunette, judging by the shade of red lipstick. Or a blonde with bad taste."

"Oh, she's got very good taste," said Sam, clearing up the cups.

"I really don't know how you do it, Holmes."

"Finding you was pretty damn smart, wasn't it though?" Once more Sarah had transformed in an instant from adult chic to a little girl, eager for praise. Sam poured them both coffee and sat down.

"Well?", Sarah was impatient. "Aren't you going to ask me how?"

Sam tilted back in her chair, folded her arms and raised an amused eyebrow at the other woman.

"Spill it," she said in her best Philip Marlowe impression.

Sarah pulled a ten by eight photograph out of a huge envelope. It was a head and shoulders of Sam at the meeting the previous night, leaning forward chin on hands, listening intently. She had no idea it was being taken.

"You didn't tell me you were going to be there last night," Sarah added, aggrieved.

"How remiss of me not to phone through my schedule."

"Apology accepted. Anyway, I had photos taken of everyone at the meeting. Not mugshots like this, twos and threes mostly. And I got most of the prints through at six

142

this morning. I'll pick up the rest later. He fell asleep over the last reel," she snarled contemptuously. "No stamina."

"Good photographer though."

"Yes, he does a lot of work for me," she said casually.

"So, anyway, I went and knocked up Dippy Don, who's the world's worst writer but he never forgets a face, which is the only reason they keep him on the Herald. He's a walking reference library on East Sussex and its residents. He knew you immediately. You threw a pint of beer over him and stole his tape recorder!" Sarah chuckled at the thought.

Sam vaguely recollected the incident, which must have been all of six years ago. She had been in private conference with a client in a pub when she had spotted a microphone behind a plant pot. It was so like something out of The Man From UNCLE that she had laughed out loud. But that hadn't stopped her teaching him a lesson.

"It was half a pint and I confiscated the tape, not the machine. So," Sam passed the photograph back across the desk, "I presume it wasn't just for the thrill of the chase that you tracked me down."

"Oh, you can keep that," Sarah passed it back, "I've got another one," and suddenly, unpredictably, her face flushed blood red. Feeling the tension in the room, but keeping her voice light as she slipped the photograph into her drawer, Sam said, "Thanks. It's a good one, though I say it myself."

"I've got the rest here," Sarah was busying herself, pulling out more prints, pushing them towards Sam.

"If we need more detail I can have them blown up."

"We?" Sam looked bewildered.

"Oh, didn't I tell you yet," Sarah had recovered her old self, "I'm making you a proposition you can't refuse. We join forces and investigate together."

Sam swung herself slowly from side to side, the tips of her fingers together, her lips pursed.

"Let's get a few things straight, shall we. Number one – what makes you think I'm interested in anything to do with the Hunt?"

"Oh, that's easy. You were at the meeting and …"

"As were two hundred or so others."

"And you gave me the third degree yesterday about what I'd seen there. And you're working for Jenny Fenton," (it was a long-shot, that one, surely, and Sam made no response), "and you think the murder has something to do with what they're doing up at the lab. I'm right, aren't I?" Sam ignored that one too.

"Number Two – even if I am working on a case … a private and confidential case, what makes you think I need the help of someone who not only is unable or unwilling to separate fact from fiction but who makes front page headlines of it?"

"I swear to you, cross my heart and hope to die."

Sam laughed, but Sarah was absolutely serious,

"or if you don't believe me I'll get Hugh to draw us up a legally-binding contract, (he's a solicitor in his spare time), that I only divulge things we both agree on beforehand."

"And Number Three," Sam was merciless, "I only ever work solo. No partners," she spelt out.

"Maybe you do too much alone." The response was totally unexpected, as well as uncalled for. Sam's muscles tightened. Back off, kid, she thought. You're getting too close. Sarah, for once sensitive to the chill factor, backed off.

"Why don't you just look at the prints. No strings. If you're interested we can talk. If not …," she shrugged, "I'll go meekly away, like a little lamb."

Like hell she would.

"There's a shot of everyone at the meeting. Or will be, when we get the other reel. So, we'll have a picture of the murderer."

"You reckon?" Sam leant back thoughtfully.

"Oh yes. If I'd done it I would've been there. Def."

"Well, that's only one hundred and ninety nine suspects we have to eliminate," she added.

"A hundred and ninety six, not counting you, me and Hugh."

"Hugh?"

"The photographer. He's a friend of mine," Sarah hesitated imperceptibly over the word "friend." "And anyway, I've got an alibi for him."

Sam looked through the prints. They were good. Clear. A group of her own friends and some other women she did not know. New to Brighton, perhaps.

"The women's libbers," said Sarah.

"Feminists," corrected Sam automatically.

"Whatever you say, boss."

Ellen and her friends, Beamish's lot. Sam stopped in her tracks. It was the head and shoulders of a man, taken from the back. She knew that silhouette, or did she? Was she just becoming obsessed with the man, seeing him everywhere. Sarah was looking at her, enquiringly.

"Seen someone interesting?"

"Oh, just this bloke here," she pointed to the other man in the photograph, large, shambling, fortyish, his face to the camera, in earnest conversation with his companion.

"I've seen him before. I don't know where," she lied, keeping her voice disinterested.

"Oh yes, you would have. That's Gatwood. His daughter found the foetus. Didn't you know?" Sam had not known and felt she should have done.

"Was he with the church brigade?" Sam asked. Sarah studied the photograph.

"Yes, I suppose he was. And now I come to think of it, I saw him at a demo against the Glenning Clinic the other day. Although I suppose he could have just been passing by. Do you think it's significant?"

The problem with this case, thought Sam, is that I haven't a clue what's significant. The whole thing seemed to be a mass of, at the moment, unrelated details that could or could not have any connection with each other. Nothing leapt out at her and said with an inviting smile, 'follow me'. She felt angry and frustrated with herself. The one person who had seemed to offer any lead at all she had lost. Not once, but twice! He had been there, right under her nose last night! But then again, was he important at all? A nasty line in sadism didn't necessarily mean you were a murderer. If it did, there would be a hell of a lot more dead bodies around. There were a lot of people

145

doing bizarre things, but did any of them have anything to do with the murder of Cynthia Fenton?

"Could be," she replied, non-committally.

"Well," Sarah demanded, as they lay aside the last of the prints,

"I think we'd make a good team? What do you reckon?"

Sam was doing some pretty fast reckoning. She had to admit that, as a particularly inquisitive member of a bullying fraternity and under cover of gathering news stories, Sarah was well-qualified to pick up a quantity of information that Sam would be best not seen in pursuit of. She could also check out what was red herring and what was not. This connection, if it existed, between Gatwood and the Born Agains. She had a feeling she had a number of the ends right there already and, with the help of a few more, she could start tying them together, but that was a part she did not want Sarah's help with. It was the part she had never shared, not even with Julia. It was the best part. Besides, she reasoned, Sarah was an unknown and unpredictable quantity. Someone who was waging a vendetta a mile high against her own mother was obviously not as cool and objective as she tried to look and definitely could not be trusted with anything like the whole picture. But, given a segment, with enough responsibility to keep her happy, she could be a useful assistant, besides being fun to have around some of the time. That this was rather unfair, she readily admitted. It was, also, a hell of a lot safer for all concerned. They were, after all, dealing with a murder.

"So?" Sarah pressed, "Partner?"

"No." Sarah's face was instantly crestfallen.

"Assistant," Sam corrected. Sarah's face began to register rebellion, but thought better of it.

"And, under the strictest confidentiality," Sam added. "Here's what I want you to do," and she began to give Sarah a list of instructions that the other took down diligently in her notebook. To only one did Sarah object.

"I can't go back on a story. It'd be like saying I made it up in the first place."

"Which you did. Just say, 'in the light of further evi-

146

dence' or something. I'll leave the wording to you. You're the writer."

Sarah opened her mouth to remonstrate, "Or no deal," cut in Sam, and Sarah closed it again. The rest of the instructions she took down without resistance. Had Hugh, seated at his desk two miles away, his eyes blurring with fatigue over a new government directive on Probate, witnessed this scene, he would not have recognised his Sal at all in her new garb of submission.

After Sarah had gone Sam had a pleasant call to make. Probably one of the few last pleasant things she would do all day, she thought.

"Hello, Glenning Clinic. Can I help you?" came a severe voice over the line. Sam smiled, having a mental picture of a vast peach bosom jutting beneath a permed head of stern and majestic carriage.

"I'd like to speak to Dr Shilpa, please."

The voice was suspicious: "Can I ask your business with the doctor?" it asked, protectively.

"It's Sam Carter, tell her."

There was a pause and at last the doctor's voice sang along the telegraph wires, causing something in the pit of Sam's stomach to do a double back flip. Whatever it was landed badly, teetered wildly, but recovered its balance superbly.

"Hi," she said, with a nonchalance that amazed her, "I've got you a piece of good news, a recant in the Herald. It might stop short of a public apology, but it should take some of the heat off the clinic."

"Sam, that's wonderful," there was a rush of relief in the voice.

"I've been so worried. How did you manage that?"

"Oh, you know, a word in the right ear."

"I'd no idea you had so much influence," the voice was impressed. Yeah, thought Sam, a kid reporter with a crush on me, some influence. But the doctor was continuing.

"So you want to cancel your visit on Monday? I suppose you won't need to come over and see the place now."

"No, I'd better still come," Sam cut in, she hoped not

too hastily, "just to be on the safe side."

Sam sat for a moment after putting down the phone, enjoying the pleasurable sensation that was suffusing her body from the top of her scalp down to her toe ends.

"Dream on, baby," she said wryly to herself. No time for that. It was going to be a busy, tangled sort of day, she could feel it in her blood.

Her next phone call was a short one.

"Fats? It's Sam. Hi. That guy I was tailing yesterday, has he been in again?"

"Lost him, eh?" Fats sounded amused. Don't you start, thought Sam.

"Another exit out the lavvy, was there?"

"No, out the football pitch."

"Eh?" But she did not stop to explain.

"Look, if he comes in again will you page me?"

"Sure, as long as it's not this evening. I've got a thirtieth birthday and a wedding anniversary, so I won't have a hand free."

"So what are feet for?" she demanded and hung up. It was 9.20.

Chapter Twenty Five

At that very moment, Sarah's mother, flanked by a heavy police cordon, rowdy demonstrators and curious onlookers, and running the gauntlet from her car to the Hunt's front entrance, was cursing the fruit of her loins with every vilification known to her. In the firing line, also, came her partner, Roger, as well as the great mass of public in general, ignorant, impressionable, ill-informed, (by her daughter, principally), as they all were. Did they not want to be helped? Did they not want to take responsibility for themselves? For that is what it amounted to. Would they rather remain, for ever, a prey to the foibles of nature? She glanced at the faces pressing close around her. Red, angry, hateful faces. Or stupid, open-mouthed, fish faces. They would do nothing to help themselves, these people. It would have to be done for them. With or without their permission. Left to the likes of them, Science would have remained in its infancy, human advancement reduced always to its lowest common denominator. Riddled by diseases that could so easily be eradicated, wracked by preventable famine and sickness and deformity, they would merely have bayed at the moon in their agony and taken counsel from the stars. Always emotion took the place of reason, paranoia ruled out calm assessment. Judith did not think highly of the common man. Or woman, for that matter. The vital decisions could not be left to them. Were too important to be in the power of mob veto. She shivered and put her key in the front door. It would not turn. She twisted it this way and that in a growing panic. She took it out, looked at it. It was the right one. She jammed it back in, conscious of a hundred eyes at her back. Unreasoning fears rose into her mind. They had come by night and changed the locks, had taken over her holy of holies, were at that moment trammelling her test tubes and microscopes and specimens, smashing the sacred relics of her calling. Suddenly the door swung open and Roger was standing there.

"Oh, hello. It's you. I changed all the locks yesterday. Didn't you remember?"

She had not. Yesterday seemed a long time ago. Before that awful television programme, before they had become national property.

"Roger, this is all your fault!" she blurted out.

"What?" He looked taken aback.

"What do you mean 'what'? All that lot out there," she waved an arm towards the crowd, "that's what," her grammar had deserted her along with her patience.

"I didn't ask them to come," he was aggrieved.

"You said just about everything last night that gives people like that the screaming abdabs about us. You might as well have frothed at the mouth and eaten a few babies, why didn't you?"

"I was only trying to tell people what good we were doing for them. How was I to know they'd be so stupid about it?"

"I could have told you."

"You didn't want to know about it, remember? Count me out, you said."

"You didn't have to go on telly in the first place. It was only because you love being in the limelight. You have to perform, don't you? Like some child who wants attention all the time." She knew she was being unreasonable but her resentment had risen and brimmed over and was unstoppable now.

"I think you're getting the whole thing out of proportion, Judith," his voice was cold.

"Is that mob out there out of proportion? Are the phone calls from lousy tabloids at three a.m. out of proportion? Is the fact that our backers might get cold feet and pull out all their money out of proportion?"

"Look. I think we should calm down. The staff will be here in a few minutes and ..."

"If they can get through the barricades. If they haven't been scared off by the death threats."

"I think it will all die down in a little while," his voice was soothing now, like a parent with a fractious child.

"And what's a little while," she demanded, not wanting to give up, refusing to be soothed.

"A week? A month? I've got work to do, Roger."

"We've all got work to do, Judith," he reminded her. One day he would allow himself the luxury of telling her what he really thought of her "work", but not now. Not while he was still dependent on her capital and collateral.

"How is anyone going to be able to work with that lot going on?" Someone in the crowd had set up a chant. The words were indistinct but the sound had a rhythmic, staccato quality, like prolonged bursts of machine gun fire. Judith felt besieged.

"God! Haven't they got anything better to do? They're obsessed!" And, striding off at last, in search of her white lab coat and the comforting cocoon of her laboratory, she called back, "God! If only people could see themselves."

"If only," reflected Roger, looking at her retreating back.

"And if there's a gene responsible for self-perception its discoverer will make himself a million."

At 10.15 that morning Jenny Fenton paid a visit to St Saviours. It was perfectly natural that, as a Christian, she should seek the sustenance of the divine form in her hour of torment, but after a sketchy genuflection in the direction of the altar she ignored the waiting rows of pews with their hand-embroidered hassocks, passed the tranquil haven of the Lady Chapel and, traversing the nave, entered the vestry, where the object of her attention, clad in human form and a pair of paint-streaked overalls, was applying a coat of emulsion to the walls. "Bill, what the hell is going on?" The man sprang back from the wall like a startled rabbit, splattering tiny white dots over the silver of the communion cup, and turned a frightened face in her direction as she closed the door behind her.

The Reverend Beamish entered his church a few minutes later, come to avail himself of a few moments of his Maker's time, his own time having been almost constantly occupied by the telephone from 5 that morning. He had answered calls from, among others, a Canadian Sufi-dancer who had converted from Judaism three years ago and now wanted to be baptised by him into the Church

151

of England (and did he do total immersions on Brighton Beach?), a woman calling herself the Virgin Mary who ran a massage parlour in Hove (he could have a year's free membership), and the bishop of the diocese, full of dyspepsia and scathing comments, the one as scaldingly acidic as the other.

Moving up the main body of the church toward the altar steps, the priest was taken aback by the sound of heated words emitting from behind the vestry door. He strode forward toward it, angered beyond measure at such discourtesy in God's house, albeit in only a minor room of it. His hand poised on the doorknob, however, he paused, listening. And, hearing, paused longer. It was five minutes before he finally straightened and, with a grave face, began to walk away, almost colliding with the outstretched zimmer of Mrs Beaver.

"Sister," he said, his voice troubled, "did you hear what I heard just now?"

"No," her voice, though cracked and wheezing, was adamantine in its purpose.

"I heard nothing. And nor did you."

"But," he began but she motioned him with her head to the porch door and commenced to push herself slowly and painfully towards it. He followed her out into the sunshine. When they stood on the steps at last, he said, "Those words would change everything."

"Which is good reason not to have heard them," she answered, her face as unyielding as a rock in his lashing sea of confusion. They stood there in silence, side by side, the tall, hale middle-aged cleric and this frail, bent member of his flock, as she poured the liquid steel of her will into the open caste of his mind, until, his vigour renewed and the silent pact between them having been signed and sealed, he said cheerfully, "With all the new recruits, it'll be a full-house this Sunday morning."

"And more," she agreed.

"I'd better get Malcolm to bring over extra chairs from the hall."

"They'll need a dust," she pointed out.

"I'll get one of the women to do that," and so they

152

chatted together, the sun warming their backs, two friends anticipating a happy event, two trusty conspirators in conference, living proof that what is heard can be unheard, what done undone. The twin poles of their religion – a baffling birth and a violent death – had stood others like them in good stead for two thousand years. It was, publicity-wise at least, a fortunate combination and one not to be sniffed at.

"If it should ever come out that …," he wavered.

"We never heard it," she stood firm.

"God works in deep and mysterious ways," murmured the vicar and she nodded, neither desiring any greater acquaintance with the unfathomable channels of the Almighty.

Chapter Twenty Six

Sam went first to Norfolk Square to track down Jerry. He was nowhere to be found in or around his usual haunt of the bus shelter or the little park behind it. Enquiries brought to light only the information that he had been seen early that morning stone cold sober, walking briskly in the direction of the Clock Tower. But neither hide nor hair of him had been sighted since. She began walking towards Churchill Square, through the throng of Friday shoppers on Western Road, but holding out little hope of finding him alert and attentive. Sober by seven, pissed by eleven, if she knew Jerry. She stopped on hearing her name shouted from across the road.

It was Jerry, standing beside another man, much younger, broad shouldered, tanned, resplendent in a beige silk suit and open-necked brown shirt. Gold flashed extravagantly from rings and Rolex. It was Stevie, a local crim she knew by sight. He padded leisurely away into Virgin Records as Sam crossed the road. "As Sam could see, he had been busy," Jerry said. Yet, so far, nothing, had been seen of the girl. If she still was in Brighton, (and there was, after all, a definite possibility she was not) she had melted away, gone to ground somewhere, well out of sight. Would Stevie and his ilk be likely to declare her, if they had got their paws on her, Sam had asked. For she was young enough to be hot property on the streets. Oh, yes, Jerry had assured her, Stevie was not bullshitting him. Stevie owed him one. What that one was Jerry did not elaborate and Sam knew better than to ask. He would keep looking, Jerry had told her. Yes, he had her pageing number about him … somewhere. He plunged his hand into his jacket pocket and scoured around energetically, then pushed it deeper, into the lining and repeated the exercise, retrieving, at last, a small, scrunched up scrap of paper, with a triumphant cry. Sam wrote it again on large foolscap and tucked it neatly into his top pocket. He saluted her smartly, (he had been a sergeant in the Scots Guards, she remembered hearing once) and marched away, a flap of material from the tear in the seat of his pants bobbing rhymically up and down as he went.

She had no news to tell Jenny. She consoled herself that the East Sussex police and Scotland Yard together had fared no better. She had scanned the early editions and there had been only a repeat of the girl's description and the police hot-line number to ring in case you saw her. There were sure to have been hundreds of calls by now, most from cranks and practical jokers and others, maybe a third, from people who genuinely believed themselves to have seen her. Each call would have to be assessed, each likely lead followed up. At least she did not have that kind of boredom-defying routine leg work to do. She was a free agent, had bits of the puzzle the police had not, while, at the same time, being denied access to sources of information available to them alone. Put like that it was evens-on who would get there first, but the reality was she had not yet managed to find two pieces that appeared to belong to the same puzzle, let alone be adjoining.

Jenny's face, when she opened the door, looked ravaged. Sam was shocked by the greyness, by the sudden addition of ten years or more to her appearance. She had obviously not slept and her eyes were sunken and dark with pain, the shoulders slumped, unable to support a burden too heavy for their slenderness. She raked a hand through her hair.

"Come in. I must have fallen asleep in the chair." Sam followed her in and closed the door.

"No sign yet of Jo, I'm afraid," she said when they were both seated at the kitchen table.

"Who?" Jenny looked blank, her eyes not quite focussing, her mind seeming unable to grasp Sam's words.

"I haven't been able to trace the girl Cynthia was with the other day," she explained slowly.

"Oh," Jenny stared down at the table, "I see." This flat acceptance was so much in contrast with the desperate urgency of the day before that Sam was puzzled.

"You still want me to find her, don't you?"

155

"Yes," Jenny seemed to rouse herself with an effort.

"We have to find her," but it was as if the thought came from a far-off place, that she could find no connecting emotion for it.

"You wanted me to find her if only to eliminate her from the enquiry," Sam reminded her.

"You know, that afternoon, before she .. she died, Cyn was saying to everyone that she'd seen the wicked experiments. At the Hunt. Those were her words."

"Do you think she had?"

"Oh Christ," Jenny's face contorted suddenly, her teeth biting into her lower lip till the blood ran.

"Oh Christ! Maybe they thought she was spying on them or something. She was always hanging out round there, but only to see Maurice. He was her friend."

"Wait a minute," Sam needed to have this nice and slow, "are you saying that someone from the Hunt .. (she had to be brutal here, to get some sense out of Jenny) .. killed Cyn because she saw this foetus experiment."

"No!" It was almost a howl. "There wasn't any experiment, any Frankenstein Foetus!"

"A lot of people seem to think otherwise ...," Sam stopped suddenly, a tiny piece slotting into place, was it?

"... unless you know different. Unless you know for certain."

Jenny looked away, her eyes haunted by things unnameable.

"Jenny?" Sam touched her hand gently, "Jenny, tell me what you know."

It came at last in a voice so hoarse with pain that Sam could scarcely catch the words, but the meaning was clear. It had been Bill's idea. Bill? Gatwood. Jenny looked surprised, like a child who expects you to be familiar with all the people, places, circumstances that she knows. She had always voiced her opposition to the Hunt, had tried to get other members of St Saviours as indignant and outraged as herself, but it was the Glenning Clinic that was their particular bête noir. The clinic was, after all, an easy target – with its abortions and, till recently, virgin births and lesbian insemination. Genetic experimentation

156

had not been on the agenda. It was Bill who had finally begun to take an interest. It was he who had come up with the plan to throw the lab and its work into disrepute, to galvanise the whole community against it. They guessed that Beamish, seeing its publicity value, would make it a cause célèbre. Which he had. It had worked like a dream. The Hunt was a pariah and her daughter was dead.

"But," Sam explained gently, "if there never was a monster foetus, never was an experiment to create one, then why should anyone want to kill Cyn for her make-believe?"

"Because they've got other things to hide, other skeletons in the cupboard they're afraid the world will see."

"You mean this search and kill mission on the so-called lesbian gene?"

"No, I don't care about that. I'm not a lesbian any more. They can take care of themselves. It's people like Cyn, who have no say at all in this society. Beautiful, trusting people who never do anyone any harm, they're the ones who always get hurt, the ones the Hunt are trying to eliminate." Jenny's eyes blazed hatred and rage. Watching, Sam thought, she has made a monster out of the Hunt, out of all the people connected to it. A monster quite as terrifying as the one she had helped to engender. I'm in danger of doing exactly the same, she told herself. In my mind, too, the Hunt has become a chamber of horrors, peopled by demons bent on my destruction. Yeah, but was that too far from the truth? This ain't paranoia, baby, it's having a sense of reality. Think of your worst nightmare then multiply it to the power of ten. To Jenny. she said, "But what about this girl, Jo? She's still the police's prime suspect." But Jenny had already forgotten her in her obsession with the Hunt.

Sam stayed another half hour, out of compassion or solidarity or guilt, or all three. As she left Jenny said, "It's either Hunt himself or the Ginsberg woman, I know it. Find out, Sam," and Sam had nodded. You didn't contradict someone who was inches from the edge and leaning right over. She would phone just as soon as she had anything to report and would be back tomorrow afternoon.

"Tomorrow afternoon I'm going on the march," and, as Sam looked questioning, "it's a coalition of everyone who's against the Hunt. Ellen came round and told me about it. She asked me to march with them. There's going to be a lot of people in wheelchairs. They'll need some support." Bless Ellen, thought Sam. It was typical of her. Not only to reach out to this woman in her agony but, spanning the seven or eight years of Jenny's absence from them as though it had been a day, to recognise, too, the difficulty of marching with the group she had joined in such close proximity to old comrades she had deserted. So Ellen had offered her an alternative, whilst, at the same time, disguising the fact. Sam vowed to ring her very soon.

She gave Jenny a hug and then moved to go but the other woman clung to her. Sam stroked the tousled head, the burning neck.

"You should get some rest. Why don't you go to bed now?"

"Come with me," the voice was muffled but the words and their meaning very clear. The arms around Sam tightened, the body pushing against hers.

"I need comfort so badly, Sam. Physical comfort, to take the pain away. It's been so long."

Sam did not alter the pressure of her arms around Jenny, neither drawing away nor moving into closer embrace.

"Jenny, it wouldn't be a good idea. I'm much better for you as a friend than a lover, believe me."

"I need you, Sam. I need to be touched," Jenny locked her body into Sam's.

"But not like that. You need a lot of love right now from people who care about you. What you definitely don't need are the complications of a sexual relationship."

Jenny pulled away roughly, as though the contact burnt her suddenly. Her eyes were hostile. That was one way of dealing with rejection.

"You mean you don't want me! So why don't you say so? You're as two-faced as the rest of them. I don't know

158

why I thought you were any different. Get out and don't come back!"

Sam heard the door slam shut as she walked off down the path. She didn't look back. What a godawful mess it all was! As she drove back to Brighton she rehearsed the scene over and over in her mind. She had been right not to sleep with her, she was sure of that. Even if she had wanted to, had felt an answering arousal. But she hadn't, so wouldn't it have been better, more honest to have said so outright? Rather than pretend she was doing so for Jenny's own good? Jenny was right. She was a hypocrite. But then how do you tell someone in crisis that you just don't desire them? With difficulty, with tact, she told herself. If you're not a coward, that is.

By the time she arrived at the sea front she had flagellated herself nicely to a pulp. She needed a drink. No, she didn't. That was the one thing she did not need. She should probably eat, but her insides were in revolt. She drummed out an irritating rhythm on the steering wheel. She was in danger of driving herself to distraction in this mood, she knew it. That old trapped feeling was rising within her, threatening to pin her in an arm-busting half-Nelson. Drastic action was needed. Immediately. She turned round and addressed the, by now, permanent residents of her back seat.

"Your time has come, baby. I need you. Bad!" The trainers winked back at her and smirked in an 'I told you so' kind of way.

In a public toilet on the promenade she changed into her track suit. It fitted. Just. Hard to believe she had been quite a sportswoman in her day. There had even been mention of the All-England, but the urgent need to sort out her burgeoning sexuality had drained some of that vital energy, that total concentration needed for training. Then, on discovering she actually was a lesbian, as she had suspected, she, typically big-mouth, felt the need to announce it publicly, shout it from the roof-tops. Consequently, she had been quietly dropped from the "Ladies" competition. That was a long time ago.

Now she headed down to the beach. The tide was out

and a long, narrow strip of sand lay wetly golden in the afternoon sun, its edges licked by a gently lapping sea. She jogged along the sand, past the sad skeleton of the ruined West Pier, the sea sucking around the massive wooden pillars of its legs, the flocks of starlings darting in and out its eyeless windows. There had been plans to rebuild it, to make it, again, a place of evening strolls and music and laughter. But, as the years, and the tides, washed by, more and more bits of it strained and cracked and snapped off in the wind and the waves and, slowly, the great spine of it was crumbling and being reclaimed by the sea.

Sweat trickled freely down her face and she could feel it begin to run in rivulets along the folds of flesh inside her T-shirt. God, she was out of condition! Reaching the Hove boundary, she turned and started the long haul back. Her legs were leaden, her chest ached with the unaccustomed demand on lung and heart. The last quarter mile she put on a spurt that almost finished her off and arrived back at the car gasping for air. Another jogger, loping easily past her, asked should he call her an ambulance?

"Go harden your arteries!" she called at his receding back. Or would have done if there had been breath enough in her body.

She had gone home and showered then and, feeling an appetite rekindling, flipped open the larder door. Still only sardines and cat food. Did nothing ever change? And why sardines? She couldn't stand them. "God, but that housekeeper's a slut," she muttered. "I'm sacking her on Monday!" Deciding she needed an emergency intake of cholesterol after such a dangerously high level of exercise, she wandered round the corner to her favourite chippie at Seven Dials.

She was seated at a table and applying salt and vinegar liberally to golden brown cod and chips when her pager bleeped. Cursing, she left her food on the table and walked the twenty yards or so to the public phone box. It was Sarah. Sam listened to her report, jotted down a few things and said she'd be in touch later. On her return to the restaurant she found her table empty.

"I put it in the oven for you," Enrico's bulk materialised from behind the counter with her plate.

"Big case you got this time?"

"Fairly," she speared a chip.

"So what's cooking?"

"I'll let you know when I find out," which both knew was untrue. He sniffed lugubriously and wandered off. Girlfriend trouble again, thought Sam, too hungry to enquire.

She had put paid to a half dozen chips and the first few melting mouthfuls of batter when her pager went off again. This time it was Fats. Her man had been in again. Great! She would be there right now. No point. He was sorry, when he had first spotted him he had been up to his eyes, an unexpected office party. The next time he looked over the bloke was gone. He had enquired of the rent boys but they didn't know where he had gone. He had been high they said. High? Yes, well, that was their interpretation, but then they were forever high as kites. He could have just been excited about something. Maybe he'd had a windfall, anyway he had to go, there was a queue a mile long at the bar that would take at least five minutes to shift. He'd try and let her know immediately next time.

Enrico handed over her plate at the counter.

"You want I should eat it for you too?" he asked and picked his teeth morosely with a match as she plunged once more into the delights of things fried to a golden turn. This time she had not the heart to refuse a solicitous enquiry. It was, as she had prophesied, girlfriend trouble.

"Pff! This woman, she take all my money and come back chomping for seconds."

"So, get rid of her," Sam managed through a full mouth.

"I done that. I get another."

"Nicer?"

"No, I go out of the frying pan in the fire." Enrico's metaphors were always culinary.

"She won't do anything I tell her."

"Sounds healthy."

161

"She won't let me look at another woman."

"Why do you want to, if you like her?" said Sam in astonishment.

"It's the principle, ennit? A man don't want to be tied," he gave a melancholic sigh and shovelled chips to a hot plate.

"Women! What a sex!" he said, temporarily excluding Sam from membership of it.

"If you can't stand the heat get out of the kitchen," she said, unashamedly borrowing one of his own clichés.

"You know, Sam, I was most happy when I didn't have no women. Before women. Life was simple then. Football, that was my passion. All the time football. Down the wing. The guy tackle, I feint, leave him behind. Speed I got, you should see me. Pass across the centre, I move in, ball comes back, I shoot. Best player in Luka, me. And I was a good boy. I go to church. To confession. My mama liked that. I go off the football field and into church. What's a matter. You no like my fish or my story?" for Sam was up and starting to walk out.

"I like both fine, Enrico. In fact," she came back and wrapped the remains of the cod in a napkin, "I'll take the fish with me. The story I'll come back for another time. You just gave me an idea. You've inspired me."

"I did? I wish I could do the same for myself," he scratched his large belly despondently as the door swung shut behind her.

Chapter Twenty Seven

All that Friday when Ian had been at school, Jo had stayed in the attic. Best not to venture down into the hall, he had warned her, in case one of his father's congregation should happen by on some errand or other. And, as for going beyond, into the town, that would entail certain and sudden arrest, for the streets were full of police cars and her description everywhere. He had brought her food that morning, sandwiches, pies, chocolate and coke, as well as his cassette recorder and a pile of books and comics that he had somehow managed to sneak out of the house. For the first part of the day she had felt herself to be in clover, a queen residing in her palace, surrounded by all the luxuries she could desire. She had been content to lie at her ease, to listen to music and stuff herself with sweetmeats.

But by mid-afternoon she was restless. Having, for almost three months, spent her days and nights beneath an open sky, whether in a city street or a farmer's field, she had lost the taste for enclosure. By the time Ian arrived back, still breathless from running, the four walls and low, sloping roof were beginning to seem to her like a prison. He had realised it and begun immediately to entertain her. He had brought cakes and a flask of tea. He had bought presents, perfumed soap and toothbrush and paste from the chemist. He had stories to offer her, from school. He could do excellent impressions of the teachers, like a cartoonist, emphasising the weakness, caricaturing it till it overrode all else, became the sum total of the person. He made her laugh. She forgot her fretfulness and he, seeing this, relaxed visibly. Mid-evening he had to go home for his supper. His father was very strict about meal-times, he told her. And also his mother, she should not be abandoned, left alone with them. He did not explain the "them" and she did not ask. Nor did he ask her about her own life, what had brought her here, to this town, to this point in time. It was as though they had made a secret pact to blot out the past and live only in the now.

He returned after his meal with food for her and they had played draughts and chequers till the patch of sky above them had long darkened. He would teach her chess, he told her. She would enjoy that – the strategies, the master plan for survival, for winning. You sacrificed a rook or a bishop, something important, as a necessary part of the plan, all the time keeping your eye on the prize, on your opponent's queen. But suppose they, (Ian and Jo had begun to talk naturally together in terms of "they", as of a common enemy), just suppose they, she had argued, had seen your ploy, were letting you surrender your own best pieces and then, when you were weakened and unprotected, moved in for the kill? But that's where the master plan comes in, he had countered. From the opening gambit to the final check mate, you had to have it always in mind, had never to let it out of your sights. If only life were like that, she had thought, a sequence of controllable moves, a game of skill and flair that led towards one achievable goal, instead of this series of accidents and errors, where people blundered helplessly around, ran amok in each other's lives and almost all were losers. But yes, she would like to learn chess, learn the master plan.

He had left her at 10.30, for he dared not stay any longer than that, he said. After his departure the restlessness had returned. She needed to stretch her limbs, to feel earth or concrete beneath her feet, a cool breath of wind on her cheek. She opened the trapdoor and climbed down the ladder. In the hall, branches of trees tapped against the windows and their shapes bent and twisted across the floor. So dark and solid had they looked that she had, at first, attempted to step over them, mistaking the surrogate shadow for the real. Piles of clothes and books were crouching forms in the corners. She avoided them, keeping to the centre of the room. She was not afraid of the dark outside but, in here, it was different. There could be no quick escape from anything that leapt or slithered or dropped from above. Here she would be trapped. The need became pressing. She had to get out. If only for a short time, had to feel space and dis-

tance before her again. Surely, by now, by this time of
night, it would be safe. And she had different clothes on.
Ian had burnt her old ones in the school incinerator. Of
course, her body itself could not be changed, but clothes
could disguise its shape. She picked a couple of old
jumpers from one of the stacks of jumble and put them
on. They smelt of damp and dust and piss but they would
pad out her thinness. She put on a trench coat over them.
She looked broader now, surely.

Her hair. The long tangled curls. Would the police have
described them too? She went into the moonlit kitchen, to
the drawer beneath the sink. Knives, plastic spoons, tin
opener and, yes, here a pair of scissors, stiff and brown
with rust but still serviceable. They would do. She pulled
a matted chunk of hair away from her head and hacked
at it, half an inch from the scalp, shearing it away in great
hanks, till the floor around her was covered in dark curls,
like a thousand leggy spiders.

When she had done she ran a hand over her head,
feeling the bumps of her skull, the velvety fleece that was
left of her hair. Then, satisfied, she put back the scissors
and went again into the hall. The window through which
she had first entered she remembered to be the third one
on the right. She stood on a chair and pulled the pane
towards her. It would not yield. She tugged again, harder,
at the handle. It had jammed. She pulled as hard as she
could this time, still it did not move. She had got the
wrong window, of course. She dragged the chair to the
next one along. It would not budge. She tried another.
And another, both sides of the hall, but none gave. She
was locked in. At last realisation came to her. Ian had
done this. Forseeing her wish for escape, even before she
had herself, he had devised a master plan, had closed off
all exits. She became afraid now. That he had, so far,
done her no harm, had, in fact, shown her more kindness
than most people she had met in her life, did not matter
any more. He wanted to pen her, like an animal. And that
was the worst thing he could do to her. She looked up at
the windows. She could pick up a chair and smash it
through the glass, then she would be out. But once out,

165

she could not return. And out there? What was waiting for her? Another prison if she were caught. And from that she could not escape. They gave you life for murder, didn't they? A life for a life. She paced up and down the empty hall, back and forward, back and forward, between jumble and stacked chairs, till the moon dropped beneath the trees and the sky began to lighten. Then, dead tired, she climbed back into the attic and as the square of sky above her makeshift bed changed from dark blue to white, she fell asleep.

Chapter Twenty Eight

There were only a few young lads on the playing field this time, shooting balls into a makeshift goal of piled jerseys. Sam stopped to watch a moment. A long shot, taken from the side looked set to go impossibly wide but, at the last moment, arced inwards, straight past the outstretched hands of the goalie.

"Beautiful ball", thought Sam, admiringly.

"Yeah! Suck on that!" yelled its sender.

"Pity about the player," she added.

The recreation ground was bounded on one side by the cemetery wall and on the other three by high iron railings, backing, for the most part, onto private gardens. There was no gate or other exit out of the field, as the cabbie had said. Not officially, at any rate. But, thought Sam, show me a park that doesn't have at least one hole in the fence for dog-walkers and the rest to get through when the gates are shut. And, walking round the perimeter, she discovered four or five places where a single bar had been removed or two bent apart.

She almost missed it at first. The gap was masked by wild briar, and high chestnuts kept the steeple from view. But, eventually, through a small parting of the trees, she saw the grey stone of the church and, squeezing through a refractory clump of blackthorns, she came out at one end of a church hall. To the left of her was the church. She sketched a quick prayer for Enrico as she walked the length of it and made her way around to the entrance, to the big square notice board that announced, (yes, there it was), 'St Saviours. The Reverend Harold Beamish'. This was where Richard disappeared to yesterday, she was sure of it. Whether to accomplish a spiritual or a physical escape, she did not know. The former, she hoped fervently. To have blown it so early in the game was too painful to contemplate.

She looked up at the sound of approaching footsteps and recognised the man immediately. Even without the dog collar, there would be no mistaking the wide, fleshy face and the folds of skin splaying over the starched, white band.

"Extra services this Sunday," he smiled at her.

"Goodee!" she crooned back. "Isn't it terrible, all that business at the Hunt?"

He was immediately sombre, his face settling into a grimness that befitted the seriousness of the subject.

"A terrible business, as you say," he agreed. HIs voice rose in volume and emotion.

"Man, in his infinite wickedness, attempting to pierce God's mysteries ... ," but here he stopped abruptly, mindful of the fact that this was the opening to his first Sunday sermon and one did not want to loose one's finest cannonade on an audience of one. "Yes, Man," she echoed, encouragingly, "he's got a lot to answer for."

"Steeped in sin and wallowing in wickedness," he affirmed.

"Still, if he wasn't," said Sam cheerfully, "you and I would be out of a job." And with a wave of her hand, she strode off down the street.

"Bill Gatwood," began Sarah, "is your original road to Emmaus." They were sat in Sam's office that evening for Sarah's first report-back. Something she was obviously taking with professional seriousness, for she had very carefully arranged her notes in order on the desk and was ticking off her list of intructions one by one.

"Meaning?"

"Emmaus? I'm Jewish and even I know that. Comes of being a reporter. You need an extensive education or none at all. Either will do. Anyway, Gatwood saw the light three years back and converted to Christianity pretty much overnight. Before that he played the horses, got pissed regularly, beat his wife, not quite so regularly, but every so often the neighbours would get woken up with a lot of screaming and shouting as she walked into a door. So she left him and went to her sister's in Angmering. But not before most of her savings had disappeared down his throat or on the back of a horse. He went to pieces, apparently, lost his job, had something of a breakdown and went into a bin. Enter God. In the form of a nurse. She gathered up the pieces, put them back together again and carted them off to St Saviours."

"Get a man when he's down, eh?"

"Right. But he became a different person by all accounts. Gave up the booze, the gees, helped old ladies across the road."

"You're bringing tears to my eyes."

Sarah looked up from her notes.

"You don't believe people can change?" Sam thought about it.

"Yeah, I do. But not without a lot more pain than you're describing."

"Mm," Sarah's head was in her notes, "What about sexual preference?"

"Has Gatwood changed that too?"

"No, I was just meaning, you know … generally."

Sam knew and didn't believe it was meant in the least bit generally.

"I mean," Sarah pursued, still not looking up, "are you born gay, for instance?"

"I guess it's like gender, isn't it? You learn the rules at your mother's knee and it's up to you whether you break them or not."

"I wouldn't know. I was never allowed near my mother's knee or any other part of her body for that matter."

The sudden bitterness in the young woman's voice took Sam by surprise. It seemed to have had much the same effect on Sarah too, for she laughed and said in what was intended to be throwaway but which carried too much dead weight, "The only sexuality I learnt about from my mother was cell division. Anyway, back to Gatwood. Where were we?"

"New conversion job, top to bottom."

"Right. Well, it was prodigal son, return of. Much joy and feasting and slaying of fatted calves. Beamish made him church warden in the first few months. Of course then there was a whole lot of pressure on his wife to trot meekly back to him. Which she eventually did. He having sworn everything would change."

"And did it?"

"Oh yes, more than she'd bargained for. In the past she'd enjoyed a tipple now and again, a flutter on the National, liked to watch those do-it-yourself sex videos that are all the rage with boring, middle-aged married couples who want to revitalise the bits they can't, but when she comes back even these mild pastimes are strictly verboten. Your man won't have anything stronger than a lemonade shandy in the house and nothing more steamy on the telly than the 9 o'clock News. So she hightails it out one night."

"And leaves the kid?"

"She wanted to take her with, apparently, but he wouldn't hear of it."

"Didn't she go for custody?"

"Not immediately. When she did he threatened to fight it, with all the might of the church behind him."

"And all that was when?"

"About two years ago."

"And he's kept up the holier than thou ever since?"

"Apparently. Except for a minor fling with another Born Again, which, of course, no one was meant to know about, being strictly secret and which was almost the first thing my informant told me. And," Sarah added with relish, "want to know who his ex-fancy woman is?" Suddenly Sam knew and wished she didn't.

"Jenny Fenton," Sarah pronounced and waited for a reaction, but got none.

"Don't you think that's interesting? That it tells us something?" Only, thought Sam, that Jenny must have been feeling very lonely and wretched at the time.

"No. Nor is it anything to do with the case." And her voice had the temperature of ice cold water.

"What about male friends?" she continued briskly.

"He's a Seagulls fan. Goes to a home game now and then with a couple of other blokes from the church." Football again. Richard was interested in the game apparently. But then so were at least half the male population of Britain.

170

"But no special buddy?" she persisted.

"Why don't you tell me who you're talking about, Sam? I've told you everything I've found out. Why don't you tell me at least one goddam thing you know? You warn me off Fenton. You're following your own private line on Gatwood. You're full of hidden agendas!"

"So what? That's my business."

"No, it's not! It's mine too if it's to do with this case."

"I said you could help ..."

"Yeah, be your assistant, not your dogsbody. You want I should just make the coffee? Is that your idea of team-work? You don't give anything, do you?"

They stared furiously at each other for several moments. It didn't help Sam to realise that at least one half of her anger was directed towards herself. Why? She was not playing fair, she knew that. But she had reasons to justify it, like a whole career of working solo and keeping her cards close to her chest. That would account for a lot of her instinct for secrecy. But was the baseline of her present anger something as shamefully scuzzy as the fact that Sarah had produced a deal of good quality information in record time? She had come up with the goods whilst Sam had got, almost, exactly nowhere.

"OK, you're right. I'm not being very democratic here."

"No, don't sell yourself cheap. Mussolini couldn't have done better!" Sam found herself laughing in spite of herself. It broke the tension.

"Look, the reason I want to keep Jenny's love life out of this is that she was ... is a personal friend." Sarah's face registerd a startled and then a knowing look.

"Not that personal," corrected Sam. "But Gatwood's connection with her isn't important." Oh no? It produced a phantom foetus, didn't it? Which started this whole business off. But she had to protect Jenny from anyone knowing that.

Sarah reached into a large envelope, drew out some photographs and spread them fan-shaped across the desk.

"But his connection with this guy is? Right?" Sarah drew out the print of Gatwood talking to the man whose

171

back was to the camera and looked remarkably like Richard's.

"You're looking for a man, I know that much. Is this him?"

It was a crying shame, thought Sam, to have an assistant that smart and not be able to trust her. She said nothing.

"Why won't you tell me?" Sarah urged, "I've promised not to tell, haven't I? Not to publish anything you haven't agreed on. What more can I say?"

Sam looked at her thoughtfully for a moment, trying to come to a decision one way or the other. At last she said, "OK, I am looking for a man, who might be connected with the case and might not. There are two reasons I haven't told you. For one, he came to my notice through a client who approached me on a different matter and, for reasons of confidentiality, I can't tell you about that."

"Why not? I wouldn't know your client from Adam probably." Sam was silent.

"Or would I?" Sarah stared at her, racking her brains through a list of possible candidates. She came up with no one she could imagine sitting at this desk.

"Ok, what's the second reason?"

"He's a nasty bit of work and I don't want you involved with him."

"That's bloody patronising! If you can take the risk, why can't I? What's the difference?"

"The difference," said Sam slowly, "is around fifty pounds and a black belt in judo."

"That dangerous, eh?" Sam nodded.

"Maybe."

Sarah thought a while.

"Well, you're going to have to tell me some time. Or I'll find out. I've got the rest of the prints here," she drew another large envelope from her bag. "Shall we see if he's in these?" He was.

Sam pointed him out, identifying him only as someone she wanted to investigate, her reasons she was not, without a thoroughly unprofessional breach of confidentiality, at liberty to disclose. Sarah stared at the picture.

"But that's Vanessa's little glamour puss," she said. "Vanessa Hunt. Has she been to see you then?"

Sam sighed and gave a mental shrug. Seeing as Sarah had most of the picture anyway, the rest was shading. She filled it in, swearing Sarah anew to secrecy.

Chapter Twenty Nine

Malcolm was excited. Today he was going to meet a very
special person. And if this were not joyful enough, he
was to bring that person welcome news. As everyone
knows, the bearer of tidings is often credited, in the mind
of the recipient, with having caused the event. Which, in
this instance, was absolutely true. Double joy! Particularly
as he had been out of favour of late. But all that would
be forgotten. Gratitude was due. Praise even. "Praise my
soul the king of heaven ..." rose from within the church,
for the choir was practising for its big day tomorrow.
"... at his feet thy tribute bring ..." His soul soared heav-
enward as he unlocked the door of the hall. Love and
longing filled him, their swift alchemy coursing through
his veins. In just over an hour he would leave for
London.

His father had been deeply disappointed that, because
of work commitments, he would not have his son's presence on the march, but he had a great respect for
Malcolm's work, without in the least understanding what
it was. Once mention of the Official Secrets Act had been
made, all questions were discreetly dropped. His father
was a good patriot. And now in fifty seven minutes
Malcolm would be on the road. He wanted to hug himself with excitement and pleasure.

Fifty five minutes. He began to stack the chairs. Light
metal and canvas, he could take eight at a time. No, ten.
He wanted to feel the play of his muscles under his shirt.
Hard, lithe muscles. He heaved a stack against his chest
with ease, (next time he would take fourteen), and started towards the church, his feet crunching reassuringly on
stone and gravel. He had, for years, given himself the
firm, crisp tread of the soldier, leather impacting on hard
earth and concrete, the sound of his own boots ringing in
the air, announcing his existence. "Man is a rope
stretched betwixt beast and Superman." Since childhood
he had trained his body relentlessly, cleansed his mind
too, eradicating any last trace of cowardice and fear.

"Man is a thing to be surmounted." Time after time he had put himself to the test, willingly undergoing dangers that would have set the the other boys gibbering. Their daredevil games of chicken were just that – games, children's pastimes, a matter of nerve and timing, nothing more. Kindergarten stuff compared to the trials through which he had put himself. One day he had walked blindfolded along a narrow ledge high above the school playground, where a temporary loss of balance or direction would have meant certain death. And he had laughed aloud at the terrified faces of the other boys, gawping up at him. "I teach you the Superman." Thus spoke Zarathustra.

It was a hot morning. He was sweating freely now. Good. Good, hard work, but he needed a drink. He went into the little kitchen and turned on the tap. The water had a heavy, metallic taste. He threw back his head and gargled, rinsing it around his mouth. It was then he noticed the trapdoor. It was not quite shut. He wondered why anyone should have gone up there. To his knowledge it was never used. They had never stored jumble up there. Too much trouble to get up and down. His eye went to the floor. Immediately below the trapdoor was a chair. Somebody had been up there quite recently. It occurred to him suddenly that that somebody might still be there.

Ian had said nothing about her chopped-off hair, but the significance was not lost on him, she saw that. Almost on arrival that morning he had set about enumerating the treats in store for them that day. It was a Saturday, a free day, with another free day ahead, (except, of course, for Matins, Eucharist and Evensong). He would teach her to play chess. Just an hour at a time. Learning should not be a chore, he said. Also, he had brought his paints and crayons. She could help him with the design of a new romper suit. Yes, he always made children's clothes, nothing else. But he did not explain. He had brought a new board game too and more magazines. He was like a mother, filling her child's school holiday jam-pack with golden treats, whether out of love, or fear lest, with the cessation of activity, a hole should appear in the fabric of the day and both slip through. As a child, she had never had a day planned for her, for her alone. Days were adult affairs and you fitted in as and where you could. It occurred to her, though, that never once had he asked her what she would like to do. Perhaps he was afraid of the answer.

He would have to be gone for a short time in the middle of the morning. A little over two hours, that was all, on an errand for his father. He was clearly anxious at this intended absence, leaving her with a large slab of chocolate, presumably to dull the pangs of a hunger that food could never satisfy. She must, on no account, venture into the hall, he had told her. Someone, (and here his face twisted slightly), would be coming to collect the chairs. He left her with a troubled backward glance.

She had heeded the warning for the first hour. By standing tiptoe on his work desk, she could see out of the skylight. Not a lot. A couple of chestnuts, (full of conkers!), and shreds of white cloud. Nonetheless, she had stood like that till her neck and calf muscles ached. It was then she had gone down into the hall. Again that same striding backward and forward brought her calm. And brief forgetfulness. So much so that the sound of the heavy key in the lock caught her completely by surprise. She had had just enough time to run up the ladder and pull the trapdoor to behind her. She had waited, making no movement. She had sensed him below in the kitchen, her eyes going even at the same time his must have done to that small crack where the trapdoor had not aligned flush. She was not surprised when the door opened and the head appeared in the gap. Was relieved, almost.
The wariness in the man's eyes turned into amazement and then into a slow smile. She smiled back, nervously, hoping thereby to ingratiate herself a little. The man hoisted himself through the opening and stood before her.

"What have we got here? A little love nest? So this is what my baby brother gets up to when I'm not around. I didn't think he had it in him."

The words were so unexpected, so incongruous to the situation that Jo could not at first comprehend them. Then the man began to pull down the zip of his fly and move towards her, his hand slowly caressing his groin.

"Let's try you for size," he grinned.

She had no premonition, no thought whatsoever in her head of it. It was as though her foot lifted of its own volition, kicked forward into empty air and made contact in the region of the gaping zip. She saw the man double over, his mouth opening in what must have been a scream. Then she was away, past him down the ladder, knuckles and shins scraping on the iron rungs. To the door. Shut. It was locked. The key in his pocket. But no, she wrenched, it gave. She was out. Running, down the gravel path, into the street. She dodged, tripping over push chairs, cannoning into passersby, almost sprawling headlong, but the momentum of her flight was unstoppable. She was free. And this time no one was going to catch her.

Ian must be his father's messenger. To those members of the congregation too poor to enjoy the benefits of fibre optics, he must go on his bike to spread the word, spread the gospel of the extra services. This Sunday of all Sundays the faithful must make their way thither. Strangers there would be aplenty, the converts, the curious and the cracked, but Beamish wanted his flock around him. For one thing, they would know the hymns. And details like that were important. There was as much stage management to be done in a church as in a theatre, even more so. For the principal actor, unfortunately, would not be putting in an appearance.

It took Ian one hour and thirty six minutes to cycle the ten miles and alert the twenty odd parishioners on his list. His heart was pounding wildly as, at last, he wheeled his mountain bike up the drive to the hall. Something was wrong, he could feel it. The door to the hall was open, but there was no sound of shifting chairs. He dropped his bike and ran. Malcolm was in the kitchen, at the foot of the ladder. The trapdoor was open. His brother's face was

177

drained white with fury. A hand lashed out and caught him a smack on the side of his face, then another, then another. A fist drove into his stomach. He felt the air forced out of him, fought for an ounce of it, as though his lungs were punctured.

"Where is she?" he gasped out, "what have you done with her?"

The blows stopped abruptly.

"Her? Was that a girl?" Ian said nothing. He had said more than enough already. 'Was'. She was no longer there. She had fled. Left him.

"So, you've been having it off with a girl up there," his brother's voice held a note of respect almost, if that were possible.

"No, I haven't!"

"Little liar!"

"I didn't! We played chess, that's all." Malcolm stared at him in astonishment and burst out laughing.

"Man, you're soft as shit, you are!" The laughter stopped.

"If I ever see her again, I'll kill her!"

Ian turned and ran. Picking up his bike, he raced off into the busy street. Traffic moved up and down. It was Saturday morning, with incoming shoppers from the out-lying villages, day trippers from London, all advancing on the town centre. Somewhere in this throng was Jo, escaping, but not from him. From Malcolm. She was running from his brother. He must find her. He looked up and down the street. Northward to Lewes and the long ridge of downs, southward to Brighton – to the sea. She had talked of the sea. Only once, but there had been something in her voice. He crossed the road and headed south.

By that Saturday morning, Detective Sergeant Walsh was forced to admit that the police had drawn a blank so far. Not that it was his responsibility, thank God. That was one compensation for not attaining higher rank. At least his head would remain firmly on his shoulders. But he felt frustrated with himself. The Chief had agreed with him that the Gatwood girl was lying through her teeth, though without accepting his theory of her motives. Psychology was not the Chief's strong point. So, attention had centred on the runaway girl. Description on national radio and television and in all the papers. To no avail. Not a dicky bird. They had checked the missing young persons list (which wouldn't have given much joy, anyway, the computer having mislaid half the database), sent the word out to children's homes, detention centres, halfway hostels. Still nothing. If she had run away, it would seem it was from her own home and a lot of parents never bothered informing the police. Glad to see the back of them very often. It was one less mouth to feed.

Of course, it could be that the girl had nothing to do with it. But then why didn't she show? Prove her innocence? (Walsh retained a touching faith in the public's confidence in the Force.) But they were keeping an open mind. They still had an eye on Maurice, the caretaker. He had been on the premises all the time. (He had been taken into Brighton General after a mini heart attack, but that didn't stop him from being a suspect.) Then, of course, there were the locals to investigate. But the girl had not been interfered with, that had been established. Was a virgin, in fact.

But it was motive, that's what he couldn't fathom. Everyone in the neighbourhood seemed to genuinely like the kid. Both her purse and person intact, the main motivation nowadays seemed to be absent. So why? She had been stunned first, perhaps even rendered unconscious, by a blow to the head, prior to strangulation. He had seen that syndrome before. Usually some kind of sexual assault occurred in the interval. He had always seen it as a form of necrophilia, the inert victim having all the outward appearance of death. It was a particular taste, unlike most rapes where the attacker actually enjoyed the struggles and fear of his victim. But, here again, Cynthia Fenton had not been touched, sexually that is. Unless, of course, the man had been unable to carry out the act. In which case they should be looking for someone who suffered from impotency. The idea sparked him. He thought of Bill

179

Gatwood, of the man's almost Victorian preoccupation with his own daughter's virginity. Repression, prohibition, obsession – it was all present in cases of that kind. And what of Gatwood's wife? He had failed to find that out. Had she died? Or left him? And, if so, why? These things would have to be investigated. That is, of course, if the Chief agreed. As four wasted days had gone by and his chief was totally devoid of any better ideas, he agreed.

Malcolm, driving to London at that moment, was flagged down by a motorcycle cop at a road block, just outside of Hassocks. No, he had not seen or given a lift to a young woman, sixteen or thereabouts. Yes, if he saw anyone answering to that description he would notify the police at once. He forgot the encounter almost immediately, his thoughts straining towards an apartment just off the Kings Road and the beautiful eyes and lips and hands of its resident. It was these he saw etched in minutest detail in his mind's eye, not the rather vague outline of a pathetic teenage runaway. It was not until he hit Purley Way, on the last stretch into London through suburban Croydon, that another picture formed itself in his mind and superimposed itself onto the description the policeman had given him. A thin, tanned face and savagely-cropped hair, a pair of wild, fearful eyes. The two cross-faded as though across a video screen and settled into one. That was very interesting. He would deal with that. At a later date.

Chapter Thirty

Sam arrived at Palmeira Square as the marchers were gathering, spreading out languidly picnic-style on the grass or marshalling their groups and unfurling banners, according to their own modus operandi. She strolled from island to island of people. If Richard were at that meeting then two to one he would be here too, especially if he were anything to do with St Saviours. On her progress around the lawns she encountered many greetings and felt again the rekindled warmth of old friendships. Ellen was very busy and looked exhausted even at this stage, but she spared five minutes to give Sam a fond hug and an invitation to a drink that evening. Jenny was with her and markedly avoiding Sam's eye, so she did not dally long. Give it time. Jenny had had more than enough to cope with in the last week.

She spied Sarah on the other side of the square, dressed in jeans, Levi shirt and DMs. In spite of the gear, or perhaps in sheer contrast to it, she looked remarkably vulnerable, a fact which surprised Sam. The girl stood looking around her in bewilderment, almost in shock. Her first demo? wondered Sam. But no, even if she had never participated in one, as a journalist she must have covered them before. Then it occurred to her that Sarah must be looking around her in apprehension at these several thousand people who were all gathering with one purpose in mind, to converge on her mother's workplace and voice their bitter opposition. Thanks to her. For she had started the whole thing. Few of these people had even heard of the Hunt a week ago. It was one thing to have a bitter personal vendetta but quite another to realise you'd opened it out to half the nation. Revenge, thought Sam, could be just as crushing to the perpetrator as to the victim. Sarah spied her and waved. As they made their way towards each other Sam saw her rally visibly, as though closing off all the chinks in her not inconsiderable armour.

"Quite a surprise for my dear old mum," she said

nonchalantly. Behind her and obviously in tow was a plump, pleasant-faced, but very hot and bothered young man wearing a heavy Nikon camera and a put-upon air.

"By the way, this is my photographer."

"Your photographer does have a name," he remonstrated.

"I'm Hugh, Hugh Manders. You must be Sam. Sarah's told me a lot about you." Has she, thought Sam? Bit difficult considering she doesn't know the first thing about me.

"About what a top-class detective you are and all that," and with what he lacked in enthusiasm he made up for in politeness. Sam found herself liking him a lot. He had charm and Sarah had not yet quite broken his spirit.

"I like your photographs too, while we're at it."

"What is this? A mutual admiration society?" Sarah cut in,

"Hugh's going to take some shots of the demo."

"Great."

"He'll develop them this evening."

"Sal, we're going out this evening."

"We'll cancel it."

"It's been arranged for ages."

"Work comes first," she flung him an exasperated look.

"Look, there's no hurry," Sam stepped in hastily. "Take your time, Hugh."

"Thanks," but he was not mollified. Nor was Sarah inclined to give in with good grace.

"We'll have to cancel it anyway."

"Why?"

"Because Sam and I will probably have work to do." Hugh looked indignantly at Sam. Uh-oh, never get caught between two lovers.

"No. I'm taking the night off myself." Hugh's face registered relief, and Sarah's disappointment.

"Then you can come to this dreary cocktail party with us. It'll be alright, won't it, Hugh?" Hugh looked as though it would be far from alright.

"No, I've already got an arrangement, thanks." She needed to put a stop on this one fast and, gratefully, left

182

them still arguing. When alone and envying couples, as she had been these last eighteen months, it was easy to forget the downside of a twosome.

And so she went on her way through the crowds, in pursuit of a blonde head and tall, muscular figure but having always, too, in the back of her mind, another, darker, softer face, a body infinitely more attractive. She found neither. At the absence of the first she felt frustration and irritation with herself, at the absence of the other she felt a more complex amalgam of emotions that she hadn't the time or the inclination to disentangle. But, overriding all, was one of disappointment. The woman could at least have put in an appearance, as a gesture of solidarity to all those whose genes were at risk of manipulation from Hunt et al. Sam had expected better of her.

She almost did not recognise Gatwood. The man's face was literally grey and, within the space of a few days, lines not evident on the photograph had appeared round eyes and mouth. He was ill at ease, his eyes flicking from one to another of the knots of people around him. She allowed them to rest on her, flick away, come back, move and return again as she observed him.

"You're Bill Gatwood, aren't you," she asked pleasantly.

"What of it?" The tone was belligerent.

"I just wanted to ask you a few questions, Mr Gatwood."

"Leave me alone."

"You seem a bit on edge, Mr Gatwood."

"I'm sick of you lot, that's all," his voice was harsh with tension. His hands were curled into fists. They were big hands, hairy and thick-fingered and she didn't like to think of them moving over Jenny's body. The woman deserved better than that. "I've got nothing to say to the Press. Nor has Sandra. So just piss off!"

He turned to walk away.

"I'm not a reporter, Mr Gatwood," she called after him, "I'm a detective." That brought him to an abrupt halt. There was fury in his eyes. But something else too.

"Look, Sandra's told you what happened twice now,"

so he thought she was police. Good. She wouldn't disillusion him. And they had thought fit to interview the girl twice. That was interesting.

"What more do you want?"

"The truth would do, Mr Gatwood."

"It is the truth, I tell you!", it came out as an explosion of frustration and helplessness. A man wrongly accused, unjustly persecuted. He was very convincing.

"But I happen to know she didn't see any foetus that night. She didn't see one, because there never was one. It was a total fabrication, to get everyone worked up about the Hunt. That's the truth, isn't it, Mr Gatwood?"

"No!" This was almost a shout. Heads began to turn.

"That's a lie," he was whispering now. "Don't you try to pin nothing on me. You couldn't prove it, anyway," he was gathering some shreds of confidence now, "even if it was true. Which it ain't."

"I think we could prove it, Mr Gatwood. If we wanted to."

"Set me up, you mean. Yeah, you do it all the time, don't you?"

"That sounds like slander to me, Mr Gatwood. Still, I'll ignore it this time. But we'll be keeping an eye on you. Just in case you or your daughter come across any more stray foetuses on your travels. We wouldn't want that now, would we?"

It was akin to tormenting a cornered animal. His spirit crouched at bay before her. Fear came off him in waves so strong she could smell it and sweat was trickling freely down his face and onto his top lip. It was the kind of baiting in which some took pleasure, she supposed. She had no stomach herself for the sport, but still she did not let up. So he had played a trick on the police, the public, his own church. No real harm had been done. The most he would get would be a fine for wasting police time and causing aggravation. The man's reaction was so excessive, so disproportionate to the actual incident that she had to get to the bottom of it. He was the one real lead she had that might possibly connect to Cynthia's murder. That was the reason she toyed with him like a cat with a mouse, she told herself, and not because she felt angry and frustrated with herself.

"You hot, Mr Gatwood?"

"No."

"You're sweating."

"I'm hot. Why don't you leave me alone?" It was a plea for mercy and it had been wrung out of him. She had had enough. Suddenly felt sick with it.

"If you've done nothing wrong then you've nothing to worry about, have you? But if you have, we'll find out. Goodbye, Mr Gatwood." And she left him, feeling his eyes boring into her back until the crowds swallowed her up. The man was terrified and she was going to find out why.

Chapter Thirty One

Lionel Kramski was a U.S. citizen and he was drunk, two facts which, though not at all mutually exclusive, should have had no intrinsic interconnection. That they did was entirely due to the fact that he was driving, that he had already had two fines for motoring offences that year, that he was a commercial traveller and that he was eligible for British citizenship in exactly six months time. All things which sprang immediately and vividly to mind as soon as he heard the smack on his front fender and saw the kid go flying onto the sidewalk, rather than the more appropriate concern for a fellow human being. Not that Lionel was a monster. He just didn't want to be returned to the States, for a number of reasons. Not least of which was the back payment of four years maintenance he owed. He had tried to keep up the instalments, but with a wife and kid to support over here, there was no way he could deliver, not out of the £12,000 basic plus commission he earned with this outfit. So when he rushed to the kid's side the prayer on his lips was as much for himself as for the body skewed across the sidewalk.

"You bloody madman! Couldn't you see him crossing the road?"

"What's the matter with you? You blind or what?"

"Go and call the police!" a woman in a red and gold headscarf commanded the man she was with. He trotted off obediently.

People were gathering now, crowding around, like vultures wheeling in an ever-decreasing circle. He had the urge to break through them, jump into his car and put his foot on the gas. Get the hell out of here. But someone would be sure to take his number. Then that would be that. With a hit and run to add to everything else he might as well book the first plane out. He would have to stay and face the music. And Lionel had never been very good at doing that.

The kid opened his eyes and looked around him.

"You alright, love?" a woman bent over him.

186

"There's no blood," said a man.

"Yes there is," proclaimed a youth, with ghoulish relish, "on the side of his head, look."

Yes, there was blood, but very little. The body was not twisted into any awkward angles that would have indicated hard things fractured inside. Nor was there any blood issuing from nose or mouth that would have meant those hard things had punctured soft things inside. In fact if he had not been lying at the kerbside, the boy might well have been awaking from a sound sleep in his own comfortable bed.

"Did you phone the police?" the red-scarved woman demanded of her man as he shuffled back into the circle.

"Phone box is out of order," he mumbled.

"Then go into the Co-op, Arnold. They'll do it for you," she tut-tutted impatiently and looked around her for common condemnation of his startling lack of initiative. Arnold moved off again through the crowd, as he was bidden.

Suddenly the boy on the ground sat up, rubbing his arm and looking around him, as if unable to comprehend this amount of attention.

"Look, there is blood. I told you," the youth pointed triumphantly. Heads craned instantaneously and in unison, like a covey of crows intent on their dinner.

"We need an ambulance," someone suggested.

"We need the police," insisted Arnold's line manager, her scarf slipping from her head to reveal newly-permed curls the shade of cochineal. She hoiked the scarf up again but it slid back down to her neck.

"No! I'll take care of him," Lionel was suddenly and resolutely stirred to action.

"You?" the woman's voice held contempt, "You've half-killed him already. Now what you going to do to him?"

"Take him to the Royal Sussex. I'm a consultant there," he added, throwing in an impossible wild card. Who would believe that? Not the newly-coiffeured woman with the recalcitrant head scarf and the submissive husband, that's for sure.

"Then you should be struck off!" she declared. But the

187

others moved back a pace. There is still, in the national character, an ingrained deference towards the professional, particularly the medical professional, thought Lionel, so that it is just possible, when necessary, to pull a monumental fast one on the British public. Now he stooped over the boy, running his hands gently over the outstretched limbs with what he hoped looked like practised skill.

"Any pain? Here? Here?", the boy shook his head.

"OK, I'll take you into X-ray anyway, just to make sure."

He helped the boy to his feet and led him to the car as the crowd parted to let them pass.

"Don't worry. He'll get the best treatment available."

"Oh, well, it won't be on the NHS then," someone joked and there was general laughter. The boy would be alright, it had been decided. It had all been taken out of their hands now anyway. People drifted away. There was, after all, shopping to be done and lunch to be made, all the chores of an ordinary Saturday to get through.

It had been a close one, Lionel had to admit as he drove away. This time he was stone cold sober. Fear did that to you. Adrenalin displaced the booze. He looked across at the boy. There was colour coming back into his cheeks. The blood on his head was just a graze, Lionel could see now. There was another on the elbow. But the eyes. They were still unfocussed, as though not yet able to place his surroundings. Shock. Or, Christ, maybe he was concussed! Now that he was well past the onlookers he could put the kid out onto the sidewalk. No one would know. They were already busy with other things and would have forgotten the whole incident by now. But the state the boy was in he might just wander out onto the road again and this time really get smashed to bits. So, what the hell? It wasn't his problem. He had enough of those already, didn't he? He stopped the car and got out. Several minutes later he returned, carrying two polystyrene cups.

"Here, son, have some coffee. It'll clear your head." He certainly needed something to clear his own. What the hell was he going to do? The only decent thing was to take the kid home, but how to do that without running into his parents? They sat sipping the sickly sweet liquid. Suddenly the boy looked up.

"The gulls!"

"Hm? Yeah, sure, Gulls. We're at the seaside, ain't we?" A thought occurred to him.

"Don't you come from round here?" The boy shook his head.

"Here for the weekend, hey?" That was better. Much better. No parents, for a kick off.

"Come to see friends?" Again the shake of the head.

"Where you staying?" The boy shrugged.

"Got money?" Head shake again. Yeah, wouldn't you just know it? But things were getting clearer.

"Look, I got an expense account with a little bed and breakfast down at the seafront. Want to stay there the night?"

"I haven't got any money."

"Don't worry about it. I'll pick up the tab, OK?" The boy looked uncomprehending.

"Have yourself a nice day. Relax, go to the beach, have a drink later on." Did kids that young drink these days? He couldn't remember a time when he hadn't drunk.

"Or a coke and ice cream. Here, here's a couple of tenners. Go ahead, take 'em." For the boy was staring at the notes. Not moving.

"What's the matter. Ain't it enough?", he demanded. Was the kid going to lay a blackmail number on him after all? That's just what he needed.

"No, I'm sorry. I don't do it for money." It was the longest sentence to come out of the kid's mouth and it knocked him for six. This time it was his turn to stare in incomprehension.

"What … you think I want sex? What, you think I'm queer or something?" Lionel didn't know whether to feel relieved, or aggrieved at the slur on his manhood.

"No, you got me all wrong, feller. You had a little argument with my fender back there and came off worst." He had to be careful not to take on too much of the blame.

189

Particularly as the kid didn't seem to remember a thing.

"It was both our faults, I admit that, but I'm offering to call it quits and give you a night at the seaside. On me. Free. Gratis, alright?" for the kid was staring at him still.

"Deal?" The boy nodded. At last!

He drove to Kemp Town, to the little side street off Marine Parade, and parked. He hadn't expected to be back so soon. The sound of hoovering several stories up ceased when he pressed the buzzer at the desk. Footsteps came down the stairs. She was wearing a flowery pinafore affair, something she never wore when he was there.

"What you doing back?" her hand pulled at the knot tying her apron. She was pleased, but embarrassed. Taken off guard. He gave her a swift kiss.

"I'm not staying." Her face fell. "I just picked up this young feller on the way out of town." She looked over at his companion for the first time.

"He needs a bed for the night."

"He got money?" her voice was suspicious. You didn't last ten years in a seaside B and B unless you had a nose for what was inside a person's pocket. That kid's pocket smelt distinctly empty.

"Put it on my account," said Lionel. She looked at him in astonishment.

"Well, he kinda reminds me of me, when I was that age. Taking off for the weekend, without a cent in my pocket. Relying on the kindness of strangers."

"You're crazy," she said, but it was a caress.

"No, just getting sentimental in my old age, I guess." They smiled at each other in a sort of two-way invitation. He was sorely tempted. But he had already lost close on an hour and had two customers yet to see in Hayward's Heath so that he wouldn't get back home before five and he had promised Maureen he would take her to her mother's ...

"Coming upstairs? For coffee?" she added, for the sake of the boy. Her eyes were an open door beckoning him in.

"I can't, baby. I'm late as hell already." The door

190

slammed shut and a key turned in the lock. Ah well, he would open it again with ease when he came back in a week or so. Renee never held out for long.

"Be seeing you," he grinned and she turned away.

Chapter Thirty Two

The march, though hastily arranged, had been organised with commendable thoroughness by representatives of a coalition of local groups. A moderator had been engaged to calm qualms, soothe tempers and smoothe over tricky conflicts of opinion so as to produce, for two hours at least, a united front against a common enemy. As a couple counsellor with Relate, it had been this woman's job for some years to reconcile the mis-matched and incompatible, tasks with which she had had some modest degree of success. Up till now she had maintained, with rugged sanguinity, that no poles were too far apart to see eye to eye (being in the habit of mixing her metaphors indiscriminately). But by 1pm on Saturday her air of insuperable cheerfulness had become more than a little forced and the mellow tones of her voice had acquired a harshness hitherto unknown to it. After two, glorious, nicotine-free years, she chain-smoked shamelessly as she fled from group to group. However, her achievement must not be minimised for, on the surface at least, all was concord and conciliation. The St Saviours contingent had, against massive protest, agreed to refrain from the singing of hymns. In return for this compromise there was to be no "Pride" sloganising. As both groups expected large reinforcements from elsewhere, it was their sworn and solemn duty to alert visiting comrades to these strict regulations. Beside the two superpowers, there were also a number of other local groups represented: Disabled Power, Animal Rights, the Tibetan Buddhist Society, the Lesbian and Gay Christian Group and the SWP, to name but a few. This latter spent a great deal of time in earnest discussion on how to lay the blame for genetic engineering unequivocally at the door of the Tory government and were attempting a rehearsal of relevant slogans in a corner. This was abruptly brought to a halt by the moderator, (now on her third pack of Bensons), with a snarl of such vituperation as had never been heard in her soft-spoken, soft-sofa'd office, nor, in all probability in the homes of any of her clients, and which brought a gentle suggestion from one of the Tibetan Buddhists (from a monastery in the foothills of Arundel) that she was, perhaps, in need of counselling and meditation.

Having established the rules of play, ensured goalposts remained in place, and obtained from all combatants a promise to refrain from kneecapping, elbowing, mutual insults and any other forms of foul play, it fell to her to coordinate the trickiest moment of all – the kick off. It was a position of such media advantage that no mere flick of a coin could decide it. Who should lead the march? Matters left to chance were sure to be challenged immediately afterwards and so it had been debated bitterly through half a long night. The Reverend Beamish declared that no member of his congregation would walk behind a godless Sodomite, whilst the Lesbian and Gay Coalition refused point-blank to follow in the wake of homophobes. The SWP offered to lead the way but were shouted down in the only demonstration of unity theretofore exhibited. Ellen was asked whether Disabled Power would like to take the vanguard but she declined. The two miles, at least partly uphill, would be exhausting enough for their members as it was. So the evening wrangled on. Finally, in her most fatigued but finest hour, the counsellor made a daring but deft suggestion. Why not have the Lesbian and Gay Christians lead the march. Many were Sodomites, but none godless, or homophobic. The suggestion left both major powers without a serviceable argument.

Come the day, as the diverse marchers gathered, it became clear there were many possible flashpoints of rebellion that would need discreet defusing or controlled detonation. But the murmurings of discontent began eventually to die down, due as much to the determined optimism of the weather, as to any human endeavour. It was a beautiful September day, the last fling of summer in an irridescent blue sky. There was a feeling of anticipation, of festivity and fellowship, as old friends re-met and exclaimed, congratulated or commiserated on new babies or old lovers.

And so it was that at 1.30 on that Saturday afternoon, as diverse an assortment of people as one could hope to see, of all colours, creeds and catechisms, some in wheelchairs, some in pushchairs, others on crutches, stilettos and even stilts, all gathered together behind one banner. The wind caught the sheet, which flapped, bellied and was held taut in a wide straining arc. The sail of the flagship hoisted, the first of the procession began slowly to move off. At its head, like twin prows of a great galleon, walked Doreen (Dr Shilpa's invaluable aide de camp) and her friend, bedecked extravagantly, the one in lavender, the other in emerald green, their combined colours recalling the glories of the Suffragette Movement and their combined ages probably well pre-dating it. Fair stood the wind. The crowds of curious onlookers parted obediently before them and they set sail.

But a calm sea and a steady one was not destined to last long. Storm clouds already gathered on the horizon and the first flurry came when the police abruptly and summarily changed the route of the march. The shipping (or rather, shopping) lanes were too busy that afternoon, they said, and a more uncluttered course could be found by diverting to another route, one running parallel to the main thoroughfare of Western Road, but which guaranteed far more peace and quiet. But that, said the organisers, was what they definitely did not want, the whole point of a march being to peaceably pass on your own disquiet to the maximum number of people. The police, however, would not budge, so the marchers were forced to. The new route skilfully evaded the Saturday shoppers but led right past the Glenning Clinic, which is where the trouble began, as anyone could have told the police it would. It was just a question of who would hurl the first insult. And as one comment breeds another, giving birth to a veritable brood of sibling insults, it was not long before a battle of verbal abuse was in full swing, with first one side and then the other gaining ground in decibels, and each in turn being drowned by the chant of an atrocious rhyming couplet which included "church". "state" and "inseminate" within its straining, overburdened

194

metre. The SWP had triumphed at the last. The fragile, custom-built peace had crumbled, shattered by pressures too mighty for its own internal contradictions and by the sheer weight of its private agendas.

Chapter Thirty Three

Jo stood at the window of her hotel room, looking out at the backs of high houses, many-storeyed seafront dwellings, with spiral-staired fire escapes and narrow, dark back-yards. Somewhere beyond them was the sea. She had not yet seen it, not glimpsed it even, but she could hear the cry of the gulls. It was a strange, high, lonely sound, the cry of the sea itself. And now that she was so close, she was afraid. Afraid to go further, to go that last few hundred yards or so to the shore.

The woman, Renee, had bathed her cuts and grazes with warm water pungent with Dettol, and a swab of cotton wool, all the time grumbling that he took her for granted, her man, (Lionel was his name), that he would have her take in any old stray. Not that he would stop and look after it himself, oh no, he was hot-footing it back to Croydon and that hard-faced bitch of a wife and the squalling brat of his. She had gone on in this vein, all the while dabbing at the raw places on Jo's forehead and arm, smoothing in ointment, attaching squares of lint and strapping them in place with strips of pink plaster. Jo had not minded the words. They were, after all, not directed at her, but rolled over her and onwards towards a small blue Toyota heading along the M23. And, too, there was no actual malice in them. They were merely a bubbling overflow of frustration and disappointment, seeking drainage.

Jo even began to enjoy Renee's ministrations. The feel of the cool fingers on her skin, the impersonal touch of them, neither intruding nor claiming unwanted intimacy.

"Once every ten days I see him. That's no good, is it? That's not enough to go on with. I should kick him out once and for all, that's what I should do. Give him the boot."

"Why don't you?" asked Jo, curious.

"And do what?" came the reply. Jo didn't know. What did you do? It was an adult world she had yet to explore, if ever.

"Find someone else, I suppose." But Renee snorted.

"Like who? Want a cup of tea?" she fetched the polished silver kettle to the sink. "I always have one about now. Peps me up." She poured in water.

"Like who?" she demanded again. "What else is there?" she asked, punctuating the question with a flick of the kettle's switch. Jo wracked her brain for an answer, but need not have bothered.

"They're all married or wasters, or both," Renee went on. "Look at my sister. Married to a bloke who hasn't had a sniff of a job for ten years. Won't get off his arse to look for one. Ten years! She works from 8 till 5, brings up three kids and gives him his spending money. She should leave him." She spooned coffee into pink flowered mugs.

"Why doesn't she?" asked Jo, already knowing the answer.

"What else is there?" Renee negotiated the pouring of boiling water, leaving Jo to ponder the female condition.

"She leaves him for another bastard, pardon my French, and what does she do then? Milk? Sugar?" Jo nodded.

"How many men will take on another man's kids? Three of them at that."

"Maybe she loves him," Jo ventured. Renee's face registered amazement at the very idea.

"She can't stand him! Hates the sight of him! But it's the next best thing to love, I suppose. At least it's something to hang on to, keep you going. Better than being on your own."

"Is that so bad?" The woman looked at Jo over her coffee cup, a moistness that could have been steam in her eyes.

"You're young. That's how you can ask that. See if you still think that in twenty years. But then, men are different. They don't get lonely. And if they do they just pick up a woman. A young woman, if she's daft enough to have him. Which she usually is. Got a girlfriend?"

The question came as a shock to Jo, before she remembered. Take care of the boy, the man had said to Renee. And she had accepted it. Jo was a boy as far as she was concerned. As far as she could see. And the police were looking for a girl.

"No, I haven't," Jo replied.

"Don't tell me you're a virgin," the woman looked incredulous and laughed as Jo blushed and looked away.

"Yeah, pull the other one, it's got bells on! I know all about teenagers nowadays," she patted Jo's arm indulgently.

"Well, so long as you respect the girl and don't make her do anything she doesn't want. And just you make sure you use something. Know what I mean?" Jo nodded, still not looking at the woman. She felt her cheeks glowing a fiery red.

A buzzer sounded so loudly that Jo jumped almost out of her chair. Renee peered through the open door into the hallway.

"They'll be a one-night stand," she whispered, "grumble about the hot water and the mattress, have cereal, juice and full fried, then take all the bread and marmalade in a serviette for lunch. I know the type. Bloody cheapskates!" she heaved herself up.

"Your room's number eleven. The key's in the door. I've just finished cleaning it." And with that she departed to welcome her pair of cheapskates, a young couple in matching green jogging suits. As Jo mounted the stairs she heard them querying the tariff.

The room was bare but quite pretty, with light blue flowered wall-paper and matching blue coverlet on the single bed. There was a small bedside table with a lamp, a wardrobe and a chest of drawers, on which were two fresh white towels and a small bar of wrapped soap. Jo fingered the towels shyly, as though intruding in a stranger's room, expecting its occupant to appear at any moment and challenge her presence there. She tried the bed, perching gingerly on the edge. The sheets were crisp and clean and smelt of sea air. It would be the first night in many months she would sleep in a proper bed. Her head still throbbed from its summary encounter with hard pavement and she was tempted to steal awhile between those coolly inviting covers before the three bears returned to expel her. But she was restless. Outside lay the lapping sea of her dreams. She had reached its edges, almost, and was impatient to come to it at last.

She got up and opened the door into the corridor and at that very same moment, emerging from the room next door, came a very thin, very frail, but extraordinarily upright old woman. Seeing Jo, a golden smile began in the crinkly eyes and spread quickly to the mouth, illuminating the aged parchment of her face.

"Arthur!" she said, "You've come. I've waited so long," and she moved slowly towards Jo, her arms outstretched.

Chapter Thirty Four

After the march was over Sarah found Sam.

"Not a sign. You?"

"No, me neither."

"No, me neither probably," cut in Hugh, "if I knew what you were talking about," he grinned but Sam could see he was only half joking.

"This doesn't concern you, Hugh," said Sarah.

"It obviously concerns me enough to take pictures for you," Hugh objected.

Sarah sighed volubly. "This is detective's business, Hugh. And detective's assistant's."

"And seeing as I'm only the assistant's assistant, nobody tells me what's going on."

"The thing is, Hugh," Sam felt she had to intervene to avert another domestic dispute, "the more people who know, the more dangerous it becomes."

"Dangerous! Sal, you never told me it was dangerous!" He was appalled.

"Oh, Hugh, don't go all big and butch on me. It doesn't suit you. Anyway, what did you think we were doing? Playing tiddlywinks?"

"So until he shows I'm going to switch tack," Sam cut in hurriedly. "I'm putting Gatwood under surveillance."

"Gatwood?"

"Yeah. He's got something on his mind and it's giving him a first-rate migraine. I want to find out what it is. So I'm going to sit tight this evening outside his door."

"But it's a small village. He'll know you're there."

"Exactly." A grin spread over Sarah's face.

"Putting the screws on him, huh?"

"That's right."

"I'll come too."

"Sal!" It was a cry from the heart.

"No, it's a waste of person-power to have two of us there at once."

"I'll do the night shift then." Hugh looked horrified.

"No need. We both need our beauty sleep. We'll make a rota for tomorrow, from morning onwards."

"Sal, I won't let you do it!" They both turned to stare at him. He blushed.

"I mean, please don't, Sal. Suppose you got hurt." He looked miserable.

"Sam's going to show me some self-defence. Aren't you?"

"Yeah. But the best self-defence is get the hell out fast at the first sign of trouble. And that's what you're going to have to promise to do, or no playing."

"I promise. I'm no hero."

"OK, meet you at Preston Park in an hour and we'll go over a few moves. I've got to go and see someone right now." And she left them. The one high as a kite, the other in deep dejection. She headed off toward Norfolk Square, in search of Jerry.

As she reached Western Road a car stopped beside her and a man called out. She turned, ready with a mouthful if he were a kerb-crawler. It was her cab driver of two days before.

"Hey, you know what? I found out." He leaned out of the car window. "Your man, he was going to that football game all along. Asked to be put out there, so he could catch the end of it, he said. Never knew we were behind him."

"Well, that's good news," she felt immense relief.

"Yeah," he grinned. "Been hoping to see you, so's I could tell you. Put your mind at rest." She drew out her wallet.

"Here, take the rest of the fare now."

"Nah. Just make sure you ask for me if you're doing anything like that again. My name's Mick. Mick Connors." And he drove off.

Chapter Thirty Five

Judith stood at the office window and watched the police herd the ragtag crowd of demonstrators past the gates of the Hunt. She had the ridiculous feeling of being in a film. the evil mill owner looking down on a thousand extras rhubarbing in obedience to some command from behind the scenes. Soon someone would say "cut" and all this angry incoherence and muddle would cease and this faceless tide of raging humanity would shuffle off and become individuals again, drinking coffee and smoking cigarettes and chatting about dogs and money and marriages, until summonsed for the next take. Alone in white muslin, she too would await her cue. Have make-up and gown adjusted. Receive direction.

But there would be none. No one was going to come along and put a friendly arm on her shoulder and say, "Wonderful darling but I want you to..," to do what? What was there to do when you were literally besieged by an angry mob? Who was going to be there with a paternalistic arm around you, or a maternal bosom to cry on, for that matter. Roger had been worse than useless. It wasn't just the thought of the whole building going up in smoke, though God knows, things like that were happening in the States. An old colleague of hers just this week had had his hands blown off by a letter bomb from some maniac accusing him of genetic genocide. The new catch phrase. These people were capable of anything. No, it wasn't just the fear of an imminent physical danger, (all incoming mail was carefully vetted now), it was this being so universally reviled, this being the object of such loathing and revulsion by one's fellow human beings. And for what? For trying to make their pathetic lives a little better. That's what was so unfair. Not that she really cared about what people like that thought of her. Their crassness was self-evident. Still, it bruised the spirit.

A few of the staff had elected to stay with her in the building throughout the day. The police had advised a presence, even though they would have men stationed around the perimeter fence all weekend. Roger had offered to be there, but had done so with so little enthusiasm that she had declined. She still felt furious with him. That he had allowed his overweaning self-importance, his puerile desire for attention to get the better of discretion was something she could not readily forgive. Especially as they were in such dire financial straits. Not that that was so very unusual. They had had many a bumpy ride in their time, with bankruptcy looming around the corner, but Roger had always managed to pull off some deal at the last minute. Had seemed to prefer waiting to the last minute, enjoying the brinkmanship. It was this particular combination of being on a financial knife edge at the same time as getting such concentrated bad press that was preying on her nerves, feeding into the anxiety of her work, making her head throb continually.

The crowd had almost passed now, hurried on by the police escort. She would stay one hour longer, perhaps, do another tour of the building and then go. She would be unable to work, she knew that. She walked up the broad main staircase and worked her way slowly along the corridor, throwing open the door of each lab in turn, inspecting the insides of cupboards, the undersides of work benches, for .. what? For whom? She had no clear idea. For anything "untoward" the police had said. As if the whole damn business wasn't untoward. As if there was anything "toward" about having first a murder, then a mob at your gate. The store room, the toilets, her own lab. No alien body or bundle secreted in any of them. She felt as she had done as a child, having to check all corners of the room for bogeymen before finally leaping into bed at night. And even then she would lie there, the blankets up to her nose, watching in fright the shadows of branches flitting in through the open window. And with them, what else?

She paused at Roger's door. It was locked, she knew. He had expressly forbidden entry, claiming an important experiment that would brook no interference. What the hell did he think she was going to do to it? Swipe it off the work bench as she went past? Irritation with him rose in her anew. The police had advised she check everywhere, leave no hiding place unturned. Very well, she would do just that and damn Roger! She put the key to the lock. And froze. There was a sound from inside. Just the slightest of scufflings. And then silence. A silence in which she could hear the whole building, like a heavy sleeper, shift and sigh. She had imagined it. But no, again, from inside, a furtive scrabbling.

She should run downstairs immediately. Liz and Owen, two of the lab assistants, were in the basement. There was a uniformed bobby at the front door. It was the wisest course. She did not take the wisest course. As someone who had never thought of herself as possessing anything as uncerebral, as visceral as physical courage, she amazed herself. She turned the key and opened the door. And screamed.

Small brown eyes stared, mesmerised, into hers. A moment later they were gone. The tiny brown, velvety thing shot off the bench, landed at her feet and was off down the corridor. Her legs, drained suddenly of adrenalin, buckled under her and she sat down heavily on a stool. For a minute or two she was aware only of her own heart battering against the sides of her chest. When it had subdued itself to a manageable tap tap, she looked around her.

The work bench was empty. No experiment. No paraphernalia in sight that heralded even the advent of an experiment. Only a plain black file. She picked it up. There was no identifying label on the front – a breach of lab procedures. Everything had to be documented and labelled accordingly, that was official practice. She opened it. Inside were no notes, no results, no formulae. Only letters. In the front was the draft of a letter with Roger's signature attached. The gist of it was that he felt it only fair to inform them of the difficulties the Hunt was having at the moment, what with adverse publicity and subsequent attacks by the local community, and that, although this was not posing a major problem at the moment, he could not absolutely guarantee that in the

204

future it would not disrupt their work. Why the hell did Roger have to be so scrupulously honest, for God's sake! Why couldn't he just leave it alone? Hope it all passed as quickly as possible? Was he hell bent on professional suicide? Behind a pale pink divider were the replies. All the companies on their books and many they were trying like mad to get on their books. The replies were, with a few exceptions, entirely sympathetic. They deplored the persecution of the Hunt, thanked Roger for his honesty and promised more business in the future. Thank God! She felt weak with relief. Bless them! And to reply so promptly. She looked at the date of the first one. No, that could not be right!

Outside, the roar of the crowd still drowned all other sounds, all normal, everyday sounds. Inside was a thick, tangible web of silence. Yes, the mill owner in her mansion, the queen in her high tower – attacked simultaneously by the invader without and the enemy within. The one shamelessly manipulated by the other. She looked about her, suddenly stricken and very alone. Treason ran riot over the ramparts, its swords sharpened and pointing at her.

Chapter Thirty Six

So what do you do when you've just kissed someone who obviously did not want to be kissed by you? It had never happened to Sarah before. Or, at least, it had only happened the other way around. Plenty of slimeballs thinking they had the right to an intimacy they were never even in the running for. She had given them short shrift. "Stealing a kiss" it was called, wasn't it? Something covert, something clever. Like the sleight of hand she had used as a child to nick chocolate bars from Woolies. On the counter one minute, up your sleeve the next and you out the door and down the street. Except stealing a kiss was different. There was no quick getaway, no easy exit. There you were stuck face to face with them, with her.

They were sprawled together on the grass, Sam demonstrating an arm lock leading to a submission, only Sam had not submitted, not to the kiss anyway. Their faces had been only inches away and she had felt Sam's breath hot on her cheek, could smell it, sweet and inviting, as fragrant as ripe corn on a summer's day and she had been seized by a sudden desire, (No, come on! She had fantasised about it for two days now!), had been seized by a long-cherished desire to taste it too. And Sam had neither responded nor pushed her away, but merely said quietly, "That's not on the agenda." Seeking desperately in her mind for a face-saver, Sarah could think of none. And so she picked herself up and dusted herself down, both literally and metaphysically and said as lightly as she was able,

"It's just that I'd never kissed a woman before and I wanted to know what it felt like, that's all." Which both knew to be palpably untrue.

"Wine, Arthur?" Candlelight flickered deep in the heart of the string of amber round Sophie's neck.

"No, mother! He's too young," the other woman had snapped, exasperated.

"Nonsense! If he's old enough to fight, he's old enough

to drink," and the old woman had poured the clear, green-tinged liquid into the frosted, long-stemmed glasses and beamed at Jo in delight.

"There's no money, if that's what you're after," the other woman had hissed at her earlier. Hermione was Sophie's daughter and as fat as her mother was thin. Strange, Jo had never before thought of elderly women being daughters. Hermione was old and Sophie was, of course, even older. But had Sophie's skin been less wrinkled, (for her face was furrowed into a hundred crinkly lines), and her joints more supple, Jo would have taken mother for daughter. A daughter still young, rushing towards life with eager hands ready to clutch at any new adventure.

"What fun!" Sophie had cried on seeing the bungie jumpers throwing themsleves into empty air eighty feet above the promenade. And Hermione had looked askance, had put a hand momentarily on Sophie's shoulder, as if her mother were then and there about to strap herself into the harness and leap into the great blue yonder and, breaking the cord, dolphin-dive into the green-grey ocean below. You got the feeling with Sophie that she would if she could. If only to shock Hermione.

"Let's have some candyfloss," she had cried as they passed the stall.

"Oh mum, no! It gets stuck in your dentures," Hermione had protested.

"Good, maybe it'll keep the damn things in!"

And so they had proceeded, slowly, along the front, with Jo pushing the wheelchair, (at Sophie's insistence), with every new thing being exclaimed upon with an excitement Jo shared. For, (she would admit it now), she had been afraid to come alone to this place of old memories, to seek the ghosts of the dead in the land of the living. But to re-visit it with Sophie, that was different. She was a mate. They were like two chldren discovering a world together, giggling with barely-suppressed hilarity beneath the disapproving gaze of the adult. For poor Hermione was her mother's mother. From the joyless look of her you wondered if she had always been, even as a child.

Sophie would burst suddenly into song, in a thin, quavering soprano. "Remember this one, Arthur. Oh you do! Of course you do!" And she'd sing, there and then, as loud as possible. About remembering someone called Jeannie, with brown hair. Or about a boy called Danny. Comic it was. Old-fashioned. And Hermione would glance around, fearful, embarrassed. "Ssh, mum," she'd whisper, "people are looking at you."

"Ooh good. Put the hat out, Arthur, we'll get us some tea money!" Sophie would say and sing louder. And then she and Jo would break into peals of laughter, laughter made all the funnier by the look on Hermione's face.

They had had tea, scented, in little china cups, and triangles of rich, dark chocolate cake. And Sophie had fallen asleep. So suddenly it had taken Jo by surprise. With her eyes closed, that wicked, laughing look in them gone, her mouth slightly open and her head lolled to one side, she looked at once very old. And frail.

"Is she alright?" she had asked, afraid.

"Oh yes," Hermione sighed, "she just nods off. Just like that. In the middle of talking sometimes."

And that's when she had told Jo, in no uncertain terms, there was no money to be had, so it was not worth her while hanging round.

"I'm not a thief," Jo had protested, though colouring a little, for she had stolen food and money to buy it, that was true.

"I wouldn't take money from an old lady," which was also true. But Hermione's face had set hard. It was a face where nothing much moved, where the features seemed welded together, into a mask of generalised disapproval, of irritation, of … what was it? Disappointment, she supposed. Hermione was someone who had been forbidden, or been unable to get what she wanted and the lack of whatever that thing was had grooved itself into every nook and cranny of her face.

"I'm not saying you'll nick it from her purse," she said, though, Jo noticed, she did not let Sophie's shiny black leather handbag out of her sight.

"It's the will, isn't it?"

208

"Pardon?" Jo was completely baffled.

"That's what you're after. Getting her to change the will. Well, she hasn't got a bean. There's only our pensions and we're using her bit of savings on this holiday. It'll be her last. There's only the bungalow and you're not having that."

Hermione had faced her across the table, her eyes pinched tight with suspicion, her jaw jutting and a little dollop of white spit forming at the corner of her mouth.

"I don't want a bungalow," Jo was distressed. "What would I want a house for? I just like your mum. That's all."

"Why?" the other had demanded.

" 'Cos she's nice. She's fun to be with. She makes me laugh."

"She's gaga you mean. It might be fun for you. You don't have to live with it." And suddenly the features had relaxed a little, the antagonism gone. And in its place something new, something more frightening – vulnerability.

"It's like being with a child," she had gone on, almost ignoring Jo now. Just wanting to talk.

"She can't keep anything in her head for more than five minutes at a time. Let's go to Selfridges, she'll say to me, all excited. That's what I want to do today. Are you sure, mum, I'll ask her. Of course I'm sure, I know my own mind, don't I? she'll say. And so I'll get the car out and bring it round the front and she'll be sat there, in front of the telly. I'm ready to go, mum, I'll tell her. Go where? she'll say. I'm not going anywhere. I'm watching Neighbours. You go out if you want. And that's how it is. All the time. And the worst is the gas ..."

And so it had gone on, the words welling up, spilling over, pouring out, like a dam burst. All her pent up anger, frustration and grief.

"She never used to be like that. She was the manageress of a shop once. Had twenty people under her. You should have seen her then." Perhaps not, Jo had thought. She would probably have been a little afraid of Sophie then.

"Who's Arthur?" Jo asked as they wheeled the still-sleeping Sophie out into the sunshine. Hermione sighed heavily.

"Arthur! They were sweethearts in the war. The First World War. He got sent to France a few weeks before Armistice and was blown up by a land mine on their way home. Never saw any fighting. He was seventeen."

Jo said nothing. It was a long time ago.

"I'd seen photographs," Hermione continued, "but she'd never talked about him till these last few years. It was when she started forgetting what happened an hour ago that Arthur started coming back to her. 'He'll be home any day, Aggie,' (that was her sister), she'd say to me. 'We're going to get married just as soon as I'm sixteen.' She's been looking for him ever since. Then you came along. But there's no money, I tell you!" and Hermione's eyes had become a barricade of bristling steel tips again, in defence of her mother's savings, of their bungalow.

"I don't want any!" Jo had tried again to convince her, but it was no use. The suspicion, now there, lay like an ugly growth between them.

"I'll be moving on soon, anyway. Tomorrow I've got to go." Because she had no more money after that, but she wasn't going to tell Hermione that, to fan the uneasy flames.

For her part, Jo would be sorry to leave Sophie. But that was life, wasn't it? You moved through it, meeting, touching a moment and moving on. Like walking through the fields in the morning, the dew and tiny insects and the scents and pollen of wild grasses clinging to your clothes and your bare skin. So you collected bits of people, some part of them attaching itself to you as you went your way, so that you became not just yourself alone, but composed of a hundred little wisps of others' flesh and dreams. And they must take you with them too. The thought was new and strange to Jo. Parts of you existing on and about another, the memory of you on another's mind and skin.

"Mind you, I will say you're doing her good." The voice was grudging. "That's the first thing she's eaten in three days."

And now this meal. In a fish restaurant. Not the kind her grandparents had taken her to, where they'd had rock salmon and soggy chips and pickled cucumber, with plates of bread and marge and cups of hot sweeet tea. This one had waiters. It was a proper restaurant. They wore white shirts and little striped waistcoats and called her "sir"! And you drank wine, not tea. She felt shy and clumsy. Faced with a veritable arsenal of cutlery, afraid of snapping the slender stem of her glass, anxious lest she slop wine onto the dazzling snow field of this table cloth.

"A toast, Arthur. To your homecoming." Sophie lifted her glass and Jo, in wonderment, had done likewise. And the two beakers of pure light had collided, spilling a little of their contents onto the cloth. But Sophie had only laughed.

"A baptism," she'd said.

And as Jo drank, the whole room seemed to fill with light from different sources, each reflecting the other, back and forth from eye to glass to candle. And the body of Sophie herself semed to emanate light, as though the tiny bones and paper thin skin had lost all solidity, had become a transparency, offering no obstacle to the path of light. A waiter, passing by, observed to himself that the old lady and (must be) great-grandson were held all evening in a circle of dancing crystal, the brightness and fragility of which disturbed him. (But then, he wrote poetry in his spare time, so that could explain it.) Jo enjoyed that evening more than any other she could remember and even Hermione, when she ventured, as she did at times, into that magic circle, could not help but smile.

Chapter Thirty Seven

Sam stopped off at her office on the way to Lower Hannerley. As she unlocked the door she reflected that the pangs of unrequited love were hard enough to bear at any stage of life, let alone during that painful, confused scramble for identity that marked, well, her own early twenties, anyway. She had been a seething mass of contradictory yearnings and she guessed Sarah was pretty much the same, for all her brat pack exterior. Well, when they had got this business out the way, if the kid did think she might be a lesbian, Sam would offer support, introduce her to some friendly faces and steer her clear of rattlers.

There was a message from Jerry on her answerphone. Apologies he had forgotten her page number and he hoped she would get this alright. There was no news of the girl, even though he had the whole of Brighton on the look-out for her, but he would continue searching, don't worry. Oh and this may not be … what was the word? .. it was on the tip of his tongue … no, it had gone … of any importance, shall we say, but a mate of his, one Phil Sparks had been panhandling down by St Peters this morning when he'd witnessed an accident, a kid run over, or at least thrown down by a car. There had been a big kerfuffle and everyone saying the boy should go to hospital, at which point the driver says he's a big doctor at the Royal Sussex and he'll take the kid there himself. (Yes, come on, Jerry, old son. Get to the point, thought Sam, with amused impatience.) So, anyway, the point was, Phil had thought it was a girl at first. 'Cos he'd been watching her, him, and thinking she was like the girl everyone was looking for. Sort of tall, skinny, neglected-looking, like Sam had said. 'Course, it was so hard to tell nowadays, but once someone started calling the kid a boy, everyone did. Did Sam catch his drift? Yes, she did. It was easily done. Once someone had been identified as such and such, that's what they became in people's minds. And if their young runaway looked androgynous

212

enough to pass for a boy, then the whole red alert she had sent out via Jerry could be a total non-starter.

The tape was continuing. Another male voice, younger, awkward, with the pomposity of extreme discomfort.

"Hello? Miss Carter? This is Hugh Manders here. I ... I want to talk to you about something very important. I think you'll know what I mean when I tell you that I happened to be in the park this afternoon and I saw .... well, I saw it all."

Saw what all? What was there to see? Oh hell, yet another complication. The betrayed lover. Didn't he know that listeners never heard any good of themselves or whatever it was? As if she didn't have enough to be getting on with.

"I would like to talk to you at your earliest con .. as soon as possible," the voice was doing its best to assert itself.

"Please." Even in extremis Hugh was polite.

"So I'd be obliged if you could ring to make an appointment," there was an audible gasp as if of relief, of an ordeal over, a mission accomplished. Poor Hugh. But he had carried it off with as much dignity as he could muster. Then ... "And please don't tell Sarah." The phone went dead.

It was farcical. She could have laughed at the ludicrous position they were all in. But she didn't. The misery in his voice could not be ignored. No, jealousy was a gutful of broken glass and it gave no rest, no peace of mind or body. As well she knew. Hugh, then, would be another thing on her list to deal with. But first there were other priorities, and, anyway, he would be with Sarah right now.

She rang the hospital. No, no young person of that description had been brought to casualty. No, (the voice was icy), none of their doctors would have treated a patient without entering it in the records and having proper nursing support. They had procedures for patient care, didn't she know?

So, either Jerry's mate had got the story wrong, or the kid had been O.K. and the doctor had simply returned him (or her) to the parents, or he wasn't a doctor at all. In which case, there was a kid out there in danger. And if she was alone and on the run, she would be even more vulnerable. She put a call through to John Street police station. An accident this morning? They would want more details than that. The voice didn't sound like it wanted anything but for her to get off the line. She knew only that it had happened outside St Peters and that the description matched the one being circulated in connection with the Fenton case. The voice if not the tone promised follow-up action. She was probably the two hundredth caller that day to have news of the elusive Jo.

She flipped through the mail. Bills and circulars, circulars and bills. Amongst the drab bundle a lavender envelope, addressed in elegant black copperplate, written with a fountain pen. Did people still use them? She tore it open and unfolded the single sheet of, (surely not!), scented writing paper. The name and address were embossed in gold on the top left hand corner of the page – Vanessa Hunt. Inside was a newspaper cutting.

"I found this in my car, on the floor of the passenger seat. Richard must have dropped it yesterday. I thought I'd share it with you, detective. Happy hunting!"

Two smiling, besuited men in the middle of one of those staged handshakes that politicians call "photo opportunities." Across the body of one of the men was scrawled in red biro the word "Ungultig." She placed both letter and cutting carefully in her filofax. It would be a task for Sarah, tracing the source of the original article and the meaning of the single word, ungultig.

It was 6.30, time Gatwood was back home, time to give another turn of the screw. He was in the phone book. 8 Meadow Cottages, Lower Hannerley. The village was typical of many of its kind on that stretch of the Sussex downs. The centre had a handful of olde worlde, chocolate box cottages, a pub and a post office cum general stores. This one also sported a green and a duck pond, the rustic charm of which made up for the rash of new developments that fringed the centre. Meadow Cottages was one of these. A row of plain, square bungalows erected by a rural council that had sacrificed aestheticism to utilitarianism and achieved neither. They were only thirty or so years old, Sam guessed, but already looking shoddy and beaten-down by successive weather fronts that pitched inland over the North Sea.

A girl of about twelve or thirteen swung aimlessly to and fro on the gate of the pinched, angular front garden of number eight. She looked up eagerly as Sam parked her car opposite, but then appeared to lose interest almost immediately, on seeing that its occupant was not male. A few moments later, Gatwood came out of the house and said something angrily to the girl. She protested but he pulled her off the gate and hustled her back indoors, with a backward glance at Sam over his shoulder. He never lifted his hand to his daughter, Sarah had said. He had better not. Would certainly not dare to while he thought himself under police observation. Let him sweat it out in there. That was the whole idea. And when the heat got too much he would be driven to take action of some sort. Contact an accomplice? Make a bolt for it? Confess? This was all assuming he had something to confess, something more than a silly hoax to feel guilty about. From the sick way he looked this afternoon, there had to be something.

Sam flipped through her tapes, preparing to settle in for a good long time. There was a tap on her window. She grinned as she rolled it down.

"Good evening, constable," she said. The "constable" scowled, being now a non-uniformed DC in the CID.

"What are you doing here, I wonder?"

"Detective constable to you. And that's exactly my question to you?"

"Just taking the country air. No crime in that, is there?"

"You just *happen* to be parked outside the Gatwood place, do you?"

"Am I? Goodness me. Isn't that a coincidence?"

"Isn't it just?"

"I've often wondered about the role of coincidence in modern life."

"Yeah, well you can go and wonder some place else."

"Not treading on your toes, am I, detective constable?", she smiled up at him.

"You're illegally parked. I'll give you ten seconds."

"I didn't see any yellow lines."

"I'm just about to paint them."

He was still scowling when Sam drove off with a little wave. So they were interested enough in Gatwood to stake him out. The difference was they had not wanted him to know. How on earth they expected to secrete two hefty rozzers in a village this size, God only knows. News of the surveillance was probably up on the parish notice board within minutes of their arrival. If Gatwood had not known before, he would now. He would have been watching from a window and seen the conversation. She grinned to herself. She had blown their cover but it meant that now the police were saving her a lot of time and effort. With them kindly doing her job, she could give herself the night off.

There had been talk of women meeting for a drink at the Wishing Well. Maybe now was as good a time as any to break the ice. She would go home first, get showered, changed, tarted up. She wanted to look her best. Not to attract, nor yet to impress, simply as protection. Why protection, she asked herself? They're my buddies, women I've known years, and loved, some of them. What was she worried about? Well, a report back to Julia, for one thing. Julia, who now lived in the big city, with half a mortgage, half a cat and, (she had been told acidly), at last, a full-time lover. Thank you, Julia and goodnight. Yes, there was an ugly raw spot somewhere in the region of her solar plexus, which she had attempted to pickle in alcohol and which was still, after all this time, suppurating unhealthily. Well, she would deal with it some time. Tonight she needed plenty of front.

When she got to the pub at nine there were only two women there. She almost turned right around and walked out again. Viv was one of Julia's old cronies and there was no love lost between Sam and her. She was sitting at a table with a very young woman, the kind that Sam was beginning to feel maternal about. Christ, when you

216

stopped looking at a certain age of women as potential lovers and saw them as might-have-been daughters, it meant you were getting old! Viv, as old as Sam, obviously did not feel that way yet, because she was giving her companion the kind of look that wasn't in a mother's repertoire. The look was being returned a hundred-fold, and more. The kid had that kind of "go fuck yourself" face and aggressive, strutting posture that Sam had seen a lot in the clubs, an intense vulnerability zipped tightly into chain and black leather.

"Well, look who the wind's blown in!" She didn't need to add the "ill," it hung there in the air. Viv had the kind of smile that could turn milk sour as you were pouring it. Always had done. The young woman beside her twitched her lips in a clone sneer, like an understudy looking to get every detail of the part right. "Viv, what a nice surprise!" Sam smiled sweetly as she set her grapefruit juice down on the table.

"Juice! After all that homophobic shit we went through today, I needed something a whole lot stronger than juice!"

The inference being, thought Sam, that a lesbian worth her salt would be drinking herself under the table right now. To prove her point, Viv swallowed down her last quarter pint in one gulp. Her doppelganger did likewise.

"Get me another, will you?", Viv pushed forward her glass. Still no name. No introduction. The nameless one rose immediately, with an eagerness painful to witness, and took the glasses to the bar. Where was Nik, Sam wondered? She had always had time for Nik, at least when she was out of Viv's company.

There was a pause, neither offering to fill it. Viv stared at her with a slight smile. The kind that stayed on the lips, but never wandered up to the eyes. Sam stared back. Yeah, she could play that one too. Viv broke first, picking up her Rizlas and busying herself rolling.

"I saw Julia last week," the fingers moved back and forward over the cylinder of tobacco.

"Oh yeah?"

"She's doing really well."

217

"Good."

"Got a new job."

"Terrific," Sam would keep the smile on her face and the pleasure in her voice if it killed her. Viv flicked open her lighter, the flame catching a glint in her eye. It held the kind of look a lion gave an antelope just before it sprang.

"Yeah, she and Stel are just back from Greece. Spent three weeks on ..." she blew out smoke slowly, "... Naxos."

Where else? Sam could see the little harbour with its fishing boats, the taverna on the quayside where they had whiled away sunbaked evenings sipping retzina under a cloudless blue sky.

"Fantastic! Did they have a good time?" The great beast faltered in mid-stride, collected itself and prepared to lunge again.

"Brilliant! Absolutely brilliant. And you know what? They even managed to get that same room again." Their bedroom, hers and Julia's, the three summers they had been there.

"Now isn't that great?" Sam picked up her juice with one hand, while the nails of the other dug into her palm. Let Viv say one thing more about Julia and fucking Naxos and she'd get this in her face. But the big cat had struck and missed, the quarry slipped past. Viv snapped off her lighter and the flame went out. There was another silence.

She was suddenly sick to death of Viv and her games. She would keep the conversation general until other women arrived. And if they didn't pretty soon, she would go.

"It was a good turn-out today at least. Shows people care."

"Shilpa was noticeable by her absence."

"She may have been. Too crowded to tell."

Jesus, the woman had an uncanny knack of finding every raw nerve. And savaging it. But that last one had to be pure coincidence. She had not admitted this attraction to anyone, scarcely even to herself.

"No. No one saw her. That's Shilpa for you. All right-on

218

words and no action."

"In my book providing undercover AI for lesbians at the risk not only of losing her job, but facing criminal prosecution looks like pretty brave action to me." Damn! She had not meant to sound so vehement. Let Viv see one little chink … but no, it was alright, Viv was off on her favourite subject.

"It's typical of middle-class hets. When the chips are down, you just can't trust them."

Some years back, at a time when white, middle-class domination of the women's movement was being angrily resisted and the politics of exclusion rightly challenged, Viv was somebody who exploited the rifts, denouncing the Brownie-pointless with McCarthyite zeal, turning what should have been an open and (yes, of course), painful debate into a crazed witch hunt. Sam had known many a good woman cowed to submission by Viv's kind of tactics. The pain was still there. You could see it in women's eyes. Pushed back deep, but there still. The fear of speaking out. The tongues that should have spoken against Thatcher et al had already been ripped out. Silenced. Censored. Who needs a police state? We can manage very well ourselves, thank you.

Class was Viv's trump card. Her father having worked in a sweatshop factory up North. It was not till some years later that they discovered he was the owner. By then it was too late. The damage had been done. And, anyway, fiction is stronger than truth and Viv's working-class cred had, somehow, remained intact.

Viv II returned with the drinks and Sam wondered again about Nik. Had she been thrown over for a woman half her age? Or had she made a dash for freedom and succeeded?

"Where's Nik tonight?" Two can play tactless. But Viv, lager froth on her lips, was unruffled.

"Indoors. Feeling sick again." And you left her alone? Nice one Viv.

"Yeah, she's sick all the time now." Sam was shocked.

"What's wrong? Is it something serious?"

Vivs One and Two looked at each other in amusement.

"Yeah, you could say that," Viv chortled into her lager.

"She's pregnant," and she winked at the younger woman who gave a proud, proprietorial little smirk. What the hell was going on? Was she the father or something?

"Well, tell her congratulations from me. I'm really pleased for her."

"Yeah, so are we," once again that look of, almost, conspiracy between them. Sam was puzzled. The "we" seemed to include the sidekick, although the "we-dom" didn't extend to staying home and looking after a bilious partner.

She drank down her juice and was preparing to leave the two to whatever lousy game they were playing, when some more women arrived. Rose was a big-boned, amiable woman with a soft Dublin accent and a long plait of hair halfway down her back. She held her partner, Ruth, by the hand.

"Sam's here!"

"Great!" Ruth stretched out a hand that Sam took and squeezed affectionately.

"It's been too long, Sam." More women joined them. More old friends. In a larger gathering, Viv took something of a back seat and Sam could almost forget her. The talk turned inevitably to the Hunt.

"The thing is," said Ruth, who lectured in anthropology at the university, "it's not just an isolated lab. In the States they've started a massive programme of testing for Fragile X Syndrome."

"What's that?" Sam asked.

"An X chromosome with a bit missing. Its presence can cause learning difficulties, anything from a serious lowering of the mental age to just a few problems with reading and writing. What they're doing is picking out any kids not doing well at school and giving them the test."

"Isn't it best to know, though? If you've got it?"

"Why? What do you do when you know?"

"Well, you give them special help."

"But, if they're not doing well they should be getting it anyway. Once you've labelled a kid as imperfect, you've down-graded her. It'll be on her records. Her I.D. card.

220

When she goes for a job, when she wants insurance, when she wants kids."

She felt along the table for her drink.

"Is this mine? I certainly wouldn't be encouraged to have kids. They'd have imperfect genes, a 50% chance of being born blind." Rose stroked her lover's cheek tenderly.

"There's an awful lot of perfect people with imperfect genes," she said and Ruth smiled and took her hand. A moment of intimacy passed between them, travelling via fingers not eyes.

"It sounds like a kind of ... quality control," said a woman who worked in marketing.

"Everything's got to adhere to the British Standard. But they can't measure a human life by BS150!"

"They can try," said Ruth grimly.

Chapter Thirty Eight

"There's been another homicide, sir," Detective Sergeant Walsh had the none too pleasant task of getting his superior out of a bed complete with second wife, (fifteen years younger), croissant breakfast and Sunday papers. The response was predictable.

"Bloody hell! Why couldn't they wait till Monday morning?"

"Inconvenient, isn't it, sir?" But restrained sarcasm was lost on the chief.

"Bloody inconvenient! What happened?"

"Young white male found dead in a hotel bed early this morning," Walsh liked to summarise. Terseness was a great quality in a copper he always thought.

"In *an* hotel bed, Sergeant. Or, even more correct, in *his* hotel bed."

"Oh no, sir. It wasn't his bed, nor even his hotel."

"Alright, alright. What happened to him, anyway?"

"Strangled, then stabbed."

"In that order?"

"So forensic say, on preliminary examination."

"Wanted to make sure, did he?"

"Possibly. Or there could have been other motives. The knife was uh .. inserted into the back passage."

"Up the arse, Edward II-style, eh?" the chief whistled. Walsh, who was rather fond of the monarchy but whose grasp on royal history was tenuous, had believed that particular Edward to have abdicated over a minor matrimonial unpleasantness. He, wisely, did not comment.

"So what do you make of it, Walsh?"

"Well sir, it could be a nutter with an anal fetish. It's usually found in men with a complex about ..."

"Bugger your complexes, Walsh!" the chief snapped, unwittingly apposite. "Just find out who and why!"

Thank you, sir, and good morning! So, while the boss tucked into his second pot of coffee and the colour supplement he was to get on with it, was he? Typical. Walsh was feeling more than a little put upon at the moment.

He had been harassed all yesterday evening by a middle-aged harridan with hair the colour of beetle juice who had insisted on reporting an accident – had she been involved? (indignation) of course not! She and Arnold had never owned a car. And the accident was ..? At exactly 11.35 that very morning. Could she not have seen fit to report it before 9.30 at night? Well, that was the thing. She had been lulled into a false sense of confidence by this man who called himself a doctor and and by everyone else believing him. But, left alone, her own instincts had come to the fore. Doctor indeed! He didn't even have a sticker on his windscreen. Nor did he ever take out the tell-tale black bag. *And* he didn't speak English. Was American. Well! Say no more.

Had she taken the number down? She had, and produced a battered BT envelope. No, she hadn't written it down at the time. Who carried a pen with them? She had written it down as soon as she'd got home. Well, after her son had phoned from Australia.

Three phone calls and a lot of police time later, the owner of F 456 IMX had been tracked down to Hartlepool. Yes, he had an XR3 of that number, which was up on a ramp in the local garage. Had been for two days. The woman had the courtesy to blush. It clashed horribly with her hair. It might be her Vs, she explained. She needed a new prescription but now this government made you pay for eye tests ... Her belligerence returned and she glared at him accusingly, at this organ of a penny-pinching state.

A further set of phone calls established that F 456 IMV belonged to an invalid lady in Dorset. The car had been parked all day in her driveway. She was sure it had been there all day because it was blocked in! By a transit van with no tax disk. She had called the police several times. When was he going to come and remove it?

So that was that. Or would have been, had not another member of the public rung in to report the same accident, but this time suggesting the victim was not only a girl, but *the* girl, the one they had been looking for. He had been hoping the chief would allow them to ease up on that search and concentrate their attentions on Gatwood, but now there was a possible abduction case they'd have to instigate a whole new set of enquiries. It was everything coming at once, that was the problem. No time to sit and think it all out. So many ends. Was it fanciful to suggest there was some connection? The chief would scoff at the idea. But this new homicide. Two attacks, with an interlude in between. Same as the Fenton case. One attack involving strangulation. Again, the same. They would know soon, from the lab report, whether any sexual penetration had taken place. Whether there was any trace of semen with the small amount of blood found in the anus. If so, it fitted in well with his theory of necrophilia. There was a connection, he could feel it. Something ticking away in his unconscious was busy tying those elusive ends together. Which was not something he could let on to the chief.

"Give me one good, logical reason why," he would say. And, of course, Walsh could not. The unconscious was not governed by the laws of logic. Nor was murder. But you couldn't tell the chief that.

Chapter Thirty Nine

Tap tap tap. Sam had strangled Julia, placed her in a rough wooden coffin and was even now hammering nails into the lid. Tap tap tap. It had not been a gory death. No blood, no struggles even. Julia had been very co-operative, been perfectly willing to die quietly. And Sam had been equally as willing to oblige. A proper gentlewoman's agreement. Yet, there was some haste involved in getting the coffin into the earth as soon as possible. She knew that a deep hole had already been dug for the purpose but a thick writhing mist obscured it from view. Tap tap tap. She woke up. The morning sun was wriggling its way through slits either side of the curtains and processing in narrow bands across the floor. Tap tap tap. What the hell! She got out of bed and drew back the curtain. A furry black face with dolorous white whiskers and one ear stared back at her.

"Do you know what time it is?", she growled, opening the window. The cat observed a dignified silence as he followed her into the kitchen.

"Chicken and rabbit or rabbit and chicken? Or any combination of the above?" She took the tin out of the cupboard and applied an opener.

"I didn't buy any more because I thought you'd stood me up."

The cat winked bright yellow eyes, "Excuses excuses."

She was ladling pale slimey pink chunks of something that seemed to have only a nodding acquaintance with either a chicken or a rabbit and that many moons ago, when the doorbell rang.

"Friend of yours?" But the cat was attending to his breakfast.

"Hi, it's Vanessa," the voice drawled over the intercom. Vanessa!

Sam just had time to throw on jeans and tee shirt before Vanessa appeared at the door in an emerald green silk track suit.

"Just jogging past the door, huh?"

"Jogging!". Vanessa looked appalled. "God no! What on earth gave you that idea?"

She cast a critical eye around the kitchen. It came to rest on the sink. It would.

"I didn't get round to doing the dishes last night."

"Last week, you mean. Where's your dishwasher?"

"Well, I don't know where it could've got to. Seems to have done a runner, doesn't it?" Vanessa opened the fridge and shut it again quickly. Her eyes lingered on the top of the cooker.

"Look, is this just a routine hygiene inspection or do you have a more sinister reason for calling at quarter to eight on a Sunday morning?"

"I couldn't sleep."

"Sorry to hear it. I could."

"I brought breakfast," she tossed a large paper bag onto the table. The smell of fresh-baked croissants hit Sam's nose and stomach in quick succession.

"Any coffee?"

"Now that I do have."

"Hallelujah!" She even managed to unearth a pot of Tiptree jam she hadn't known she possessed.

They sat in the living room, over the last few pieces of unsullied crockery. The croissants were delicious.

"Where did you get these from? Harrods?" she joked.

"Of course." Sam stared. Vanessa was serious.

"I de-frosted them before I came. I didn't think you'd have a microwave somehow."

They ate in silence after that, looking down over the wide, elegant sweep of Montpelier Crescent, the gulls wheeling and shrieking overhead. It was a perfect, sun-filled Sunday morning. She had spent a number of them sitting here at the table, dawdling over breakfast. But it felt good to share it with someone for a change. From downstairs the smell of garlic and fried meat drifted upwards.

"Mrs Jablowski," Sam explained, through a melting mouthful.

"She makes real Polish sausage. From scratch."

"I like this flat," Vanessa said sudddenly.

226

"But cleaner, huh?"

"Who the hell cares? At least it's alive!"

"That could be true. I haven't had the courage to look lately."

But Vanessa was on her own inward journey.

"I mean the people here are alive. We live in a commuter village where all the real people have been pushed out. It's full of accountants."

"They're real enough. I've got the bills to prove it."

"But we might all just as well live in Clapham. Everyone came to find the real countryside, but it's not there any more. It's moved away. And left us, with our gin and canapes and nothing to say to each other."

Poor little rich girl, thought Sam. Vanessa pulled out a pack of cigarettes.

"Do you mind?" she said, but put them away when Sam grimaced.

"I've got some news for you."

"Richard?"

"Sort of. I mean, yes. Except I don't know how exactly. Last night Roger and I went to London for one of his business dinners."

"Bit difficult for him to get called back to the lab for half an hour if you're in London." The tone was light but Sam's face was serious.

"No, it wasn't like that. I wasn't called upon to do my duty for God and Queen Judith. This one had his wife there. Or at least, that's how we were introduced, but I could have sworn they hardly knew each other."

"Newly-married?"

"Maybe. But even so ... " Vanessa fell silent, staring out of the window, a frown across her brow.

"You know when you live with someone, even for a short time, you start to sort of ... slot into each other. And then there are the little signals that go on all the time between two people who are intimate. Do you know what I mean?" Sam did.

"Did they talk about their life together at all?"

"Oh yes. A lot. Too much. Their house in Dusseldorf and how she's just had it re-decorated, (he owns three research labs and an expanding new chemical company in Germany), and where they went for their holiday and what he likes to eat for dinner and all the time I kept thinking, "I'm listening to a script."

She was silent again. Sam waited. Was this the news? An interesting little enigma to puzzle over if you felt inclined, bit like a rubric cube, but hardly worth the ride over to Brighton on a Sunday morning.

"And Roger was trying to get money out this bloke?"

"Well no. That was the other odd thing. I mean, they went out and talked business on the terrace, but Helmut had obviously come with the intention of making Roger an offer."

"An offer?"

"For the lab?"

"Without Judith being there?"

"Well exactly. Roger said she was just leaving it all to him. Which she does. All the money side. She hates it. But as a major shareholder I couldn't understand why she'd leave a decision like that to Roger. Anyway, in the event, there was no offer."

"Why not?"

"Because Helmut was expecting to buy a company that was pretty much on the rocks, whereas the Hunt has never had it so good. In the last few days Roger's been inundated with work. All the bad publicity has been incredibly good for business."

Yes, of course. They might have known. Roger's search for the able-bodied, heterosexual, perfectly symmetrical, preferably male clone would endear him to many. They had succeeded in merely boosting his business. She had a desire to be with someone like Ellen or Ruth, someone who would share her own anger and frustration. Vanessa's cool detachment, amusing up till now, had become suddenly irksome.

"So, anyway, I'll come to my news."

"You mean that wasn't it?". What more could there be?

"No, just a snippet I thought might interest you." She automatically picked up her cigarettes and put them down again.

"Oh, go ahead," said Sam. "I can't have you do a cold turkey on me. I'll open a window."

Vanessa sat beside the open window, funneling the smoke out into the morning air. It blew straight back in again, but Sam soon forgot about it.

"This man .. Helmut Schneider is his name – is one of the men in that cutting I sent you."

"Which one?", Sam reached for her pocket book and drew out the cutting.

"That one, on the left." So, not the one with the word across his chest.

"You're sure?"

"Oh yes. I asked him about it. Said I'd seen his picture in the paper."

"Did he tell you who the other man was?"

"Yes. A man called Bill Hutchinson. He owns a lab like the Hunt in Cambridge. Or. at least, he did. It was in schtuck and Schneider took it over, lock, stock and bar- rel. That's what the photograph was about. New anglo- german merger and all that."

They both looked at the photograph, the hearty hand- shake, the smiles.

"I bet the poor sod had to force that one out. Apparently Schneider picked it up for a song."

Chapter Forty

Malcolm woke that morning with a sense of blank misery. Misery had a rhythm, it occurred to him, it was the rhythm of the sea. It washed over him, waves of it, drenching him to the core, then ebbed away, sucking his spirit from him, leaving him beached, stranded. He had spent the night on the shore, up by the Hove lagoon. He had wrapped himself in his car blanket, but still it had been cold, with a sharp wind rising just before dawn. The sun had thawed out his stiffened limbs and brought his body back to life. But this frozen block inside his chest had refused to melt.

He had been spurned. His labour of love refused as dismissively as if he had been proffering a cigarette. Somehow, afterwards, he had got back to Brighton. He could not remember the drive, half-crazed and ripped apart as he was, till there was no single cell of him that did not scream in agony.

He had sought release in sex. The sheer, hard, physical violence of it had brought a measure of relief. And then the disgust followed. As it always did. "Man is a rope stretched betwixt beast and superman." It was not only the lack of control, when body took over governance from mind. It was this corrupting of his flesh with another's that always appalled him afterwards. And the boy had been unworthy. A piece of trash, culled on the street. He had debased himself rightly enough. And all the time yearning for the other, for the one person he exalted and with whom he felt exalted. Together they could have, should have, attained the high peaks. "I teach you the superman." But now ... He shivered.

He had bought hot tea from a stand on the promenade. No food. His stomach revolted at the idea. There was no going home. Not yet. To put on an act in front of them, to try and camouflage this despair would be impossible. His father would see instantly that something was wrong. He needed to be alone. But that thought, too, was unbearable. He needed to be alone with someone.

Someone who would be there but ask nothing of him. With whom, or near whom, he could lick his wounds in peace, if not in total isolation. Who would offer him that kind of dispassionate friendship? It was then he thought of Bill. He wouldn't ask questions. Wouldn't be interested. Would give him the offer of one of those poky little rooms in his house and leave him to get on with it. Yes, that's exactly what he needed, Bill's brusque indifference. No cloying embrace. That had been the boy's mistake last night. He had noticed the sob that Malcolm had tried to disguise and pulled him close. But it was not those arms he wanted. A spasm of self-pity claimed him. The arms that should have enfolded him had kept him at arm's length. And then the boy's terror, that had done it. Anger kindled, leapt and consumed him. It was all her fault. All of this mess he was in. It was her dumb, pig-ignorant fear of him all along. Couldn't she see, hadn't she known? The worst thing you can do to a child, to anyone, is show you are afraid of him.

Chapter Forty One

After Vanessa had gone, Sam had put through a series of calls. The first was to Sarah. Hugh answered. There was an awkward pause. Damn love! Damn sex! Damn the unpredictable, disruptive human imperative to get oneself attracted to the wrong person at the wrong time and for all the wrong reasons! Damn Hugh and Sarah, and Sunita Shilpa for that matter! Having condemned much of the known world to hellfire, Sam said pleasantly, "Oh, hello Hugh. I got your message, thanks."

"Good." There was a pause that threatened to go on forever, then, "Look I …" they began simultaneously.

"Sorry," they continued, together.

"Actually," said Sam, "it was Sarah I was ringing to speak to. I don't suppose you want to talk with her there."

"Sarah's on a job. For the Herald. She got called before eight this morning." Join the club, thought Sam.

"There's been a murder."

"Who?" asked Sam sharply.

"Some bloke, some tourist. In a hotel room." Nothing to do with the Hunt then.

"Look, Hugh, about what you saw yesterday, (and you shouldn't have been snooping round, anyway. I'd be furious if I were Sarah … no, I'm not going to tell her). But it was nothing. Just a kiss, O.K.? It didn't mean anything."

"Oh, so you just go round kissing every woman you meet, do you?" "I …?" But Hugh's fury was pouring out now, a lorry-load of it, all dumped on her.

"Trifling with their feelings and then saying it means nothing?" "Look, it wasn't … !" Oh, what was the point? If Hugh, through some optical illusion or some distortion of the mental vision, had decided it was she who had initiated that kiss, then let him believe it. It was no skin off her nose.

"Look, Hugh, whatever it was that happened won't happen again. I'll see to that! Now, will you give Sarah a message for me? It's about the Gatwood stakeout …"

And she had proceeded to relay her instructions. He

was reluctant. It was dangerous, was it not? It shouldn't be. Not in the middle of a populated village, but yes, there was always the possibility. However, if Hugh were worried, he could have a role in this too. It would safeguard Sarah and be an extra pair of ears and eyes. By the time she put the phone down Hugh had become quite cheerful, like a brand new cadet, anxious to please.

Her second call was to Ellen. Not that it was urgent. Just that now she'd broken the ice, she didn't want to leave it to freeze over again. From the temperature of Ellen's voice it already had. To Sam's, "Hi Ellen, I wanted to take you up on that dinner offer," there came a frosty, "Well, I'm a bit busy in the next few days actually."

Sam was taken aback. The voice was tight and constrained, not like Ellen at all. Obviously Ellen thought so too, because she relented a little and the voice thawed.

"The thing is, Sam, it's the funeral on Monday, Cynthia's."

Oh Christ, of course! Somebody died, you had a funeral. Why had she forgotten about that? Not being in touch with the raw edge of it, with Jenny, she had lost all sense of the tragedy, had begun to see it only as a puzzle to be solved.

"What time is it going to be, Ellen? I'll come, of course."

Again the voice iced over, "I don't think that would be a good idea, Sam. Jenny's not very keen on seeing you. After what you did." And the ice melted again suddenly. Ellen could never stay distant for long. Not with those she loved.

"Sam, how could you do it? How could you take advantage when she was so vulnerable?"

"What!"

There was a pause.

"You didn't, did you." Sam said nothing.

"What happened? Did she want you? No, don't tell me. I think I understand. Poor Jenny."

"Look, I'll … I don't know … should I send flowers?"

"No flowers. Donations to Mencap. And I think she would appreciate a card, whatever she says now."

"Sure. Ellen, I'm doing my best to find the killer."

"Are you? I hope it wasn't that kid they're all looking for. Jenny's convinced it's the Hunt man. Well, we'd all like that, wouldn't we? I'll see you very soon, Sam. Love."

Sam put down the phone with a sigh. To be accused twice in the space of five minutes of being a slavering sexual predator was too much for any self-respecting dyke to bear.

Chapter Forty Two

Renee had heard it on the morning news. The police were asking for information about a young person, either a boy or a girl who looked like a boy, (description), who had been knocked down yesterday morning near St Peters by a dark blue Toyota, driven by a man, (description), with an American accent who had called himself a doctor. She had sat down, leaving the bacon to burn in the pan, staring at the radio. Her first thought, her only thought was that they must not find out. Lionel had to be protected at all costs. There were all sorts of charges they could throw at him, given half the chance. Failure to report an accident. False pretences. Even abduction, though the boy, (or girl, they said. No. Surely not!), had not been unwilling. And she herself had bandaged him, fed him, made him welcome, made him comfortable. But you couldn't trust the police. And if they got him on that lot it would be a one-way ticket back to the States. Away from her. And that would be it. Alone again. Only three years older. No, she had put too much into this one already.

She would let Joe stay another night. There was only him and the two old women. One was gaga and the other a mute drudge. The French family that came late had gone early and the young couple in their matching tracksuits had left (taking half a loaf of Mother's Pride and five little cartons of jam with them, as she knew they would). There was no one else. It was containable. She could contain it. Then tomorrow, early, she would ring his office. He was always there on Monday morning. And he would know what to do. She rescued the bacon too late. There were footsteps on the stairs. Joe, come for his breakfast? But no, it was one of the old ladies. The daughter. Her face was streaked with tears and she was trembling.

"Please, come quickly. It's my mother." And tears gushed suddenly from the eyes, ran down the crumpled, defenceless face.

"What's the matter?"

"I think she's dead."

Malcolm had been too pre-occupied to notice the car with the two men in it as he turned into Meadow Cottages. He wanted only to be safe in the cool seclusion of Bill's house. Its squat ugliness seemed paradise to him right now. He parked his car beside the gate and got out. The curtains of the living room were still drawn, which was strange at 9 o'clock in the morning. But, of course, it was a Sunday. *The* Sunday. Two big services. And he would miss them. But there was nothing he could do about it. He would have to find some excuse to offer his father. But not yet. Not until he had lain a long time in stillness, not until he could douse this agonising liquid fire in his chest.

He was lucky. He had got there just in time. A few more minutes and Bill and Sandra would have been leaving for church. The curtains drew apart an inch or two and Bill's head peeped through. Malcolm managed a half-smile of welcome, but it was not returned. Instead was alarm, writ loud and clear on Bill's face. A hand appeared now, waving. Neither greeting, nor beckoning, but warning. Insistently, urging him away. He paused at the gate, pretending hesitation, as if to check a house number. Discovering his mistake, he walked on, crossed the road, checked again on that side. Was he being watched right now? If so, by whom? From what vantage point? If only he knew. He must not panic, that was all. He opened the gate of a little blue bungalow with a last splash of summer's honeysuckle dying on its walls and rang the bell.

"Hello," he said to the old man in shirt sleeves and carpet slippers who opened the door.

"I'm looking for a ... Mrs Hunter."

"You're looking in the wrong place then, young man. You won't find her here."

"Any of these?" Malcolm indicated the row of houses.

"Nope. No Mrs Hunter that I knows of in the whole village," the man said with satisfaction.

"Oh dear. This is Upper Hannerley, isn't it?"

"Ah no. There's your mistake now. This is Lower Hannerley. Upper's another two mile up that there hill," he pointed.

"Thank you. Thank you very much. You've been very helpful, you've no idea," and he walked back to his car. It was then he saw the two men. Plainclothes, you couldn't mistake them. They appeared not to notice him and with a feeling of inordinate relief he pulled in the clutch and drove sedately out of the village. But they were watching Bill. At the phone box in the next village he stopped and put through a call.

Chapter Forty Three

Hugh was on his third lolly and it was equally as digusting as the last two. Not that he liked ices of any description, (too cold on the stomach. White wine was the only thing that should be chilled), but there had been nothing else to eat. He would have given anything for a quick visit to the Green Dragon for a spot of Ploughman's, but the orders had been clear — to stay in sight of Sarah and the Gatwood cottage come what may. So here he sat, beside the duck pond (three mangy mallards and a gangly goose) which was, luckily, in close proximity to his rescue station, an ice cream van, parked on the green. Marco had assured him the van would not budge till the steady stream of sight-seers to the Frankenstein Foetus Wood had trickled to a halt for the day and, at five o'clock in the afternoon, there was still no sign of that happening. The village green had been given over to a temporary car park (£1.00 a private vehicle, £2.50 a coach!) and Hugh was positive the price of his lollies had doubled over the span of the afternoon. Still, at least he had some sustenance, which is more than could be said for Sarah, who had not had a morsel since breakfast.

He had been tempted to make a rescue sortie, bent double, Marine-style, with provisions (well, a melting choc ice), but all that had been strictly forbidden. For Sarah's safety. He was only to break cover if she should be approached in a menacing manner by Bill Gatwood or anyone coming from that house.

He had to admit it was a good plan of Sam's. Hugh was to go straight to Lower Hannerley while Sarah would attend the morning service at St Saviours. She would there be able to look out for Richard and also keep an eye on Gatwood. After the service she was to approach Gatwood for an interview, intimating she understood he knew more about the Foetus affair than he was giving out, remarking by the by how strange it was that the murder had happened at the Hunt only a few days later. In full view of a whole congregation, there would be no danger to Sarah. She was then to follow him back to the village and sit tight outside his door, breaking the routine only to put her card through the letter box at hourly intervals. With the police and a determined news hound on his back, Gatwood was going to feel the pressure tighten another notch or two. Except that Hugh had seen no sign of the police. Unless they were, even now, keeping watch from an upstairs window of a house taken over expressly for that purpose. (Hugh had a deplorable taste in American cop movies.)

It had all presumably gone well from Sarah's end. Gatwood had arrived back at twelve, got out of the car and bundled a small figure in a school mac in through the front gate. The daughter, he supposed. And since then, five inexorably slow hours later, there had been no sign of movement from the Gatwood house. It was not the way he would have chosen to spend a Sunday afternoon, not by a long chalk. Still, he had been allowed into Sarah's new hobby, which was something. Not that she had wanted him in at first. Had seemed quite resentful for some reason. And his eventual inclusion had not been at his repeated requests, but at Sam's insistence. A fact which rankled deeply.

He had spent a lot of time that afternoon thinking about it all. That Sarah was somehow under the influence of this woman could not be ignored. Exactly how much and in what way he would have liked to ask, but was afraid. He would have felt a lot happier if Sarah had slapped the woman's face yesterday, instead of acquiescing to the kiss. Although it was possible that she was physically unable to, being pinioned to the ground. That was something he had not thought of. If only he could ask Sarah. But that was impossible. She must never know she had been spied on. Yes, perhaps that was the explanation. There had been an element of coercion then. He need not worry. But he did. For many reasons. The kiss. It had roused him to anger, to jealousy, to misery. It had roused him, full stop. And it was his own response to it, almost as much as Sarah's, that was at this moment causing him concern.

Lesbianism was something he had seen only in the porn mags he'd read at school. It had always held a fascination, that was true. But it had puzzled him. What was going on? As he'd heard one man say, they were missing the vital ingredient. And yet, seeing the kiss yesterday, the naturalness of it, he had felt … what did they call it now? … surplus to requirements. And he had wanted to shout, let me in, please. That attraction and repulsion, desire and jealousy could co-exist in one compound reaction was a notion unfamiliar to Hugh and did little to combat this sense of shifting ground beneath his feet that he had been experiencing all week. It was an uncharacteristically thoughtful Hugh that fed the bottom of a discarded Cornetto to the mallards that afternoon.

"Your ice lolly's dripping all over your trousers," the voice was young and female and the eyes raked longingly over the wreckage of his .. what did Marco call it? Fabbo? Whizzo?

"Oh damn!" He dabbed ineffectually at the trail of cerise stickiness down his thigh.

"Disgusting thing, anyway!" He tossed it into a bin and dipped his fingers in the pond.

"Mickey's my favourite. So's Zoom. And Zoid. And sometimes Ripple."

"You've got a lot of favourites."

"Yes," she replied sadly, "and no money to buy them." She bounced her feet rhythmically against the legs of the bench.

"Here," Hugh reached in his pocket and produced a pound coin, "have one on me." The girl's eyes lit up momentarily before the light was quenched.

"No. Can't. My dad says I mustn't take nothing from strangers."

"Jolly good advice. Still, if I happened to drop the money on the floor by mistake and you just happened to find it. It would be a matter of …"

"Finders keepers," she provided promptly.

"Exactly."

She returned a few minutes later with a Zoid or something equally foul and a large can of fizzy drink.

"I say, how did you manage to get all that? He charged me a pound just for a lolly."

"Tourist prices," she said airily. "You been up there yet?" she nodded towards a large coach party of pilgrims all attempting at that moment to clamber over the stile and onto the woodland path at once.

"No, not yet."

"I found it."

"Pardon?"

"I found the Frankenstein Foetus!"

"Gosh!" Well, on all the benches by all the duckponds in Lower Hannerley! It had been a pound well spent.

"Do you want my autograph?"

"Rather. Except I don't have a pen."

"It's all 'cos of me these people are coming here. Hundreds of them. Thousands probably."

"Probably. You should get discounts on your ices in that case." She had the grace to blush.

"Do you want the change back?" She put her hand half-heartedly into her pocket.

"No. Keep it."

"Tell you what, if you give me another pound I'll show you the exact spot and you can take a picture of me on it," her eyes gleamed with a new mercantile light.

"Uh no, I can't right now. I'm waiting for someone." The gleam disappeared and was replaced by a look of boredom. She looked around, presumably for a more promising punter. He had to get the conversation round to her father before she sloped off.

"What does your dad think about all this?" He indicated the bulging car park and ice cream van. She shrugged.

"He's fed up with it. Says he wished he'd never ... it'd never happened now. It's brought nothing but trouble."

"What sort of trouble?"

"Police been coming round persecuting us with their questions." That must be Gatwood's phrase, thought Hugh.

"Spying on us."

"Spying?"

"That's what my dad says. He says they were there all

241

night. And now there's a lady reporter wants an interview. Her over there. She's been sitting outside our door all day."

"Has she indeed? What a cheek!"

"My dad's going mad. I never seen him in such a state. He ain't slept for days now. I better go back. It's church in a minute. He'll hit the roof if he knows I been out," she got up. He must find out more, before she went. He struggled to order his thoughts. What was the most important thing? Richard.

"Hasn't your dad got any friends, anyone he can talk to about it?"

"He don't have no friends except the people at church."

"No one there who could help?"

"He's sort of mates with Malcolm I suppose. They go to the match sometimes." She was beginning to walk away.

"Who's Malcolm?"

"The vicar's son."

"At the church here?"

"No, at St Saviours of course." Like all children she assumed everyone was privy to the settings, plot and dramatis personae of her life.

"Oh, you mean that tall chap, sort of my age, with short blonde hair?" he called after her.

"Yeah, that's him," and she was gone.

Chapter Forty Four

Riverview Mansions was an exclusive, turn-of-the-century block of flats a few minutes walk from the Kings Road and, as the name suggested, within hailing distance of the Thames. Very nice, if you could afford it. And, presumably, this was just a London pied-à-terre. She ascended in an opulent Art Deco lift. Its door slid open with a self-satisfied sigh at the top floor. Flat E was the penthouse and the view from the hallway was stunning. To call it Riverview was just plain modest. From here you had the whole Thames valley spread out at your feet. On a clear day you could have seen Brighton, if the Sussex Downs hadn't got in the way.

The door was opened by a woman of around thirty, in tight leather trousers and a green silk top that yelled 'designer' at you. Her skin was lightly tanned and her hair must have been bleached each separate, silvery strand at a time. Her mouth was wide and confident and the eyes a rich emerald that sort of vibrated off the shirt. So this was the 'wife' who had puzzled Vanessa so much. It took Sam ten seconds to clock her. And from the look in the eyes of the other, about the same amount of time to do the process in reverse.

"Ja?"

"I've come to see Helmut."

"He's not in right now," the voice was husky, the accent Americanised. "Do you have an appointment?"

"No, I was just passing, so I thought I'd pop in and say 'hello', for old times sake."

"He's gone for a jog along the Embankment. You want to come in and wait?"

"If that's O.K."

"Be my guest," the ambivalence was intentional. She liked to tease, this one.

The living room was huge and south-facing, and almost empty. But the few bits of furniture it did contain were the sort they cordoned off in stately homes. A chaise longue and a couple of classy armchairs, an antique table and a Chinese-looking cabinet. There were a few Kashmir rugs scattered on the floor, just to break up that old monotony of parquet. The home contents here would be worth more than Sam's flat, twice over.

"Helmut isn't in London that much, so there's no point going to town on the decor," she explained.

"Hell, no," replied Sam, "just a few sticks of furniture, that's all you need."

"Please, sit down. My name's Irena, by the way."

"Sam."

"Would you like to … (the pause could have been a problem with the language, but Sam thought not) … drink something?"

"Sure. Got any Perrier?"

"We've got everything here," she opened the Chinese cabinet. It was stacked full of, as she said, everything. She brought ice from a little kitchen.

Irena's English was excellent, as befitted someone who had attended one of the best private girls schools in Germany. She had learnt "everything" in that boarding school, (this with a little smile). She was easy to talk to once you got used to the double entendres and other little ambiguities. They found they had a few things in common. Musik – Irena played drums in a women's band. Ja but she was not feministik. She was as good as any man so she had never had a problem with inequality. Sam refrained from pointing out that money might have helped there. And a private education. Then there were the Berlin night clubs, a liking for which they both shared. It was the politics that posed the problem. Ja, but since the Wall had come down the … what do you call it? … the character of the clubs had changed, downgraded. In a city under seige the gay clubs had been centres of an alternative culture, retaining some of the sexual extravagance of the old Kabarets. Now they were on the tourist route, full of Oestinger yobs. The East Germans? Pff, they wanted everything the West had but without paying for it. Yes, they were poor, but that could not be helped. There was only so much to go around. It had taken less than a generation, Sam thought to herself, to make a "them" out of people who were of the same race, religion, even in some cases, same family. What hope was there when different ethnicities were involved?

But Irena was good company and when Schneider arrived half an hour or so later, she had almost forgotten his existence. He stood at the door, a tall, wiry man of around fifty, with a neat greying moustache and pince nez spectacles.

"Sorry, Irena, I didn't know you had company," he said, smiling at Sam with easy charm. Irena looked at him in amazement.

"Ich verstehe nicht. Ich dachte sie vare eine Freundin von dir!"

"Von mir? Nein!"

Two pairs of suddenly hostile eyes swerved synchronistically towards Sam.

"You lied! You said you were a friend of his."

"No, I said I'd popped in to see him. You just assumed I was a friend."

"Get out of here at once," Schneider's voice was harsh, the charm gone now.

Look," she turned to him, "I must admit I did sort of gain entry under false pretences, but I've got no sinister purpose. I just have to talk to you."

"Certainly not. You force your way into my apartment by lying to my wife …," he moved towards Sam, threateningly.

"Yes, your wife and I had a very interesting chat about gay clubs we'd frequented in Berlin," Sam beamed at him. He gave a quick, furious glance at Irena.

"Warum hast du die Klappe nicht gehalten?"

She shrugged. "I thought she was a friend of yours," she said again.

"Look," said Sam, "Don't worry. I've no desire to bust up a happy closet. All I want to do is ask you a few questions. About this man." She held out to him the photograph of Richard.

He did not take it, but stood, staring at it for a moment, motionless, only a muscle in his jaw twitching from time to time. At last he passed a hand wearily across his brow and looked up at Sam.

"O.K. How much do you want?" he said.

Chapter Forty Five

"We met in a park," Helmut looked slightly embarrassed. "Frankly I just wanted sex. I had had one hell of a week at work and I needed to relax. So we went back to his place. It's in a workers' suburb so it was alright. I have to be very careful, you know. It should have ended there but it didn't. He sort of hung on. And he was pleasant company. Speaks fluent German, and has a knowledge of European culture and society, which most English people lack. And besides, at my age, there is a certain caché among your gay peers in having a handsome young thing on your arm, metaphorically. To the straight world, when we dined out, he was my favourite nephew.

But the problem was he became obsessed with me. Quite apart from the fact that I find that kind of attachment irksome, anyway, it brought out another side of him, a side I did not like. Underneath all the urbane chitchat and social grace, he has quite a tenuous hold on reality."

"You mean he's mad?"

"Let's say he inhabits a myth."

"So does most of America."

"Yes, but at least it's a collective myth, so they're all ignoring the same reality. With Richard it's the Nibelungen, you know?"

Sort of, but perhaps Helmut would refresh her memory.

"It's the old folk myth of Siegfried and the superheroes. Wagner used it as the basis of his Ring Cycle. He, in turn, was influenced by Nietsche, whose philosophical writings as everybody knows," (they do?) "rejected conventional morality and espoused the idea of a Superman who imposed his will on the weak-minded masses."

"Hitler?"

"You have it. The Nazis embraced both composer and philosopher."

"And Richard embraced..," she hesitated a fraction (Irena's habit was catching), "... all three?"

"As you say. His notion of Germany is one we left

247

behind fifty years ago, thank God. Though, of late," he looked discomforted, "a small proportion of my fellow countrymen have been flirting with those ideas again."

"So, what you're saying is, underneath, Richard is a nasty little thug?"

"No, he's far more complicated than that. You would be underestimating him."

"He doesn't seem too estimable to my mind."

"What I mean is it may be a dangerous thing to do. At the moment he's poised between the animal in him that he loathes and this desire for ... god-like perfection."

"Just being plain old human's not enough, huh?"

"Not for Richard."

There was a pause.

"Did he ever talk religion to you? Mention God, as opposed to gods, use any Bible-speak?"

"He likes high-flown language and purple prose. I remember a little phrase he'd repeat sometimes – "No man cometh unto the father except by me."

"What did he mean by it?"

"I've no idea."

"And you don't know anything about his life? His real life, not the Superhero stuff?"

"To Richard that was his real life."

"But didn't you want to know ... weren't you curious about his family, his friends, his ... job?"

"No. It didn't interest me."

Just who has lost touch with reality here, thought Sam. Everyone who came into contact with Richard seemed to suffer endemic curiosity deficiency.

"Do you mind if I ask? Did you break off the relationship?"

"No. And yes. I don't mind and I did break it off."

"May I ask why?"

"I found his views contemptible. And," he shrugged, "to be honest, he was beginning to bore me." (In reverse order probably.)

"And he was upset?"

"Devastated. He was totally besotted with me, you understand. Phoning me up all the time, at home."

"And you kept telling him to shove off?"

"Not always. Sometimes I would arrange to meet."

"Kind of you," Sam tried to keep the sarcasm out of her voice.

"As you say. But when he started interfering in my business affairs, that was it. This man, Bill Hutchinson, he owned a lab in Cambridge. I was negotiating a merger with him. Richard started making threatening phone calls to him, saying he was going to see he lost all his business. That sort of thing. Nothing mentioning me, of course, but that may have come later. Then he tried a spot of arson, but, luckily, only succeeded in setting light to an outbuilding. I didn't know this until after the merger, when Richard had the nerve to claim it was all his doing. That was it. I put an end to the relationship there and then."

"And the Hunt?"

"Again, yesterday he claimed the credit for bringing it into disrepute."

"Did he say how?"

"No, I said I didn't want to know. I told him that if he tried to imtimidate Roger I would never ever forgive him."

"Seeing as you'd already given him the push, did that carry much weight?"

"Oh, yes. Words like 'forgiveness' and 'redemption' have an intense effect on Richard."

"So he agreed to lay off Roger?"

"He said something like .. 'there was no need for persuasion where Roger was concerned'."

"Meaning?"

"I don't know. I was sick of him by then. I wanted him out of my hair. The Hunts were coming to dinner, as you know, and I hoped the whole deal would be settled by evening. Which it was. Though not to my satisfaction."

"Nor to Roger's, by all accounts."

"No. He did seem to be disappointed. But I couldn't make a big enough offer, not with the lab doing so well all of a sudden."

"I suppose Roger would have stayed on, with certain perks he doesn't enjoy now?" Schneider smiled.

"You can't possibly expect me to tell you that," he replied. "But it's a shame. Roger was so sure three or four weeks ago that the Hunt wouldn't survive all its bad press."

"Three or four weeks ago!"

"Yes. So, you see, it's ridiculous for Richard to suggest it was anything to do with him."

"But," said Sam slowly, "three of four weeks ago there was no Frankenstein Foetus, so how could Roger have known?" But she already knew the answer.

Chapter Forty Six

Bill Gatwood watched the car start up, turn onto the main street and disappear. This time there was no replacement, no changeover. The police had gone. Yes, they might be back. But, for now ... Even so, he waited half an hour then walked slowly into the village centre, as though taking an evening stroll. The tourists were gone at last. (How he cursed the Foetus now from the bottom of his heart!) The street was deserted as dusk fell. He walked the length of the village and turned back. No cars with men inside lurking in wait. He entered the phone booth. It was a machine that answered. He put the phone down. For several minutes he stood deep in thought, then he picked up the phone and dialled again. This time he waited for the message to finish, his throat already constricting in readiness. At the beep he swallowed nervously and began.

Sophie had been her friend. Like Cynthia. Sophie had made her laugh. Like Cynthia had done. And now, like Cynthia, she was dead. So Jo had fled. She was bad. That's why her mum had left. That's why they had put her in a home. It's what she deserved. And it kept people safe. From her.

She walked the length of the shore line. Past great concrete ramparts like castle walls, where sailing boats rocked and dozed in its great arms. Beneath chalky cliffs, glaring white in the sun, the town a memory behind her. When the path stopped she did not know what to do. If only it could have gone on forever and she could have followed. With its cessation there was need of decisions, which she could not make. She turned and retraced her steps, back to the place of houses, of people.

Towards late afternoon she came to a place cordoned off, the barriers stretched across road and pavement, a line of police inside, and outside, people hurrying this way and that. This was it. The decision. It had been made for her. She would give herself up. Confess. She pulled aside the metal barrier and slipped through.

"Excuse me," she said to a broad, uniformed back. It turned impatiently.

"Hey you! What do you think you're doing. Get back the other side!" And he pushed her roughly out and locked the barred, metal stand into place.

"Keep right away! You understand?"

And so she had gone on walking, the sea a constant companion by her side. She stood at last at the end of a jetty, the big waves lunging and splitting themselves against its stone sides, the spray a fine mist, stinging eyes and mouth. After almost three months and as many hundred miles, she had come at last to the edge of the world, to the point at which solid ground gave way to heaving, frothing turbulence. It would take only a small movement to pass from one to the other. She put her hands on the wet balustrade.

"Jo?" She turned, hearing her name without surprise. The man's face was puffy and waterlogged, like a river bank eroding. He held a bottle in one hand. The other he extended towards her in greeting.

"I'm Jerry. Want a drink?"

Chapter Forty Seven

From London, Sam drove straight to Sarah's flat, as arranged. She was just back from Evensong and was steadying her nerves with white wine.

"Join me?"

"No, just a juice."

"I somehow thought all private eyes would be lushes."

"I was." A pause.

"I'm sorry."

"That's O.K.," Sarah gave her a look that was a whole mix of a lot of things, touched her cheek very briefly and said, "I'll squeeze you some fresh oranges."

"And peel me a grape? No, I want to hear what happened. Just get out a carton and sit down."

Which Sarah did.

"Phew, I've totally O.D.d on religion. After two and a half hours of Beamish broadsides eternal damnation would be a welcome break." And Sarah related her day. She did it well, filling in the little details of person, place and ambience that made you feel you'd been there. Sam listened, entertained. She relaxed, stretching out on the sofa. Sarah's flat had none of the hi-tech minimalism Sam had imagined. It was comfortable. She felt entirely at home there. But that could have had something to do with the three day pile of dirty dishes in the sink.

So, Gatwood looking as though he were running a fever, but no sign of Richard. Another theory come crashing down. If Richard were in any way connected with St Saviours, he would have been there today at some time or other.

"And he couldn't have been disguised? In surplice and whatever? In the choir or something?"

"No, I gave them the once over. There wasn't a sign of him in the whole congregation. Do you think maybe Richard's nothing to do with the Hunt or the Fenton murder at all?"

"Oh, he's definitely got something to do with the Hunt. That's for sure."

And Sam recounted her own adventures that afternoon. She found herself getting quite heated about Schneider and his cosy little set-up. However much of a worm Richard was, (and she still had nothing to really link him with Cynthia's murder), there was no doubt he had been given a massive run around by Schneider. And if the man was teetering on the brink of sanity that was just the kind of behaviour to nudge him over.

Sarah listened to the account in silence.

"So what's slimeball Roger up to then? Is he double-crossing my mother?"

"Sounds like it."

"But he can't dispose of the Hunt without her say-so."

"I suppose he would have presented it as a fait accompli. They were in the shit and he'd found a way out. It seems as though she wanted nothing to do with the money side of it, so he could have done some creative accounting to make it look a lot worse than it was."

"Bastard! How fucking dare he do that to my mother?"

It was a peculiarly human foible, reflected Sam, that no matter how much you trashed a person you loved, as soon as someone else did the same thing it was unforgivable. The fact that Sarah could, by her actions this past week, have brought her mother to the point of penury and wrecked the research of years, did not detract one jot from her indignation at Roger for also attempting just that.

"But he was talking about bad press three or four weeks ago?"

"So Schneider says and there's no reason to doubt him there. And, apparently Richard said Roger ... what was it? ... needed no pursuasion."

"So he and Richard were in it together?"

"It's a definite possibility."

"Then where does Gatwood come in?"

"I don't know. Maybe he doesn't. We've got nothing to link him to Richard at the moment."

"And nothing to link Gatwood to anything but the Frankenstein Foetus. Except that he's shitting himself."

"Maybe he's defrauding the Inland Revenue. Maybe he's a dope dealer. I don't know. He could be feeling guilty about any number of things." There was a glum silence.

"But," said Sarah, "we know Richard did something to … the Hunt?"

"So he says."

"And that Roger's involved?"

"That's pretty certain, I'd say."

"Why?"

"He was counting on all the bad publicity."

"But how could he? How did he know . . ?" She stopped suddenly and went very pale. "You mean I played straight into his hands?"

" 'Fraid so."

"I'm going to go and see my mum," she stood up. It was the first time Sam had heard her say "mum" and she guessed it was one of the first times she'd used the word since childhood.

"Hey, wait a minute. Let's go easy here."

"But she's got to be warned. Roger might have more little plots up his sleeve."

"Exactly. But do you think she'll believe you? Your word against Roger's?" Sarah stared.

"Of course she will. I'm her daughter, aren't I?"

"Exactly."

"What are you saying?"

"You're the daughter who's been trying to ruin her."

"So now I'm trying to protect her! Alright?" Sam said nothing as Sarah stood and glared at her angrily. Then she slumped back down in her chair.

"She'll believe Roger, won't she? She'll believe that arsehole and not me." The thought had knocked the wind out of her.

"I just think Roger's capable of some very fancy footwork and unless you go to her with hard evidence you might find he comes out smelling of roses …"

"And me of old drains?"

The phone rang. She did not move. To the unasked question, she said, "It's on answerphone. I know who's calling."

The beep, then, "Sal please. Let me talk to you. I've got

to talk to you. I can't stand …" She leant over and turned down the volume knob.

"Pathetic isn't it? That's the fifth message so far."

"What's happened?"

"I told him it was over." A pause. Sam didn't want to ask. It was none of her business what was going on between them. Except that it had been made her business. She asked.

"I told him we were through. That I don't love him any more."

There was a pause which Sam knew she was expected to fill. She did not.

"Don't you want to know why?"

"No."

"Why not, detective?" The tone was bantering but the eyes held high level anxiety, "Thought you were curious about everything."

"This isn't my business."

"It is. You're the reason I've left Hugh."

Why had she supposed it would go away if she simply ignored it? Because it was her way of dealing. Or not. The way she had somehow imagined all the problems between her and Julia would disappear, so long as neither mentioned them. Out of sight, out of mind. She was so good at that. Yes, it was her way of dealing and it didn't work. Never had, really. Because, however hard she worked at keeping unwanted emotions neatly tucked away, other people couldn't or wouldn't oblige. So now, here she was again, as with Jenny, faced with some untidy feelings that demanded to be addressed. Did anyone know how to handle situations like this?

"Sarah, I really like you a lot. I really enjoy your company," The cadence, if not the sentence, hung unfinished in the air. Sarah picked it up unerringly.

"But?" her voice was light, but the chin quivered slightly.

But … I'm old enough to be your mother. Which was true. Or, I make it a rule never to mix business with pleasure. Which had been true until quite recently. Or, sorry, but I have a long-distance lover, which was a downright

256

lie. But all would have been serviceable, a facesaver for both of them.

"But I'm not attracted to you sexually, Sarah."

There was a silence as heavy as a slab of concrete between them, during which Sarah's face, although remaining outwardly immobile, registered some massive inner re-arrangement. She can bang shut emotional doors as skilfully as I can, thought Sam. The problem is they have a way of letting out whatever's in there. However hermetically sealed, there's always seepage. Some time or other. Sarah slipped into her jacket and swung the strap of her bag over her shoulder.

"Sarah, maybe not now, but some time, if you want to talk …"

"No thanks. No need." She took perfume from her bag and dabbed it on neck and wrists. She took out red lipstick and plied it deftly. Along with these she donned the professional woman.

"I've got work to do." She opened the door, now a smart, businesslike figure, quite remote from the proceedings of minutes ago.

"You can let yourself out, can't you?" She was gone.

Chapter Forty Eight

There was no moon. The tops of the elms brushed the clouds in a gathering wind, dark shapes against an even darker sky. Steepy Hill, the single-lane metalled road that ran from Lower to Upper Hannerly, was deserted. At this point, mid-way between the two villages, there were no dwellings, only pasture on one side and a stretch of woodland on the other. As the headlights of a car topped the hill, like twin searchlights in the night, a figure stepped out from beneath a hawthorn, a shadow amongst deeper shadows. The figure stood alert, the body tensed and strained towards the light on the horizon. The car breasted the summit and came fast down the hill, its lights doused now behind high hedges. It slowed at the sharp bend at the bottom and then, moving into the straight, instead of gathering speed, as would be expected, it slowed even further. The figure had now moved into the middle of the lane, the arms held up, as in a gesture of warning or welcome. The car, now slowed almost to a halt, gave a sudden lurch forward and accelerated, the throttle screaming. The figure stopped, frozen, like a rabbit immobilised, caught in the headlights now fast approaching, the arms still raised – in supplication this time.

A moment later flesh and metal met with an impact that sent the person flying upwards, somersaulting over the bonnet and landing with a jarring, bone-breaking thud onto the road. The car braked, came to a stop and began to manouevre back and forward in the narrow space, in a one hundred and eighty degree turn. Headlights again picked out the fallen figure, face and arms on the grass verge, body sprawled across the lane. The car gathered speed and swerved slightly to the right. There were two bumps in rapid succession as of traversing a rutted road and then it was moving on up the hill, back the way it had come, its tail lights extinguished as it crested the hill.

Darkness and stillness returned to lane and fields, their presence more tangible than before. From the trees came a rustling as stealthy as an errant breeze. The bushes by the roadside parted and a fox emerged. She halted, sniffed, nosed the dark, spreadeagled shape and began licking the wet liquid that was spreading in a puddle over the tarmac. After a while she continued her journey across the road and into the fields.

Chapter Forty Nine

Judith had lain awake all night, her body ramrod rigid beneath the bedclothes. Her mind had looped round and round that single word, "betrayal." She had trusted him, had given the reins of the Hunt, financially at least, into his hands. How he must have laughed behind her back! She had thought of the two of them as partners, for all she owned the lion's share. Had thought that, on the matter of the lab at least, they shared a common aim, a single vision. But he had tried to destroy the Hunt? Why? That's what she could not understand. Was it pure malice? Did he hate her? Enough to irreparably hurt himself too? They had never been close, that was true. And she had had, at times, to exercise her power of veto over some of Roger's wilder schemes, but surely he did not harbour resentment for that? It was, after all, her capital.

Betrayal. The word returned again and again, forming an unending circuit in her mind, like one of those awful neon tubes.

Her own daughter, bent on her destruction, on bringing the lab to the brink of disaster. Out of spite. Out of hatred. To be hated by one's own daughter. How had it happened? How had the rift between them widened to this unbridgeable chasm? Things like that happen without you noticing them, don't they? Looking back, you can't see the steps along the way. Only the before and after. But what was the before? Sarah had always been an impossible child. She had simply grown into an impossible adult. That was all. One that hated and betrayed her mother.

And so it had gone on. All night. And 4 am or thereabouts is not an auspicious time to mount a post-mortem on your life, when the body's pulse is at its feeblest and the mind a little adrift from its usual reference points. It is precisely for this reason that many people, somewhere en route between one heartbeat and the next, slip quietly from this world. But Judith was not one of these. Not yet. Though during that long night there were admittedly,

260

times she almost wished she were. And at dawn, as the sky lightened from mauve to green, she fell asleep and dreamed of addressing a prestigious and totally enraptured scientific conference on her research on Hewitts Disease, realising too late she had omitted to put on her clothes.

The following day was miserable in the extreme, dragging through hour after indecisive, angst-ridden hour. She must phone Roger, must tell him she knew everything, must insist he withdraw from the Hunt immediately. But he had built it up, through his fundraising, his deals. The reputation for "sexy" research they had got was all his doing. Even the name was his. Yes, but he had tried to sabotage it all. She looked again at the file she had found the day before, willing it to be a mistake. But there was no mistake. The dates on the letters were no mistake. She must confront him with it. But she felt so raw, so skinless. How could someone hate her that much? She wished she were not alone. Wished there were someone in whom she could confide, someone who would stand with her, stand beside her against the traitor. At a quarter to eight on Sunday evening the front door bell rang. She went to open it.

"Hello, mum."

Chapter Fifty

Sam got to the Easterner around eight thirty. She could see immediately something was wrong. The pub was half-full but someone had turned the volume down. Low. An almost silent movie. People looked up nervously as she came in, checked her out and then returned to their hushed conversations. A general unease and suspicion was writ large across the faces of the assembled company. Fats, serving drinks with the same mechanical swiftness and precision, had an expression as bland and automaton-like as his movements. Which meant he was very upset.

"A kid murdered," he explained.

"Who?"

"Young lad from London. Came down for the demo. He disappeared last night and his mate," (he indicated a tall, thin young man sitting huddled in an overcoat way too big for him), "thought maybe he'd just met someone, was having a good time, you know. He didn't worry too much till the kid didn't turn up this morning. Then he went looking for him. When he still hadn't found him by lunchtime he was at the end of his tether, so as a last resort he went up John Street." She knew what he meant. The police were always a last resort if you were gay.

"They took him straight down the morgue to identify the body. Poor sod. He's been sat like that ever since."

"Where was he found?"

"Hotel room. He went there alone apparently and rented a room, but he already had a room, at Joseph's." (One of the gay men's B & Bs along the Front). "The desk clerk saw him go up, alone. No one else around. Only the other guests."

"So they think it's one of them?"

"Got to be, hasn't it? Some queer-hating psycho. The body was mutilated."

Sam looked around her. So here was the reason for the muted voices, the constraint. It was a whole community not only grieving, but under threat.

"We're making a grapevine," Fats continued, "a sort of Neighbourhood Watch. Nobody goes off with a stranger without telling at least one other person. You see anyone suspicious around, you phone two people, who each phone another two and so on. Luckily we're small enough to be able to do it here. We mostly know each other. It's the visitors who are going be at risk."

"Fats, look, I'm still looking for that bloke."

"Oh yeah," but she could see his interest was elsewhere, on their own immediate problem.

"I haven't seen him for days."

"If you do ... It's really important."

"Yeah sure. I'll try and remember." She turned towards the door. Maybe he would remember, maybe not. A thought suddenly occurred to her.

"Fats?"

"Yeah?"

"The hotel? Which one was it?"

"Uh ... it's called the ... Graham?"

"The Gresham?"

"Yeah, that's the one."

Chapter Fifty One

The lobby of the Gresham was deserted. The guests, at least the ones allowed to leave, had all fled. What happened last night had not been included in their holiday brochures. Sun, sea and sadistic psychopaths – not quite a Thomas Cook speciality. There was a "no vacancies" sign on the desk. Neat. The hotel would be closed to visitors by order of the police, but this way it just looked like they were doing a booming trade. The man looked up from filling in a ledger.

"We're full, I'm afraid, Madam," he smiled ingratiatingly.

"Detective Carter," she flashed an old gym card at him briefly. The smile disappeared and was replaced by gloomy resignation.

"I thought you'd finished. All this has been very bad for business."

"Didn't do the kid any good either. There's just a couple of things I need to go over with you. Now, according to your statement," Sam flipped open her note book and consulted her shopping list, "you say the victim arrived alone. No one immediately before or afterwards?"

"That's what I told the officer," the man wore a persecuted air.

"Mm. You would have noticed, would you, if there had been anyone else hanging about?"

"Look around you. You can see the dimensions of the lobby. He'd have had to have been a mouse to get in here past me." He shuffled a pile of invoices as though they were a deck. Ex-casino, huh?

"Or else have come in the back way?"

The man dropped the bills. Some slipped beneath the counter and he spent a while picking them up.

"No back way in here," his head re-appeared eventually.

"Really? You must be the only hotel not to have a tradesmen's entrance."

"It's always locked."

"That's not what I've heard."

"Go see for yourself." That it would be locked now, Sam was sure.

"Key?" He gave it to her without a word.

The exit gave onto a narrow side street. The buildings opposite were all back entrances of restaurants and fast food joints. Directly across the street was a lighted window from which a delicious smell of curry was wafting. When had she last eaten? She returned the key.

"Witholding evidence is a criminal offence," she reminded him and wandered out into the night, leaving him with his depressed accounts.

The waiter beamed at her.

"Table for one, madam?" Full marks for not treating a single woman like a pariah. She'd have to come and eat here some time.

"No thanks, not this evening. I just want to see the manager."

A wary look came into the man's eyes. Was this a disgruntled take-away customer, objecting to a dish. They used nothing but the best ingredients.

"Is there anything wrong, madam?"

"No, nothing the manager can't sort out."

She was led reluctantly to the small bar at the end of the room. A woman emerged from the kitchen. Small, slim, resplendent in blue and gold sari. Sam's heart missed a beat. But, no, the woman was older, more worn.

"This lady ..." the waiter began unhappily.

"Detective Carter," she said. The wariness on the waiter's face gave way to out and out panic. He disappeared through the kitchen door. She followed him, just in time to see a young man in an apron tugging desperately at the bolts of the back door. Hampered irreparably by a pair of soapy pink rubber gloves, he succeeded only in gashing his elbow on the edge of the sink.

Sam crossed the room rapidly and laid a hand on his arm. He turned and faced her, terror tumbling from his eyes and a language she did not understand from his mouth.

"Please," she said to the waiter, "tell him I'm not

interested in his papers. I'm not concerned with his legal status. I just want to ask him some questions. About the hotel across the road." But the waiter was unable to hear anything but his own fear. The woman took control, asserting her authority, cutting through the panic and confusion.

"Your questions, please?"

"Was he here last night?" Yes, he had been.

"Did he see anyone enter or leave through that door opposite?"

The question translated, the boy nodded his head. A man went in and came out about an hour later.

"What time?" The boy shrugged. He had no watch. Time was all the same to him, the hours counted by dishes and more dishes. The woman pressed him. It had been after the big party of men came in, the ones who drank a lot and called for the hottest Vindaloo they had.

"Pub closing time?" suggested Sam. Yes, it had been around 11.30 the man had gone in. And come out? They had been about to close. He was washing the glasses. Nearly one.

"Can you describe the man?" Young, slim. Tall? Yes, so big. He held his hand 8 inches above his own head. Short hair, yes. Pale hair, pale skin. It was all she needed.

Sam thanked them. They had been very helpful. Officially, she had never seen the boy. The matter was closed. She went, leaving behind her evident relief, but feeling a bully. So many fragile worlds, forced to exist on the fringes of legality. And she had conned them. They had attributed to her a power she did not have. Had been at her mercy and she'd used it. How easy it must be, she thought, to abuse that power if you were given it. To see yourself as superhuman. Whereas, in reality, you had become less than human, half man, half beast.

Chapter Fifty Two

"Gatwood dead? I thought we had a cover on him."

"We had to take it off, sir. With the IRA alert at the Brighton Centre there just wasn't enough manpower to go round. I was going to put it back as soon as I could."

"Terrific! So in the meantime he's managed to get himself bumped off?"

"Run over."

"Accident?"

"If it was it's hit and run. No witnesses."

"Christ! That's bad luck!"

"For Gatwood?"

"For us! He's all we had to go on. Any ideas?"

"Could be an accomplice. Or, it could be revenge."

"Revenge?"

"Yes, sir. I was wondering about Jenny Fenton. If, like us, she suspected Gatwood of the murder, but couldn't prove anything ..."

"Possible. Barely. Is that all you've got?"

"It's one theory, sir."

"Terrific! Get another and we'll have two to rub together."

The chief could be very unfair sometimes, thought Walsh, who had not had a lie-in or time to read the Sunday papers.

"I found out that Fenton had an affair with Gatwood."

"Where does that get us?"

"Well, she'd know about any sexual ... peculiarity."

Walsh still favoured the impotence theory.

"It's all theory, Walsh. Have you got one, single hard fact?"

"No, sir."

"God help us!"

"Sir?" At this point a bright, up-and-coming young constable put his head around the door.

"What is it, French?"

"The vicar's here."

"Blimey, that was quick!"

267

"The one who was on telly. Beamish. He's at the desk."

"What does he want?"

"He's lost his son."

"Sounds like a joke about the New Testament."

"Says he went to London yesterday and never came home."

"How old?"

"Oh ... uh, in his fifties, I'd say."

"His son!"

"Oh? Twenty four, sir."

"Old enough to look after himself. We've got enough on our hands right now."

"Thing is, sir, he's brought in this photograph."

"File it in Missing Persons then, French."

"Yes, but sir, I recognise him. He called on Gatwood this morning. Or he would have done, but I think he got the tip off we were there. So he pretended he'd got the wrong house."

"Are you sure?"

"Yes, sir. He drove a VW Polo, registration number G 879 HNK."

With youngsters like that coming up all the time, Walsh thought sadly, his own inspectorship seemed to retreat more and more into the far distance.

Chapter Fifty Three

After leaving the Gresham, Sam sat in her car and toted up what she had so far. Not a lot. Not enough. Another day gone by and still she could not locate Richard. She knew a hell of a lot more about him now, that was true, knew his deepest, most secret yearnings. But not his address! If the murder at the Gresham was his work, then he had finally flipped over, out of reach of reason. The beast had taken over. And was on the loose. The question was, would he do it again tonight? Maybe, maybe not. She couldn't take the chance. Could not gamble another life. The only thing to do was to take the whole story to the police. At least they had the manpower to scour the town, the computers to check and cross-check. Not that that had produced Jo. Still, she could not sit on this one.

In which case it was only fair to tell Sarah. She'd been in this from the start. She got the answer machine before she remembered. Sarah was ignoring the messages. Damn! That meant a trip to Sarah's flat. She was scribbling the note when her pager started bleeping. It was Fats.

"Sam, he's here." Allelujah!

"I'm on my way. Fats, keep him there. I don't care what you do. Lock all the doors and throw away the key, give everyone drinks on the house – I'll pay! just don't let him out of your sight!"

"I've got that boy's mate to watch him. Gives him something to take his mind off things."

She scratched out what she'd written and began again.

"8.45 Gone to Easterner. Richard's there. Wish me luck. Sam."

She put it in an envelope and dropped it through the letterbox.

So this was it. This time she wouldn't, mustn't blow it. She turned the ignition. It whirred and died. Again. The same. "Oh for God's sake! After years of neglect, why choose a time like this?" She twisted the key furiously, but the engine was silent.

"Mr Connors isn't on tonight," the voice was crisp. "I'll send you someone else."

"No, just give me his home number, will you?" The voice bristled, "Our drivers aren't allowed to do private jobs."

"Look, this is John Street police station."

"Oh. I see. Wait a minute. I'll get it." Sam sighed. Did the public never think of asking for verification? Fortunately for her, they did not.

Mick was in the middle of supper and would be right there. Sam heard a woman's voice raised in protest, but this was no time for female solidarity. He arrived three and a half minutes later in a cloud of burning rubber.

"O.K. I'll pay you extra for your brake linings."

He laughed happily. "Where to?"

"The Easterner." They started at sixty.

"But I'm not paying the fines." He slowed down. Fractionally.

"O.K., this is the deal. It's a tail. The same guy. And he's dangerous, Mick. I think he's a killer." Mick nodded swiftly. She noticed, gratefully, he wasted no time on unnecessary comments.

"If he goes on wheels we keep with him, whether he clocks us or not. If he's walking I'll follow on foot. You drive well back. If you lose sight of me I'll drop a beer mat in the road."

"No need, I brought this." He handed her a small two-way radio set.

"My wife calls me on it when she wants picking up from Waitrose."

"Mick, where've you been all my life?"

The pub was busier and the general level of noise and energy had heightened. Bleak despondency had, with fellowship and alcohol, given way to anger. That's what was buzzing from table to table now. They were ready to fight.

Richard sat in a corner, alone. She was shocked by his appearance. His formally sleek hair was tousled and streaked with sand or dirt and at least a day's stubble covered his face. He sat staring into space, seemingly unaware of the hubbub around him. With a nod to Fats, she settled herself by the street door. "This time, sunshine," she thought, "whither thou goest I'll be right behind."

Chapter Fifty Four

As Hugh let himself into Sarah's apartment the familiarity of the place smote him, nearly felling him as he walked through the door. The smells. Her bath oils, the basil on the kitchen window, the waxy lemony scent of candles from Sarah's brief brush with aromatherapy. His senses recoiled in pain from them. Was all this lost to him for ever? Every inch of the place had a memory for him. The red stain on the carpet where they'd spilt nearly a whole bottle of Beaujolais. The rip in the back of the sofa where it had got caught on a nail in the door when they were moving her in. The framed portrait of Virginia Woolf – "You must read 'The Waves', Hugh, it's the best book that's ever been written!" He had never got beyond the first page. He would read the whole blessed thing twice over every day if only Sarah would come back to him.

It was so unfair! Their lives had been perfect till that woman came along, (he could not bring himself to say her name). Didn't she realise the devastation she was causing? Probably. And didn't care. He wished her into the bottomless pit of oblivion, into the deepest, hottest flames of hell, for all the hell she was putting him through now. That he had trusted her, had allowed himself to be gulled into believing her intentions honourable only this very morning! And all the time she was planning to take Sarah away from him!

It was not possible, not tolerable to think he had lost Sarah for ever. If he could just bide his time, allow her space to come to her senses – perhaps a whole day. And the woman would probably drop Sarah as soon as she'd had enough, anyway. And he would be there. Waiting. Solid. Unswerving. Strong. He, therefore, had to wipe all those awful whining messages off Sarah's machine before she heard them and threw up. There it was, the green light winking at him. Yes, it knew the depths to which he had crawled tonight. But Sarah, thank God, did not. He would erase them now and she would never know. Would think he had maintained a dignified aloof-ness. Might well worry even that he had not been in contact. Oh yes, that was more like it! The picture of Sarah sitting alone here by the phone, waiting for him to call was very appealing, made him feel rather emotional. But it instantly gave way to another picture, a jarring, disturbing one that involved another figure beside Sarah, and he hastily dismissed it from his mind and flicked on the machine.

Standing there glumly watching the tape rewind, he shoved his hands deep into his pockets. It was then he remembered the note he had found on the front door mat. Hugh was an honourable man and, besides, it had always seemed to him the height of squirminess to intrude on another's private business but, having broken one lifelong prohibition yesterday by crouching on hands and knees in dog shit spying on Sarah, it seemed but a short step from there to opening her mail. This was war, after all, and all was fair. Still he lingered, guilt nibbling at his frayed and war-torn edges. He opened it.

The brevity and formality of the note surprised him. He had expected to be hurt by endearments, those private little intimacies so treasured by two but so agonising to a third. The tape clicked to a stop. He pressed the Erase button. There, soon it would all be gone. All evidence of his weakness, his petulance. Gone forever. He watched the tape turning, eating up his words. She would never know.

A step on the stair caused his heart to lurch violently. he wanted to vomit, to run into a dark hiding place and stay there. To be caught thus! He thrust the telltale note into his pocket, flicked off the machine and waited. The footsteps passed the door and continued up the stairs. Sarah's neighbour. His knees trembled with the after-effects of terror. He had been lucky this time. But, per-haps, any minute … She could be parking her car outside right now. And then, there would be no return to a state of Grace, no eventual reunion. He crossed to the door, opened it cautiously and slipped out onto the dark stair-well. He would go home and wait for her to ring. She would, he knew it. But oh the minutes and hours ... and even days that stretched ahead of him! How he hated that woman! And had a good mind to tell her so.

Chapter Fifty Five

Richard left the pub at 10.15. She gave him 45 interminable seconds then she, too, walked out into the night. He was heading towards the sea. She nodded to Mick and began following, hearing his engine start up behind her. The wind had risen, the promised squall chasing fast across the Channel towards them. Good. A wind covered the sound of footsteps, engaged and kept your attention.

Richard turned left before reaching Marine Parade and began threading his way down side streets running parallel to the front. "Good move," thought Sam. A head wind out on that exposed coast road could slam you into a wall. He kept a steady pace, but the purposefulness of before was gone. At the small T junctions he would hesitate a moment, then go left or right, but always turning again a minute or so later to the east, keeping the sea always a few hundred yards to his right.

As they approached The Lanes, the rabbit warren of trendy tourist shops between North Street and the front, Sam looked back. There was no sign of Mick. The Lanes were mainly pedestrian thoroughfares, anyway. He would have had to make a detour. The streets were almost deserted now. Just a few figures scurrying home, bent forwards, leaning into the wind. The rain had taken hold and the north/south cross streets were wind tunnels, hurling you to one side, sluicing icy buckets of water into your face, down your neck.

A crackle inside her jacket made her jump. She had forgotten the radio.

"Where are you?" she had to almost shout to hear herself.

The wind howled in answer. She put her ear and the receiver under her jacket.

"What?"

Splutter gurgle "... Haägen-Dazs parlour ..." so he was in Meeting House Lane, immediately due south.

"We're just above you, heading towards East Street," she waited.

Wind, the whine of aerial reaching towards aerial and, eventually, "... I said, O.K.!"

Rain ran in rills into her eyes. For a moment she was blinded. When her vision cleared, Richard was gone. It had been so quick. And there were no streets ahead to left or right. Not even an alleyway. He had gone into a house, perhaps. But these were all shop fronts, hardly any private residences in this part of town. Was he sheltering in a doorway, the rain at last too much for him? She stood, caught in indecision. To wait too long, she could lose him for good. To go ... He suddenly reappeared, the red tip of a cigarette between his lips. How did he expect to keep it alight on a night like this?

He came out onto East Street, Al Fornos and the cab rank on his left. Was he planning to take a taxi after all? If so, she'd better warn Mick. But no, he crossed the road into Pool Valley, into the big square of the bus station. She passed only yards from Mick. He jerked his head towards the front. She nodded. Yes, he'd turn left onto the coast road, eastward.

There was a queue at the cab rank, she noticed. People in mud-spattered evening dress, clutching like grim death onto skybound umbrellas. Just out from a concert at The Dome.

"I thought Brunhilde a trifle homespun," a loud fruity voice called.

"Oh quite," replied a woman in a fur stole.

Richard had left the shelter of Pool Valley behind him and crossed the coast road. He stood now by the sea wall. To his left a hundred yards of winking bulbs welcomed all comers to Palace Pier. There wouldn't be many takers on a night like this. He turned to the flight of steps beside the pier and disappeared. So he was going down to the promenade. She crossed the road, a physical feat, the rain whiplashing across mouth, eyes and ears. She saw Mick drive to the roundabout at the mouth of the pier and turn into the slip road that ran the length of the beach. Good move. If Richard kept going east, that's just where they'd be headed.

The promenade was slippery with wet pebbles, hurled

up the beach by the sea. It flung itself against the steel girders of the pier, rearing and crashing against the slender supports, foaming at the mouth in its fury. The clamour of it drowned the noise of traffic above and would make radio communication impossible.

She looked around for Richard. He had to have gone left, under the pier. The promenade to the right was cut off by a stone jetty thrusting into the sea. Ahead were the boiling waves. He couldn't have gone that way. Unless he was planning on not coming back.

She turned under the pier. It was dark and cavernous, smelling of piss and seaweed. To her left the black walls slimey and running with some liquid excrescence (the sewage outlet was around here somewhere) and to her right the vaulting iron props, and the sea. Nothing else, but darkness. She could have done with more light.

Suddenly there were plenty of lights. A million of them exploding in her head. Something slammed hard into the side of her jaw. A fraction higher and the lights would have gone out completely. She fetched up on the ground, her back against a pile of girders, her hand scraping on barnacles, a smell of rust and old urine in her nostrils. He was standing straddling her, all three of him. Superhuman, human and sub-human blurred and resolved into one, only to split a moment later, then merge again.

"So you're the nosey bitch who's been snooping around!"

"Glad to hear my reputation goes before me."

A foot crashed into her ribs and she heard the crack of something delicate breaking. The radio. If the radio goes dead I'll come after you, he had said. No heroics, she'd ordered. The police then? No. I could be in the middle of something important. Give me half an hour at least. In half an hour, she could be ... So long, Mick. Nice to have known you.

"Bill told me about you." Bill. At last, the link. Sarah would be pleased.

"He said you'd threatened him."

"Now isn't that just like old Bill, always exaggerating."

A foot smashed into her belly, bringing bile to her mouth. Enough of the social chitchat. It was time for business.

"Put my mind at rest, Richard. Tell me what happened at the Hunt that night. Were you and Bill going to torch it?"

"Not badly. Just a warning."

"But Cynthia got in the way?."

"She popped up out of nowhere. What you doing with petrol cans? she said. Making a bonfire? I'll go and get Maurice. He likes bonfires. Bill grabbed her and told her to keep quiet but she wouldn't stop struggling. He must have got her carotid because she passed out. Bill thought he'd killed her. He started crying. So I sent him home." He took someting out of his pocket and began fidgeting with it. There was a dull sheen of metal.

"And then you finished her off?"

"After … consulting a higher authority." Siegfried, presumably.

"They'll catch up with you, you know. Bill's about to spill any minute."

"He already has. All over the road."

He lunged then, the knife slashing downwards. She rolled to the right, her feet at the same time opening and closing round his ankles like scissors. Like steel pincers. He fell crashing to the ground beside her. She was on him then, pinning his arms, forcing his shoulders down, getting her weight across his body. Yesterday, in this position, Sarah had reached up her head and kissed her. Most times the umpire counted three and called 'submission'. This guy wasn't into kissing right now and their was no third person around. Not down here. Not in earshot, nor eyeshot, nor any other shot. She was alone. Alone. How you always wanted it, baby. Remember? Enjoy!

He swung his hips violently to one side and she toppled over. They rolled back and forward over the pebble-strewn concrete, the blade always inches from her face, the stones digging sharply into any bit of spare flesh. Unfortunately she had too much of it. She was as big, as tall as him. But he was that bit heavier. Muscle weighed more than fat. And he was younger. Fitter. She would run out of wind soon. She had to get to her feet.

She got her knee up, connected it with groin, not hard, but enough to weaken his hold for a second. Enough to let her get to her feet. But he was up too, like a cat. Still had hold of her with his left hand. The other, the knife hand, she prised back, out, away from her face. She sank her right knee and heaved hard with her shoulder. He fell forward over her, crashing to the ground. She heard the air hiss out of him like a punctured tyre. Still he would not let go. Still he held her, as though the two of them were fused together. She braced herself and wrenched upwards with all her strength, but her feet slid forwards on the slippery stones and she toppled down, the back of her head lamming against the wall. In a second he was on her.

Fuck you, bitch!" He was panting heavily and there was blood in his mouth. Whose, she wondered, his or mine? His arm rose, the blade flashed and was gone. With a howl of pain, he pitched sideways.

Suddenly there were lights, wheeling, gyrating across the roof and walls. Real lights, not in her head this time. She heard whistles, sirens, voices calling and feet pounding past her head. A figure knelt beside her, taking her hand, fumbling, prodding anxious fingers into her wrist.

"The pulse is thumb side," she heard herself mumble, as if in a dream.

"Is it? Thank God, I thought you were dead! It took me ages to find the right pebble."

"Right pebble?" It was a dream.

"It had to be absolutely round and about eight inches in diameter. The size of a cricket ball."

"Why's that?" Her voice came from miles away.

"Otherwise I couldn't have been sure of hitting him and not you. But I found it in the end."

"Glad about that, Hugh," she said and fainted clean away.

Chapter Fifty Six

They were after him. The animals. A whole pack of them, baying at his back. At the top of the steps he looked about him. Flashing blue lights lined the road, a semi-circle of them, barring traffic from the west. More were arriving from Peacehaven, their sirens screaming. Below him, voices on the steps. He turned immediately right and ran onto the pier. Deserted. The gale hit him full in the face. At the sound of feet on the wooden boards behind him he propelled himself forwards, into the wind.

Past the rows of iron-shuttered stalls – "engrave your name," "tell your fortune," "pierce your ears" – past sideshows and fruit machines and donut stands, all empty, flushed out. The whole teeming place washed and scoured and rinsed clean by the rain.

The wind caught and tore to shreds the yelping and yowling behind him, so that their voices lost all force and authority. He laughed as he ran. They were nothing but animals. He was worth ten, twenty, a hundred of them. His muscles felt hard and supple, there was nothing they could not do. He was invincible.

He was nearing the end of the pier, that cluster of low fret-worked turrets that were Ghost Train, Hoopla stalls, and Try Your Strength. They were at his heels now, more and more of them. He could feel the vibrations of their feet pounding the wooden planks. He must be up, above them. Far above them. He swung himself onto the balustrade. It was slippery with salt water. Salt, too, in his mouth, his eyes, his nose. He tasted it, smelt it, his whole body was sticky with fine salt spray atomised by the fission, the colossal, pulverising power of water on steel below.

But from here a short leap to the rooftop, groping for handholds, clinging to guttering, hauling himself up onto the topmost point. Yes, now he could see the bowl of Brighton behind him. Its smallness amazed him. All those lighted, dolls-house windows. Little houses full of little people, of pinched domesticity, of lives led in miniature.

Eyes that never lifted above the dense smog of their own polluted breath. He had no part of their world. "I lift up my eyes unto the Lord, from whence cometh my help."

He turned, alerted by some instinct, some divine prompting. A head had appeared above the roof behind him. And another, and another. They were swarming up the drenched and slimey walls after him. He kicked hard at the face of one and it disappeared. Another lifted his arm too late in protection and he dropped backwards. But more took their place. Till the roof was covered in them, black-coated crawling shapes. He turned and ran along the spine of the roof, his feet slithering, his body twisted this way and that by the wind. Ahead, above, the winds of heaven came to snatch him away, to catch him up in their arms. He reached out towards them. "Man is a rope stretched betwixt beast and Superman." And leapt.

Chapter Fifty Seven

"Did Richard approach you or was it the other way round?"

They were facing him across the desk, she, Judith and Sarah. He resembled a cowed terrier, back against the wall. She half-expected him to start whimpering any minute. If he did she would throw up.

"He rang me. About a month, six weeks ago. Said he was going to bring the lab to its knees, or something dramatic like that. I said, go ahead. It would suit me. I'd decided the best way of dealing with a threat like that, you see, was to make light of it, to be flippant, take the wind out of his sails. He rang off. It was then I got to thinking. We'd just had a row, Judith and I. Remember? About the Hawser idea?" He looked towards her, appealing, dog-like. She made no response. She and Sarah sat side by side, presenting a blank wall of contempt. They were very alike, mother and daughter, Sam observed. There was a single-minded quality about them, a tough stubbornness, overlaying a deal of vulnerability. But that last was not in evidence right now.

"But he phoned you again?" Sam prompted.

"Yes," he licked dry lips nervously, unused to this battery of female ferocity.

"He said, did I mean what I said? That I would welcome the Hunt going under? Because if so, we could do a deal, he and I."

"And you agreed?" This was Sarah, in disbelief.

"I said I'd think about it. We were broke, you see. The money just wasn't coming in. If only we could have taken on more of the big-paying stuff, if you hadn't been so pre-occupied with the Hewitts research. It would have been different."

Judith did not rise to the gambit, merely studying him as if he was a laboratory animal, a creature in whom she had no personal interest. But, under all that, thought Sam, she must be mad as hell.

"So then he came up with this monster foetus idea. I

laughed at him at first, but he said it would catch the public imagination, that it just needed one newspaper, one journalist to fall for it. Well, then, of course, I thought immediately of … knowing how much she hated Judith." Mother and daughter wriggled uncomfortably. In their new-found solidarity they did not want to be reminded of the mess of years that lay between them. Especially by an insect like Roger.

"And the torching was Richard's idea, presumably?" From what Helmut said, he liked playing around with fire.

"Yes. I was worried about that," he looked around at Judith to emphasise the point. Big deal, a belated sense of responsibility.

"If the whole building went up there'd be nothing for Schneider to be interested in. And, besides, there was old Maurice." Just as an afterthought. "He lives on the premises. I didn't want him hurt. I said it had to be a small, contained blaze, right away from the labs, and the Fire Brigade had to be alerted within minutes."

"So when did Richard tell you about Cynthia?"

He was sweating hard now, great damp patches of it seeping onto the underarms of his shirt.

"Look, there was nothing I could do. It was out of my hands. When he rang I told him, I said it had been a stupid idea, apart from the danger of the flames, there had always been the risk of someone finding them there. I said it was his responsibilty. He had to do whatever he thought best. It wasn't my business."

Sam's head began to reel. She hadn't got this straight. Or had she?

"Wait a minute. You're saying he rang you *before* he killed Cynthia?"

"Yes. Didn't Richard tell you that?" From the look of stunned horror on the faces around him, he realised, too late, that Richard had not. His face, already a dull, pasty white, took on the colour and clamminess of putty.

"He rang you to ask what to do and you told him to get on with it."

"No! I just said I didn't want to get involved, that's all."

283

He looked around him desperately, twisting his hands, wringing them together. Pontius Pilate.

"Look, it's terrible what happened to the girl, but what could I have done? Whatever I'd have said … I mean we know the man was criminally insane."

"You should have thought of that before letting him loose."

"And, anyway, the girl was retarded. With those cases, they're very often better off dead."

Sam's fists clenched tight and she dug them hard into her knees. Either that or smash them into Hunt's face. Bust that putrid mouth right open, like a rotten melon. No, better let the police deal with him. As though reading her thoughts, he said,

"They can't pin anything on me, you know. It was Richard who did it."

There was a silence. The kind in which you contemplate maggots in a dustbin. Roger got up.

"Well, I suppose we should let our lawyers deal with the business side," he said. "I'm going to be off to Germany. Schneider's offered me a job." He looked around at them. "I'm not to blame, you know," he repeated and left the room.

"Is that true?", Judith turned to Sam. "That the law can't get him for it?"

"They'll sure as hell try. But no, they may not succeed."

"Then I'll get him. I'll make his name horse shit from here to kingdom come."

Chapter Fifty Eight

The great thing about having a swathe of bandage round your head is that it guarantees you a lot of attention. And sympathy. So when Sam walked into the Glenning on Tuesday she found Sunita all gentleness and caring itself. Those long, slender hands darted everywhere in concern, except the place Sam would have most liked them to come to rest, cool on her cheek. Or on her arm would do. At a pinch.

But Sunita was not one for easy intimacies, that was obvious.

"So Roger's gone has he?"

"Yes, though the Hunt lives to fight another day. Worse luck!"

A pause.

"I thought I might have seen you at the march on Saturday," she said.

"Meaning," replied Sunita, "why the hell wasn't I there?"

"You see right through me."

Sunita's smile lit up the office.

"I had an emergency meeting with our trustees that afternoon, otherwise I would have been there."

Sam felt relieved. It had been bothering her.

"But," Sunita went on, "I'm not entirely against genetic engineering. There are gains to be got from it too, you know."

"Perfect specimens, you mean?"

"A better chance for some people, let's say. You can't just turn your back on new scientific knowledge, pretend it's not there. You just have to make sure it's used in as responsible a way as possible."

"If you feel like this why would you have gone on the demo?"

"To make people aware of the issue, open up a public forum for debate. The problem with this bloody country is that no one wants to talk about anything any more. They think if they shut their eyes and ears it'll all just go away. It won't. It'll just happen without their permission."

A pause. Sam, aware of a sore area way down in her chest and unable to do anything about it, was staring resolutely out of the window.

"I've disappointed you, haven't I?" Sam turned her head with an effort, willing herself to look at Sunita.

"I guess this feels so important that, yeah, I wanted you to feel the same way about it, because … because you're important." There, she had said it. She kept her eyes on the other woman's face. And Sunita didn't flinch or throw up her hands in horror or say anything devastatingly polite but evasive. Instead, she gazed back at Sam thoughtfully for what seemed like a century. The silence went on for such a long time that Sam felt she had to break it, to offer them both a way out.

"Look, it's O.K. It's just something I happen to feel right now. I get like this sometimes. Don't worry about it."

"I'm not. I'm thinking about it."

"Are you?"

"Of course. You did mean me to take it seriously, didn't you?"

Didn't she just! Silence again. Sunita was obviously giving the matter a lot of thought. Or maybe just thinking up ways to put it kindly, that she just wasn't interested.

"Look, I appreciate that it's sort of out of the blue …"

"No, not really."

This woman accepted no easy options, no comfortable solutions. She could simply have accepted Sam's offer of a get-out, have done a 'Yes, this is so sudden, I'll have to get over the shock,' number and left it at that. As something they never mentioned again. If and when they ever saw each other. Sunita had an intellectual honesty, she guessed, that made it hard on herself, as well as on those around her. A relationship of any kind with this woman would be a challenge.

"I felt it right from the start."

"That I was interested?"

"That there was an attraction." Another pause. What was she saying? Simply rephrasing what Sam had said or …?

"I'd like to be friends with you, Sam." So that was it.

"Would you? Great."

Sunita burst out laughing.

"What?"

"You tried so womanfully not to show your disappointment."

"Yeah, well ..."

"Come om, Sam. Did you expect us to be passionate lovers before we're even friends?"

"That's the way I've always done it."

"Has it worked?"

"Not really."

They looked at each other and smiled. A warm comfortable smile. "And it may stay at that. At friendship. I make no promises I can't keep."

"Well, whatever, it'll be fun getting to know you."

"Want to start tonight? Over dinner?"

Before she left, Sam gave the building a once-over security check as she had promised. It was pretty tight. Sunita had seen to that after the burglary. Alarm, window locks, mortices, heat sensitive outdoor lights. But it was the small rooms, little basement windows, grills and air vents that people overlooked. In the stores cupboard she came across a white-coated figure, bent over a pile of cardboard boxes. The spikey blonde hair and jutting arrogant jaw were strangely familiar. The woman looked up, startled, as she came in. A sullen expression lodged itself on the youthful face, a near-permanent resident in all probability. It was Viv Two.

"Just doing the stock-taking, huh? Checking the sperm count?"

"Getting rubber gloves actually." The voice was cold and hard, but for all her defiance the woman was eying her nervously. So that was it. This explained the secret smirks and smug sidelong glances on Saturday night. This was Sunita's burglar.

"You should be careful, you know. The way Social are chasing up absent fathers, you might get hit with a paternity suit." The waves of resentment directed at her back as she left, gave her intense satisfaction.